CW01647145

DEVIL'S BARGAIN

NATASHA KNIGHT

Copyright © 2019 by Natasha Knight

All rights reserved.

No part of this book may be reproduced in any form or by any electronic or mechanical means, including information storage and retrieval systems, without written permission from the author, except for the use of brief quotations in a book review.

PROLOGUE

Melissa

It's past midnight when I get home, the perfect clear sky black but for the sliver of the moon. The walk from the bus stop is only two blocks, but this isn't the best neighborhood and I'm on my guard.

The one thing I can consistently rely on is that the streetlamps will always be broken. I wonder if the township even bothers to fix them anymore.

Twice on the short walk I catch myself glancing over my shoulder, the streets quieter than they should be.

When I turn onto the walkway up to my house, the motion detector sets off the light and I reach into my tote to dig out my keys.

Once more, as I climb the three steps up to the porch of the quaint, two-story yellow house, I look behind me.

But I'm alone.

And all the windows of all the houses are dark and the

only sound is that of my keys jangling as I finally find them at the bottom of the bag.

I insert the key into the top lock but when I turn it, nothing happens.

Did I forget to lock it? It's happened before, when I'm not paying attention. Although I'm usually careful.

I dismiss it, insert another key into the second lock. That one is locked.

Relieved, I push the door open and step into the house and before I've even pulled the key out or closed the door, I know something's wrong.

It's the smell of the place. It's different. Subtle, but it doesn't belong.

Aftershave.

And not just one scent.

Instinct tells me to run. To get out. But before I can process, the light goes on and it's simultaneous to someone clearing their throat.

It's only then that I manage to get my legs to work.

But I don't even get out of the house before a hand clamps down around my arm and tugs me back inside as the door is slammed shut.

I stumble, out of breath for that smallest effort, and I don't know how I don't scream.

How, with my heart hammering against my chest, I somehow don't scream as I look at the man sitting on the armchair, a worn-out antique that came with the rental.

As I take in the two who stand in my living room.

The third who's holding onto me, his grip like a vice.

"Let me go!"

I struggle.

The one in the chair watches and I can see he's entertained when his lips curve upward.

He gives a nod of his head and I wonder if he timed his order for the man to release me because the moment he does, I fall flat on my ass. I'm surprised he doesn't laugh when I do.

"Finished?" he asks when I look up at him.

He's wearing a suit and the others are dressed in black jeans and black shirts.

I don't know how I don't move or scream. It's like I can't. Like I'm paralyzed. Even my vocal cords are paralyzed.

"Ms. Doe," the man in the armchair says.

They know my name.

Of course, they know my name.

Men like this, they're not petty thieves. Not here to steal things. Not at this house anyway.

"Are you finished?" he asks.

I swallow. Nod.

He gestures to the man looming above me who once again closes his hand around my arm and hauls me to my feet before releasing me to stand on my own.

Armchair Man checks his watch. "You're late."

"Who..." But my question dies away as he rises to stand.

He's huge. A giant. Bigger even than the one beside me, and I find myself shrinking back.

"And now we're behind schedule," he says casually, simply continuing his sentence.

I spring back as he approaches.

He grins and I get the feeling he's used to this. To people being afraid of him. I get the feeling he likes it.

"Who are you?" I ask.

"I'm not the one you have to worry about, sweetheart," he says with a wink.

He gestures with a single nod to the man at the door to open it.

I look outside at the sedan that's just pulled up to the curb. It looks totally out of place here in this neighborhood. It's got to be worth more than several years of mortgage payments on any of these houses.

The driver gets out, leans against the car and lights a cigarette. A second car, a replica of this one, pulls up behind it.

"Coming?" Armchair Man asks me.

I turn back to find him watching me. He gestures for me to go to the car and he's not smiling anymore.

We both know I don't have a choice, but still, I can't just go with him.

"This is a mistake. I—"

"Hawk doesn't like to be kept waiting. Are you walking on your own or am I walking you?"

"Hawk? I don't know—"

"Walk or be walked, Ms. Doe?"

I swallow.

He gives me that grin again and leans in close like we're old friends.

But I know men like him.

I grew up with them.

And there's nothing remotely friendly about them.

"I suggest you walk. The other way isn't so pleasant."

I also know there's no benefit to doing as they say. No leniency for obedience. And so I try again to run because I can't not.

This time, I make it out onto the porch and it's when I'm setting foot on the front lawn that he catches me. Armchair Man. And his grip, it's different than the other man's. Harder.

"Please," I plead, tugging to free myself. To somehow pry his fingers from me.

"For a minute there, I thought you'd be smarter," he says, beginning to lead me down the cracked pavement to the waiting sedan, my struggles seemingly inconsequential.

When we get to the car, I set my hand against the hood, brace myself.

"Really?" he asks like I'm too stupid for words.

I meet his eyes and I try once more to free myself. He releases me abruptly, then boxes me in and cocks his head to the side. The look in his eyes is so steely, so cold, it sends ice along my spine.

"Get in the goddamned car," he orders, his voice harder.

He doesn't give me a chance to obey.

Instead, he wraps one arm around my middle and a moment later, I'm in the car and he's beside me, and when we pull away, I hear the locks click into place and that sound, it's like a foretelling of my future.

1

HAWK

I sip whiskey from my place at the back booth of the auction floor. It's the quarterly draw, a party I throw for my *associates*, for lack of a better word. We've had a good quarter, and this is their reward.

Every man who's walked into this room is captured by the many cameras. Every name noted. Every bid recorded in the ledger.

Piano music sets the backdrop, the collection of voices loud over it even though most speak in whispers during the breaks in entertainment. These, too, are recorded, and they'll be dissected later.

Pretty women serve drinks and anything else required of them as the stage is readied, the next girl taking her place on the raised dais.

This one, her name is Calla or Cara or something. She looks young, but I'm assured she's legal. They like young, the men gathered here.

She's on offer for one night only, and from the look of her, she'll bring a high bid.

I study her face on my screen from the cameras installed

behind the curtain. She's hesitant, to say the least, but Marcus handles it. Marcus' loan comes due tonight—and I've been more than patient—so he's got some incentive to make sure she gets her sweet little ass on that stage.

Besides, she'll be paid handsomely for her time. For the use of her body.

I watch as she's situated on the dais that's set at the very center of the stage. The auctioneer, an old English man, takes his place behind the podium. The gong sounds as the curtains are raised and a hush falls over the room.

The spotlight shines on the girl and she squints into the bright light, momentarily blinded. Two women peel the cream-colored cloak from her and let it drape at her feet. There's a swell of approving sounds from the men who are probably all sporting hard-ons for the pretty, young blonde.

I admit, she is magnificent. Not my type, but magnificent.

The auctioneer takes in the response and starts the bidding high.

Good.

Flesh comes at a cost. One these bastards can afford to pay.

The elevator doors slide open, drawing my attention. Axel steps out and turns his gaze only momentarily to the stage. He's about as interested as I am in that girl. These women, it's too fucking easy with them.

Calla, or whatever the fuck her name is, is probably creaming herself as she's turned, bent over, and the numbers being shouted out grow higher and higher.

I'm more interested in the woman who's following Axel.

Well, following isn't quite the word.

She's got a man on either side of her and, for as small as she is, she's struggling to free herself of them.

She turns her head this way and that as she takes in the scene. I think she gasps when her gaze falls on the exposed woman on the stage about whom the auctioneer is embellishing the virtues of a virgin ass.

He's good.

He's very good.

Because her price just doubled.

The word virgin never disappoints. I get it. There's something about being the first man to sink your cock into virgin territory.

Marcus catches my eye from the side of the stage. He raises his glass to me.

I raise mine back because this puts me in a good mood. It means I'll get my money tonight and I won't have to get my hands dirty for it.

Contrary to my reputation, I don't like getting my hands dirty. I will when I need to, but this is easier. Cleaner.

Axel reaches my table and clears his throat.

I turn to him. He gestures to the girl to be brought forward.

"Ms. Doe. Liza's sister," he says, sounding almost bored.

I shift my gaze to meet the girl's frightened one and all I can think for a moment is how her almond-shaped eyes match the color in my glass so perfectly.

Whiskey eyes.

Pretty. Very pretty.

With smooth olive skin and hair so dark it's almost black.

The photo I saw didn't do her justice.

"Let her go. She's not going anywhere, are you, sweetheart?"

I don't expect an answer.

When they release her, she brings the huge bag that was apparently on her shoulder in front of her.

She's clutching it like armor between herself and me.

"Get rid of that." I gesture with a quick nod of my head to the tote. I want to see the rest of her.

When one of the men reaches to take it, she pulls back, hisses at him. Actually hisses.

I chuckle, sip from my glass, and watch, surprised to be entertained.

In the background, I register the gavel coming down once. Twice. The number is making me very happy.

When the bag is gone, she looks back at me, her face flushed. She doesn't seem to know what to do with her hands but eventually closes her fingers over the back of the chair in front of her.

At least she's not making a spectacle of herself. Not yet, anyway. Not that anyone here would help her if she made a run for it.

She's wearing a heavy jacket. Too heavy for this time of year.

"Sit."

"Are you Mr. Hawk? I think there's been a mistake."

"Sit."

Axel mutters a curse under his breath, takes her arm, pulls out the chair she's gripping and puts her in it.

"That's better," I say.

He stands to the side, leaning against the wall, arms folded across his chest. His eyes narrow as he scans the crowd and they fall on one man in particular.

I look at the man, make note of who it is.

"Errand?" I ask him.

He turns to me, gives me one brief nod.

"I'll take care of this," I say to him. "Go."

He looks at me. "You sure?"

I glance at the pretty girl sitting stiffly across from me and give him a one-sided grin. "I don't think Ms. Doe will give me any trouble, will you?"

She just stares at me.

Axel chuckles. He makes his way through the crowd and it's like the parting of the sea as he approaches. Which is why he works for me. He's one mean son of a bitch. It's good to have him on my side.

The noise of the crowd intensifies as Calla is removed from the stage and the curtains are closed. It'll be a little while before the next one is put on the block.

I turn my full attention to the woman before me.

"Hawk," I say.

"What?"

"Just Hawk. Not Mr. Hawk."

"Oh."

"Melissa Doe. Strange name."

"This is a mistake." She reaches into the giant tote, which is lying at her feet.

One of the soldiers puts a hand on her shoulder, stopping her.

"What—"

I give him a shake of my head.

He steps back.

I don't think she'll pull a gun out of the thing. She's not the type to even own one.

She gives him a nasty look and resumes digging around to pull out her wallet. "Look," she says, opening it, taking out her driver's license and holding it out for me to see. Her hand trembles. "My last name is Chase. You've made a mistake."

When I reach to take the license, she pulls it away. I raise my eyebrows and hold out my hand, palm up.

She looks at it, and, very reluctantly, puts the driver's license in it.

"I don't know you. I don't know—"

"You'll get to know me," I say without looking up, studying the license instead, turning it over. "This isn't a very good fake. You've never been pulled over?"

"What?" She flushes, eyes huge and panicked. "It's not fake." Her voice is a little higher.

I tuck it into my jacket pocket.

"That's mine," she starts weakly.

Without taking my eyes off her, I raise my hand and one of the servers comes over with an empty crystal tumbler. I pour whiskey into it, push it toward Melissa and think how much I like the sound of her name. It's soft and sexy and her lips are full, and I can smell the fear coming off her and fuck, I take a deep breath in because nothing—and I mean nothing—gets my dick hard as that sweet scent.

"Drink," I say.

"My driver's license."

"You'll get it back. Drink."

Trembling hands come to the table, one moving to take the tumbler.

She looks at it.

I look at her. At thick lashes concealing those pretty eyes from me. A lock of wavy, dark hair falls out of its messy bun on the top of her head. She tucks it behind her ear as she brings the glass to her nose and sniffs.

"It's not poison."

She takes a cautious sip.

"And?" I ask.

"What?"

"Do you like it?"

"No."

I grin. "Drink it anyway. It'll calm your nerves."

She looks at me, then at the room full of men. The only women are those serving them and the one she just saw on the auction block.

"Why am I here?"

"Because your sister is out of commission and she owes me a good deal of money."

"My sister?"

"She's never been very reliable."

"I don't have a sister."

"Come, now. Liza Boyd."

Her face loses a little of its color. "Liza?"

"Nice girl. Until you get to know her."

She gives a shake of her head, straightens her spine. "I haven't spoken with Liza in years. We don't keep in touch. And she's not my sister." She pauses and a crease forms between her eyebrows. "Is she…is she in town?"

The question surprises me, but I know people. They lie. Anything to get away with shit they have no business getting away with.

I notice the sheen of sweat collected on her forehead. Another sign that she's lying.

I nod to answer her question.

The furrow between her eyebrows deepens. "What do you mean 'out of commission'?" she asks as if she just heard that part.

"Seems she was beaten."

"Beaten?" She looks truly caught off guard. "Is she okay?"

"She'll be fine. In time. Recovering at the hospital. Take off your jacket, Melissa."

Melissa. There it is again. The sound of that name, it's

almost erotic.

"I'm fine. I'm not staying. Which hospital?" she asks, pushing her chair back and just starting to rise.

At my nod, that same man from earlier closes his hand over her shoulder, stopping her before she's even straightened fully.

"Sit."

She swallows and is once again seated.

"I'll tell you when you can leave. Now take off your jacket."

She gives me a long look, glances at the man in her periphery, then shifts in her seat. She pulls her arms out and leaves the jacket at her back.

Underneath she's wearing a cheap pale blue sweater that's frayed, but it does hug her generous breasts so I can't complain.

"I won't be bullied," she says, and I see the effort it's taking her to keep her voice level, to keep her eyes on mine. To pretend like she's not scared shitless.

"Then don't make me bully you," I say with a smile.

"Can I have some water?" she asks.

"What's the magic word?"

Her left eye twitches and I'm not sure she's aware of her hands fisting.

I raise my eyebrows, waiting.

"Please."

I nod, call a girl over and tell her to bring ice-water which is delivered momentarily.

Melissa picks up the tall glass with both hands and drinks it all down.

"Which hospital is Liza at?"

"It's 'may I' by the way. Not 'can I'."

I know from the look on her face she's telling me to go to

hell. Not many people would dare. At least, they'd be better at hiding it.

This night is turning out better than I expected. I knew she was good-looking when I had Axel pick her up, but good looks alone aren't enough to keep me engaged.

"Centennial Hills," I say. She looks confused. "Hospital. She's at Centennial Hills Hospital."

"Did you beat her up?"

"I won't dignify that question with a response." I don't beat women. Period.

"Who did then?"

"I wouldn't know. Better?" I ask, gesturing to the water.

She doesn't reply.

I sip my drink and study her.

"You don't look much like each other." Melissa's olive skin and dark hair are opposite Liza's ruddy complexion and reddish hair. It make me think Italian. Maybe middle-eastern?

"What?"

"You look very different than your sister."

"I told you, we're not sisters," she says with a touch more irritation in her voice than I like. "I was fostered in the Boyd home. We're not related."

"Blood or fostered or adopted, I don't care."

"Never adopted," she clarifies, clearing her throat and not quite looking at me.

I just hope she doesn't think the fact that they're not related by blood means she's off the hook.

"What am I doing here?" she asks, ignoring my question, sounding more steely than I like.

"Like I said, *Liza* owes me some money." I make a point of saying her name rather than calling her her sister.

"I don't have anything to do with that."

"But you do. Given Liza's current state, well, she's no good to me." I set one elbow on the table, rest my chin on my fingers as she processes this information. "And the only name she could offer up was yours."

"Mine?"

I nod. It's quiet and I wonder when she's going to get around to asking the two-hundred-and-fifty-thousand-dollar question.

"How much does she owe you?"

There it is. "A quarter of a million dollars."

Her mouth falls open.

"Liza has a gambling addiction," I say. "And, as it turns out, a drug addiction."

"But that much money. Are you sure? I mean…that's a lot of money."

"Agree. She spent it quite nicely in my casino, though."

She's quiet for a long moment and her eyes narrow before she speaks. "So, let me understand this. You lent her a quarter-of-a-million-dollars to gamble in your casino, then you stole it back from her in that same casino and now you want her to pay it to you all over again?"

"I stole nothing. Take care with your words, Melissa."

"But that's the gist of it, right? And did you know about her drug addiction when you lent her this money?"

I lean forward and she draws back. Good because I'm suddenly not as entertained.

"When someone comes to me for money, I don't ask why he or she needs it or where he or she is going to spend it or how. I don't give a damn. All I expect is that it's paid back by the agreed upon date."

"Let me guess, with a ridiculous interest rate."

"That not asking questions comes at a price, Melissa."

"Stop saying my name."

"But I like saying it. *Melissa*. It just...rolls right off my tongue." I lean back in my seat, swirl the ice in my drink.

She flushes, at a loss for a moment. "You're a loan shark," she finally says.

I shrug a shoulder. "I'm many things, first and foremost, the owner and CEO of Hawk Enterprises, an employer of several thousand people, a lawful, tax-paying business-man with many friends."

From the look on her face, she understands what I'm saying.

"If you think that I can pay you that kind of money, you're mistaken," she says. "I don't have anything close to that."

"Most people don't. Obviously, I didn't expect Liza to pay me back in cash. We had a different sort of arrangement that suited both of our needs."

Her forehead creases, and a moment later, a look of understanding passes over her face.

I grin. "Get your mind out of the gutter. I don't fuck women like Liza Boyd. I never have. I never would. It's not that sort of arrangement."

"I don't understand what you want from me then."

The gong sounds as if on cue and Melissa turns to look over the quieting crowd of men.

I follow her gaze to where the curtains part to reveal the next beauty, this one a full-figured red-head.

I turn back to my guest, watch her in profile. I study her pretty little upturned nose, the high forehead, full lips that part slightly as she takes in the attraction on the stage.

"What is this?" she asks.

"An auction."

She looks at me with an expression of shock and utter disbelief on her face.

"So these men, they're bidding on…her?"

I nod.

She turns back to watch the girl who is ceremoniously disrobed, and I'm surprised to see she's a natural red-head. So rare these days.

The auctioneer calls out the opening number.

When Melissa looks at me again, she's flushed and picks up her empty glass of water. Realizing it's empty, she puts it back down. I raise my hand for another but when it comes, she doesn't touch it.

"Why am I here?" she finally asks me, voice higher again.

Her big eyes are filling up with tears and those tears seem to make them go a soft caramel and all I can think is I bet she's pretty when she cries.

"Have you figured out what our arrangement was? What Liza agreed to sell to repay me?"

Her throat works as she swallows, and I think I hear it even over the crowd.

"I don't…this is…" her voice breaks. "You shouldn't have lent her that kind of money," she says weakly.

"Liza's poor choices are not my responsibility."

"They're not mine either."

"Well, then we're finished here. There is another way, after all. One I was trying to avoid, considering her situation."

"What do you mean?"

"I mean, she's in such bad shape already. Beaten badly when they found her."

The color drains from Melissa's face.

"What do you expect from me?" she asks. "I don't have that kind of money. I don't even know how to get it."

"I'm well aware of that. Watch," I say, turning to the stage just as the girl extends her arms to the two women on either side of her. She's turned and bent and displayed and when the man with the strap walks toward her, the room goes completely still in anticipation.

That sound, Christ, that sound of leather on supple flesh and the red-head's sudden gasp as the delicate skin is tested, fuck, it never fails.

The red-head's skin turns crimson, the thick stripe glorious against such pale skin. It sends a deep, satisfied murmur through the crowd.

When I look back at Melissa, she's staring at me wide-eyed. I wonder if she realizes she's hugging her arms to herself.

We remain like this, me watching her, her watching me, as numbers are called out, and the auctioneer asks for more, more, more and soon, the red-head is going once, going twice, sold to the dirty old fuck in the corner.

"Lucky man," I say, swallowing my whiskey.

"I'm going to be sick," she says.

I push my chair back and stand.

She watches me walk around the table toward her, craning her neck, shrinking away.

I hold out my hand.

She looks at it like it's a hot poker I'm telling her to grab.

"I can't do that," she says, shaking her head, a tear slipping down her cheek.

"Bathroom, Melissa. So you can get over whatever you need to get over and do what you need to do to pay me back."

"And if I won't? If I can't?"

"Won't and can't are two very different things."

"What will happen to her? To Liza?"

"Let's not go there. Then you really will be sick."

2

MELISSA

His hand is huge.

Hell. He's huge.

I reach out, place mine inside it and it feels warm and rough and when he closes his fingers over mine, his grip is firm, this gesture, it's as though I've already agreed.

Because I know what I must do. I know why he brought me here. I have no doubt.

You owe her nothing.

I haven't seen or had any contact with Liza in years. I didn't know she was in town.

And she can't know that I am.

I manage to get to my feet, and he's got to be a good foot taller than me. Even with my pumps, the top of my head barely reaches his chin.

Heads turn as Hawk, his presence at my back enough to guide me, leads me toward a door at the back of the room where a man stands sentry. He opens it at our approach.

I hesitate.

"Go on," Hawk says from behind me. He's standing

closer than I realize and a shudder runs through me at the feel of his breath on the back of my neck.

I hear the faint hint of his accent. I heard it throughout our conversation, stronger sometimes than others. It's in the way he says his r's.

I walk inside and the lights go on. I realize I'm in his office.

I don't want to be impressed or amazed, but this is spectacular. The walls aren't walls at all but windows overlooking the Las Vegas strip. Tonight is clear, and the lights blink in a rainbow of colors. This view, it's something out of a magazine.

His desk is huge and modern, set at the far corner facing the entrance. There's a sitting area in another corner with sleek leather couches. Everything is top quality. I can tell.

"This way," he says, beckoning for me to come.

I follow.

He opens a door and I don't know what I expect, a bedroom maybe, but it's a bathroom. A large and luxurious bathroom and the walls here, too, are glass.

I glance back at him.

"No one can see inside," he says and when he goes to close the door, I stop him.

"Wait."

He looks down at me and I think how strange his eyes are. Different colors. One is a mossy-green, the other half green and half crystal-blue. The green is warm, the blue ice-cold.

But I know any warmth I think I see is in my head. This man, he's all sharp edges. It's like someone took a beast out of the wild and put him in a thousand-dollar suit thinking it would somehow tame the animal inside. Somehow contain it.

"Melissa?" he says my name and I realize I'm staring.

"She was going to do that? To pay you back?"

He nods.

"You want me to do that? Like those women? Because she can't?"

"I'm merely giving you an option. It's your choice entirely."

"You want to strip me, put me on that stage and sell me to pay a debt that's not my own?"

He cocks his head to the side like he's a little annoyed. "Like I said, I'm giving you an option. I thought you'd want to help Liza, considering you grew up together. She was certain if I could find you, that you'd want to help."

"How did you find me?"

He studies me and I see his eyes narrowing. He's remembering the driver's license, putting two and two together.

"Should it have been hard for me to find you? I mean, the house is under M. Doe. Although I am curious about the driver's license."

I need to relax. Think. "I just...what you arranged with Liza, you obviously took advantage of her—"

"Don't push me, Melissa. My kindness only goes so far."

"Kindness?"

"Yes, kindness. Besides," he pauses as his gaze drops to my mouth, my chest. "I wouldn't be surprised if you drew more than what's owed."

"Is that supposed to make me feel better? To make this sound somehow more appealing? Not like what it is?" My voice is quaking, it's as unsteady as I feel.

He shrugs a shoulder like he couldn't care less and checks his watch. "Let me know in the next five minutes."

With that, he takes his phone out of his pocket and turns his back to me to walk toward his desk.

I close and lock the bathroom door and lean my back against it.

Five minutes.

I have five minutes to decide this.

Liza's here and she knows I'm here. But why hasn't she approached me?

I hold my hand out and realize it's trembling.

I walk to the sink, turn on the cold water and splash handfuls of it onto my face, then dry it. The towel smells like him. I wonder when I noted what he smelled like.

I hang the towel back on its rack and looking at my reflection, tuck the hair that's fallen out of the clip behind my ear.

Those women that I saw up on that stage, they're in a league all their own. Me, the makeup I had on earlier today has disappeared, the only evidence of there having been any at all is the smudge of mascara on my temple. I wipe it away.

I look down at my sweater, at my plain skirt and boots, everything second-hand but my bra and underwear. I look around the bathroom and I've never been in a world like this before. A world of money where a quarter of a million dollars is something you loan out. Where men like Hawk rule and women are put on auction blocks to be sold to the highest bidder.

Hawk. Is that his first name or his last name? I don't even know. But I do know that I don't belong here. I don't belong in his world.

And I *am* going to be sick. Because I know myself. Because Liza was a kid when she told that lie and she was scared. As scared as me.

But it's hard to remember that sometimes.

Hell, I wish I could forget all of it, whole years of my life.

We were supposed to leave together but after her betrayal, I ran. I didn't care that I left her behind. Not then.

"Melissa," comes Hawk's voice from the other side of the door and it's a godsend, saving me from going back to that terrible time. That terrible place. "Time," he says.

I grip the lip of the sink, steel my spine, look at myself in the mirror. I just have to block it out when I'm up there. Just block it out when whoever buys me uses me. Just disappear like it's not me. Not my body.

That's nothing new. I can do that. Hell, it's second-nature.

I have no choice. I can't let him hurt her. Or worse.

I won't.

"Melissa," his voice is firmer.

I turn to the door, place my hand on the doorknob, take a deep breath in and wish I'd drunk that whiskey. I could use it now.

I open the door.

Blood flushes my face at the sight of him. He's good-looking, but rough. Rugged, like he doesn't quite belong here. Not in an office. Not in a suit.

He watches me, his face impassive, waiting for my decision, I guess.

"Will I be safe?"

He nods once.

"Can I say no? Once I'm...bought." The word sends a wave of nausea through me.

He shakes his head. "Once you agree, you're bound."

"To anyone?"

"To anyone."

God.

Can I do this? Can I even do it?

"It's one night of your life."

One night. One night when I give myself to a stranger.

"Melissa?"

One night where I prostitute myself.

I can say no. It's my choice. I can walk away.

I had a choice then, too, and I chose. I walked away. I left her behind.

Do I abandon her again?

"Decide."

I shift my gaze from his, take a deep breath in and nod.

3

HAWK

Yes.

That was her decision.

Melissa is taken backstage to be prepared.

I sit at my table with Axel across from me. He's back from his errand.

Axel Drake and I have known each other since I was sixteen-years-old. He's one of the few men I consider a friend.

There were three years when he left Vegas and went east. It's a time he doesn't discuss though, not even with me. All I know about it is that he and his brother, Hugo, a man I've never met, spent time in prison there and I have a feeling it has something to do with that errand he ran earlier.

I understand revenge and I don't care what Axel has to do to take care of what he needs to take care of as long as he's available when I need him. It's an understanding we have between us.

He drinks the last of his whiskey and I pour him another.

The gong goes off and the auctioneer announces this is the last of tonight's draw. They'll be anxious for it. I only have half a dozen girls at each party. Keeps them hungry.

"Want me to keep someone on the sister?" he asks as the curtain goes up. "I have a feeling she'll disappear as soon as she's released. If she's smart, that is."

We're both watching the stage as he speaks, as the spotlight begins its ascent up the raised dais where she stands like an offering.

It seems like it's a slow dragging of the light, like we're given an inch at a time. Just glimpses as it travels up the draped figure where two women stand on either side.

Finally, the light shines on her face and she squints, turning away momentarily.

I didn't realize how long her hair was. It falls in waves over her shoulders and thick bangs frame her whiskey eyes. They've fixed her makeup, lined her eyes heavily and put a sheen of gloss over those pouty lips.

I notice her hands are fisted and she doesn't raise them like she should when the girls draw the cloak from her, baring her naked body.

I swallow at the sight.

"Keep someone on her, but don't pick her up," I say, hearing how thick my voice sounds. "She's no use to me anyway, not in the state she's in."

I swallow the rest of the whiskey in my glass and can't drag my eyes from the naked woman on the stage. Watching her face burn in embarrassment while her eyes narrow in a combination of rage, rebellion and confusion as the men call out numbers.

The auctioneer discusses her heavy breasts—large for her small waist—and the particular shade of pink of her hard little nipples.

I myself can't look away from those breasts, can't not think about how perfectly they'd fit in the palms of my hands as I weigh them.

"Turn her!" someone calls out.

Feeling oddly possessive, I note who.

Melissa struggles against the girls who take her wrists and they're confused. The women on the block are willing. No one is made to do this against their will. Not really.

This one, though, she's not like any of those women. I knew it from the moment I first saw her.

"Turn her!" more chants come from the crowd. Her resistance will only make them want it more. Want *her* more.

The auctioneer, too, is momentarily at a loss. He glances over the crowd to my table.

I give a nod and two guards step out of the shadows and onto the stage.

The auctioneer gestures to the men. "Turn her."

By the time they get to her, she's off the dais.

"I guess she changed her mind?" Axel chuckles as we watch the scene, this cartoon as the two giants grab the naked woman who can't be more than five-and-a-half feet. She's fighting as if her life depends on it and somehow manages to knee one of the men in the balls.

Axel winces.

"Ouch," I say, pouring more whiskey into my glass without taking my eyes off the spectacle.

"Why don't you stop it. You know you're going to buy her anyway," Axel says, taking the bottle and pouring for himself.

I turn to him. Before I can deny it, he laughs.

"I know you, Hawk. You want that girl. You did the moment you laid eyes on her."

I shrug a shoulder and when I turn back, the men are forcing her back onto the platform. And when she raises her middle finger at the crowd, the bids explode.

The soldiers hold her there, and the auctioneer is looking at me again. I nod once more, and he picks up the strap and walks toward the girl.

She sees him, sees what he's carrying, and her eyes go huge as she's turned and bent at the waist. She screams when he raises the strap and brings it down hard across her ass once, twice.

"Quiet, girl," he hisses the command.

More numbers are called out from the cheering crowd.

Calls for more strokes to be laid on her beautiful ass.

When the auctioneer returns to his podium, she's straightened and turned to the room again. Her face is flushed, and I wonder if she can see me. If she knows I'm watching. If she knows it was me who ordered the strap.

I stand. The room quiets as I do, and I speak my number.

"Quarter-of-a-million dollars."

I don't have to raise my voice and I meet every eye in the place daring any one of them to challenge my bid.

The gavel comes down once. That's all that's necessary when I bid.

"Sold for a quarter-of-a-million dollars."

I look at Melissa's tear stained, mascara-smeared face. She still can't see me. The spotlight is too bright on her. But she must recognize my voice and know that it was me who bought her.

The men take her down from the platform. She still fights as she's removed from the stage. The curtain falls and the lights in the room go on announcing to everyone that it's the end of the night.

Axel chuckles. "Told you," he mutters as I resume my seat.

"Fuck you," I say, the excitement I feel in my gut something foreign. Something I'd forgotten.

One hour later, Melissa is delivered to my penthouse by the same two men in about the same fashion as when she threw that fit on the stage.

I'm standing at the window with my back to the elevator when I hear the doors slide open. I sip my drink, watching the lights of the strip in this city that never sleeps.

A city of vultures.

Hungry.

Always hungry.

Always looking for innocent flesh with which to fill their bellies.

I'm hungry, too.

I set my empty glass on the counter and turn to face her.

Innocent flesh.

I'll fill my belly with hers.

"You asshole," she says.

The men are physically restraining her. She'll have bruises on her arms tomorrow.

"You fucking asshole!"

I give a nod and the men strip her of her cloak as they step back onto the elevator.

It takes her a moment when she's naked again but then she meets my gaze and her eyes narrow as she marches toward me. It's hilarious because of the fact that she's naked, very much so, and her hands are still fisted. They only unfist when she stops inches from me and raises her right arm to slap me.

I catch her wrist, narrow my eyes, catching the other wrist too when she raises that one.

"Don't ever do that," I warn calmly.

"You're an asshole."

"So you've said." I stretch her arms wide, looking her over as she struggles to free herself.

"They took my things. My bracelet—"

"You'll get everything back. No one will steal from you." I look her over. "You'll shave your pussy."

"Like hell I will."

I give her a smirk, transfer her wrists to one of my hands and turn her, take in the two thick welts on her ass and spank one cheek.

She yelps and jumps.

I turn her back around, lower her arms and pull her to me so her naked chest is pressed against mine. I feel her hard nipples through the fabric of my shirt. I search her face, her pretty, angry face.

We stand like that for a long moment. Her breathing is shallow, her heart is racing. I can see it in the violent throbbing of the pulse at her neck. Her eyes are ringed in smeared black and she looks like she's about to cry again.

I release her, step back, look her over again. Long legs. Slender but defined. Yoga, I'd guess. Not a runner, her muscles are too lean.

"Why did you do that?" she asks when I turn away momentarily to pick up my glass.

I watch her as she stands awkwardly, not sure how to cover herself, I guess.

"Why did I do what?" I ask just to piss her off some

more. Most women are eager when they're brought up here. And very willing.

She's different.

"Why did you put me up there? Humiliate me like that when you were just going to buy me all along."

"Who says I was going to buy you all along?"

She's confused.

"Besides," I continue. "I thought you could use a little humbling."

She turns away as her forehead wrinkles and she wipes away a tear, smearing more black across her temple.

"You're a mess," I say.

"You're an asshole. An asshole!"

"And your vocabulary is disappointingly limited." I walk to the liquor cabinet. "What do you want to drink since you don't like whiskey."

"Can I just have some clothes?"

"What did I teach you earlier about 'can I' and 'may I'?"

"Fuck you!"

I decide on vodka and pour it straight. She's going to need it for what I have planned. I walk back to her and hold out the glass.

"I warn you, don't slap it out of my hand. If you do, you'll kneel in the broken shards while you suck my dick, understand?"

Her face flushes a pretty red.

It strikes me. I can't remember the last time I saw a woman blush. Not the women I know, at least. And it's not something she can fake.

She looks up at me, trying to gauge how serious I am, I guess.

I'm dead serious.

She takes the glass. Sips. Looks down at the floor or her feet or something. Just not at me.

"Why don't you have a good cry. Get it all out now because right now is when I'll be most patient with you."

"Patient? You just stripped me naked and put me up on a stage for those...those...perverts to bid on me like I'm a piece of meat!"

"Remember, it was your choice. People need to learn to take responsibility for their lives, their choices. Own their shit."

"Fuck you, Hawk!"

I step to her, and to her credit, she doesn't back away. I cup her chin, tilt her face up.

"I will fuck you. It's why I bought you, sweetheart."

She shrugs away, turns, walks to the chair and picks up the blanket draped over the arm to wrap it around herself.

The pattern of the tartan makes me pause for a moment. The maid must have put it out by mistake. It's the only thing that doesn't fit here. And I should have gotten rid of it long ago.

I sit on the leather couch, cross my ankle over the opposite knee, watch her.

She swallows the contents of her glass and stands there looking at me.

"Help yourself if you'd like more."

She shakes her head, sets her glass down on a nearby table.

I watch her as she takes in the penthouse. It takes up the top floor of my building and is situated just above my office. The room we're in is a grand room, wide-open with kitchen, living room, dining room and walls of glass. The furniture is modern, everything either black, white or gray. And as beautiful as it is, it's almost clinical. The lines clean, everything in its place, everything with a purpose.

I don't like clutter or anything messy, not anywhere in my life.

My eyes fall on that tartan again. Why have I kept it all these years? I need to talk to the maid. I don't want to have to see it every time I fucking turn around.

Melissa lowers herself into the chair nearest her and farthest from me. She hangs her head and her hair falls forward like a veil between us, but I don't miss the tear that drops.

She combs her fingers through the thick mass, sniffles and straightens her spine. She meets my gaze.

"One night," she says.

I nod.

"And I'm free and you won't hurt Liza."

"Not a bad deal if you ask me."

"You're not the one who has to fuck you."

I chuckle at that. "You could do worse, sweetheart."

"I'm not your sweetheart."

I shrug a shoulder. I could give a fuck.

"What are you, anyway? What's your accent?" she asks.

She hears it? I wonder if others do too. I've worked hard to rid myself of it. Rid myself of the past.

"Scots."

"You're from Scotland?"

"Born in the Highlands." I sip from my glass. I hear it now, too. Familiar and foreign at once.

She scratches her head, studies me, then dismisses whatever thoughts are going through her head by giving it a shake.

"What happens now?"

I uncross my legs. Point to the floor between them. "You come here."

Her eyes grow wide at the command.

"I said come."

She gets up, walks toward me like a condemned woman walking to her execution. She stops a few inches from me.

"Kneel."

I see fear in her eyes. Her breathing is short and uneven, and I notice how the light dusting of fine hair on her arms stands on end.

"Kneel," I repeat.

"No."

I reach out, keeping my eyes on hers as I slip my hand under the tartan she's still clinging to and, before she can get away, grip the patch of hair between her legs and twist. I rise to my feet, holding her where she is by that handful of hair.

Her face contorts in pain as I loom over her.

"You really think that tartan will keep you safe from me?" I ask, my voice low as, with my other hand, I drag it off and let it fall to the floor. "I said kneel."

"I said no." Her voice is high and trembles and her pupils are dilated either with arousal or fear. A combination of the two, I'd say, considering the musky scent of her.

I walk her backward, still holding onto that patch of hair between her legs. "You want me to make you, Melissa?"

"You will anyway. It's what men do, isn't it?"

My jaw tightens. "You've dealt with the wrong kind of men, then."

Her eyebrows knit together, and she studies me.

When her back hits the wall, she swallows, slaps her hands to my chest. "Stop."

"I change my mind," I say, leaning down inhaling her

hair, her skin. "Don't shave your pussy." I press my chest against her as I curl my fingers.

Her mouth opens and she makes a sound, something like a squeak.

I slip my fingers between her folds and when I do, I cock my head to the side and grin.

"Oh, Melissa," I say, drawing her name out slowly.

She squeezes her eyes shut for a moment, lowers her head. She pushes against my chest like she's trying to move me, and it's cute that she tries, but I don't budge.

"Are you wet for me, sweetheart?" I ask, tilting my hips, making sure she can feel my erection against her belly. "Because I'm hard for you."

"This is a devil's bargain," she mutters.

I lean my face down, kiss her jaw, cup one heavy breast with my free hand, weigh it like I wanted to from the first moment I saw her naked. I rub her pussy.

"Are you going to come on the devil's hand, then?" I ask.

She fists her hands, punches my chest. It doesn't hurt. I wonder if she meant for it to. Probably.

It's quiet, the only sound that of her wet arousal.

"I want to be clear," she finally says, her body giving a little jerk when I take her clit between thumb and forefinger.

"Yes?" I ask, not bothering to try to keep the grin from my face.

"I don't want this," she says as that involuntary jerk comes again.

"No. Clearly you don't want me to touch you," I say, pinching her nipple.

"I mean it."

"Noted."

I rub that swollen nub and watch her. It won't take long

for her to come. I can see it on her flushed face, see it in the dilated pupils of her pretty whiskey-colored eyes, in the panting, open mouth.

But then I draw my hand away, up toward her belly, wiping her own arousal on her as I step backward.

"You don't want it," I confirm, giving her a wink like we're co-conspirators. "Get on your knees," I tell her, undoing my belt, the buttons of my pants.

She looks down at my length pressing against the slacks, then back up at me. She gives me a one-sided grin.

"Do you usually have to pay women to suck your dick?" she asks, tilting her head.

I smile. Study her. "You're poking a bear, sweetheart."

"That's sad, really, a man like you, having to pay women to fuck him."

"On your knees. Let's put that mouth to the use it was intended for."

"Are you always such a jackass?"

"You bring out the best in me. Kneel."

"I'm not putting that thing in my mouth."

"Do you prefer to take it up your ass?" From the look on her face, it's not what she expected. "We'll get to that, I promise, but I was easing you in, *sweetheart*."

"Stop calling me that. I am not your sweetheart."

"You'll be whatever I want you to be. You're bought and paid for, remember? Now get on your knees before you piss me off."

Her face goes red and rage rolls off her.

I open my mouth to say something, but I don't expect what she does next.

I don't expect her to slap me, not after my warning.

Her gasp comes an instant after her hand collides with my face.

I force a long, deep breath, feeling the sting of the slap. Feeling the rage bubble inside me. I tighten the muscles of my gut to tamp it down, to control it.

I'm bigger than her. Stronger. I can hurt her in a way she can't hurt me. I have to be careful.

When I shift my gaze back to hers, she has her hands to her mouth and her eyes are huge. She's staring at me like she can't fucking believe what she just fucking did.

It takes me a long time before I speak.

"You want to play rough, Melissa?" The words are a low, almost whispered threat.

She swallows, shaking her head. Streaks of black line her cheeks, a trail of mascara and tears.

"Because I can do rough."

She gives a scream when I lift her off the floor, throw her over my shoulder. I feel like a caveman as I stalk down the hall, slapping her ass once as her fists pound against my back.

My bedroom is the last one, it takes up the whole of the back of the penthouse. I walk in, flip the light switch so the lamps on either side of the bed go on. They cast a warm, yellow light, as the clear glass of the windows turns smoky, darkening.

Windows for walls here too. The city lights beyond. Quiet but for the sounds she makes as she struggles.

I toss her on her back onto the bed.

She bounces on the mattress.

I stare down at her, at her pretty, naked body, small and soft and supple. I unbutton the top buttons of my shirt, undo the cuffs, taking my time as I watch her lying there watching me. Once it's half-unbuttoned, I pull it over my head.

She looks at me, takes in my chest, my arms.

On the outside, I look like a businessman. Underneath the thousand-dollar suits, I could be mistaken for the enforcer.

Her eyes zero in on the tattoo she can see.

"Respect all. Fear none," I tell her.

At least until they prove you wrong.

Her gaze shifts to my eyes.

I strip off my pants, and they move south to the dragon along my thigh and hip, and it's like she can't stop looking and doesn't know where to look, especially when I take off my briefs and she sees my hard cock. I watch her for a moment as she takes it in and when she meets my eyes again, I see a slight panic inside them.

I put one knee on the bed. "You want me to be rough with you?"

She's up on her elbows, then her hands, and inching backwards away from me.

I grab her ankle, tug her back down and lay my weight on her. With one hand, I grip the hair at the back of her head, force her to look at me and all the while, I feel her wetness against my belly, my cock.

"Some women need it. Do you need it, Melissa? You need me to be rough so you come?"

She shakes her head as much as she can, watching me, her breathing short and audible.

She looks different than I expect. Panicked.

And mute.

I have to remember she's not the usual sort of woman I bring up here. Any fear those women show is an act.

This one, I get the feeling she's not acting.

I shake off the thought.

I just paid a quarter-of-a-million-dollars for her. I'm

fucking her. And for that price, she'd better be one hell of a fuck.

Without taking my eyes off her, I open the nightstand drawer, take out a condom. What I want most is to sink my cock into her bare, but I don't need complications.

"Cat got your tongue?" I ask, kneeling up over her to roll the condom on.

She swallows, huge eyes locked on my dick.

"Please tell me you're not a fucking virgin," I ask, realizing this could be the panic I see.

She blinks, drags her gaze to mine. She's still mute.

I raise my eyebrows and she shakes her head.

Good.

I smile, lean down over her, cupping the back of her head, twining my fingers in her thick hair and holding her when she tries to turn away. I slide my other hand between her legs and bring my face to hers, inhaling deeply, turning her a little to take the lobe of her ear between my teeth.

"Think you can take it all?" I whisper when she whimpers as I rub her swollen, wet clit.

Drawing my hand away, I lay my weight on her, grip one thigh, bend her leg at the knee and open her up. She's so tight when I push into her that for a moment, I wonder if she lied. If she is a virgin.

I watch her face as her warmth envelops me, and I think yes, I want to tear into her. I want to feel her heat.

Her face tenses as she stretches to take me. She makes a sound, a whimper, and her hands are on my shoulders, nails digging into my back.

"It hurts," she says.

"You're tight." I move inside her, feel her juices lubricating the passage, pull out, thrust. "That one's for slapping me."

"It hurts," she repeats, and there's that panicked expression again, her eyes almost child-like when they meet mine.

I slow, draw back.

Her nails dig into my biceps, my chest. I'm sure she's drawing blood now.

"Easy, Melissa," I say, taking one of her wrists and drawing it to the side. "Relax."

She looks over at it, at my hand on her wrist. She makes a sound and I can hear and feel her breathing coming shorter as she tugs at her wrist.

My grip isn't hard but I keep hold of her.

Realizing she's not a match for me, she turns those big eyes back to mine and the skin around them is wet. A tear slides down the side of her face.

"Let me go."

"You need to relax. It won't hurt if you relax."

"Please let me go."

Watching her face, it's strange, like it's taking all she has not to break out into a full panic.

I pull out of her, take her other wrist and drag her arms over her head.

She arches her back, twisting to see what I'm doing, and when she feels the leather of the first cuff wrap around her wrist, the sound that comes from her is like that of an animal.

Not a fighting one.

A wounded one.

Once both wrists are secured, I take my weight off her and slide down her slender body between her legs. With my hands on her thighs, I open them wider.

"Let me loose. Please."

Her pussy's wet, dripping. She's ready. Even as tight as she is, she's ready. But I'll give her this first.

I dip my head down and lick her and hear her sharp intake of breath as she goes dead still.

I do it again, circling her clit, then taking it into my mouth.

"Please!" she cries out and when I suck that hard, little nub, it's moments before her back arches and she lets out a long moan. Her eyes are closed, face tense, hands fisted in their restraints and she's coming. She's coming hard and fuck, she tastes good. She tastes amazing.

I don't go down on women. I haven't in too long to even remember their taste.

But her. I can't get enough of her and when I ease my grip on her thighs, she bends her knees on my shoulders, squeezes and whimpers.

I suck harder, drawing out her orgasm, wanting another.

"Oh God. Please stop!" She's panting and her thighs are squeezing and she's coming again, bucking with her release even as she begs me to stop.

I taste her, relish her every breath, every whimper. I only let up when she falls limp on the bed.

I kneel up between her legs, look at the gaping pink of her dripping cunt, then at her face. She's relaxed and soft, her eyes like the color of sand on the softest beach.

"I like your taste," I tell her.

"Please take these off. I'll do what you say. Please take them off."

"Not yet."

I lift her hips, turn her over. She tries to immediately turn back, but I stop her.

She makes that sound again, that wounded, panicked sound.

"I'm not going to hurt you, Melissa," I tell her.

She buries her face in the bed.

"You're safe."

"I'm sorry I slapped you. I won't do it again. Just take them off."

"Look at me."

She shakes her head.

"Look at me and I'll take them off."

It takes her a long minute, but she turns her head and her face is wet with tears and I remember what she'd said about men. About being forced.

"You're safe. I'm not going to hurt you. It's just sex, all right? Just sex."

She nods fast but I can see she doesn't believe me.

My dick's going to go soft. I have never dealt with a woman crying in my bed.

After a moment, I reach up and undo the cuffs.

She draws her arms in and rolls onto her side, turning away from me.

I get off the bed, go into the bathroom to slip the condom off and pull on a pair of draw-string linen pants. I walk into the living room and grab the bottle of vodka and a glass. I return to find her sitting up on the bed, her knees pulled up to her chest, arms wrapped around them. Her hair is a wild dark mass beneath which her whiskey eyes track me.

I pour a generous portion of vodka into the glass and hand it to her.

She takes it without being urged to. She drinks a small sip first, then downs the rest of the glass.

"I can honestly say I've never had a woman need to be drunk to fuck me," I say. I'm serious but I also need to diffuse this. Get her out of her head and whatever's going on in there.

"I just don't like being tied up." She holds out her glass for more.

I pour more vodka into it.

She shifts her gaze away like she can't look at me and drinks the whole of the glass.

I put the bottle down.

"More," she says.

"No more," I tell her, taking the glass.

She sets her arms stiffly at her sides.

"I want to look at you," I say.

She stares back at me.

"Just look."

She nods.

"Get on your elbows and knees."

I watch her take in the instruction, pour myself a vodka in her glass while she does, slowly, turning over, climbing up onto her elbows and knees.

"Knees wider. Good. Like that."

She follows my instruction, burying her face between her forearms, her hair hiding her from me.

I take the glass, swallow the contents of it, pour another and walk around the bed. My dick hardens as I take her in, her smooth olive skin, the heavy breasts hanging down, almost too heavy for the rest of her, begging to be cupped and squeezed.

Her shapely thighs and her ass.

Fuck.

Her ass. Her cheeks are parted just enough to display her pink and glistening pussy and as I look at it, a smear of arousal slides down her inner thigh.

I want to lick it off her. Bury my face in her ass and devour her.

Swallowing the contents of the vodka, I set my knee on

the bed.

She shifts a little, tensing.

"You're fine. I'm not going to fuck you." Fuck. Did I just say that? "I just want to see, Melissa. Taste."

I widen her knees with my own, and settle between her, set my hands on her ass, open her wider.

She makes a sound. A whimper.

I dip my face down, kiss her lower back, her ass cheek. I smell her arousal and fuck, I want to bury myself inside her. But instead, I lick her again, lick that smear of arousal from her inner thigh, hear her gasp when I do.

I slide my tongue along the length of her pussy and circle her asshole. I do it again and again until she's panting and I'm going to fucking blow in my pants when I hear her come again, that sound she makes a fucking aphrodisiac.

The smell of her, the taste of her, the sight of her, all of it, it makes me fucking crazy, and it takes all I have not to sink my cock into her. Not to hold her down and spread her open and drive into her.

It takes everything for me to get up off the bed and walk out of the bedroom.

I slam the door harder than I intend to and walk with a fucking steel rod between my legs into the living room to pour myself three fingers of whiskey. I drink it in one gulp before pouring another.

I go to the wall of windows, look out onto the strip and sip my drink.

I don't know what the fuck just happened in there. Between me buying her *to fuck her*, I might remind myself, and this, me here with fucking blue balls.

The bedroom door opens, and I turn to watch her walk into the living room. She's barefoot and wearing the shirt I just took off. It's huge on her. It falls almost to her knees and she keeps having to tug it up when it slips off her shoulder.

When she sees me, she stops, hugs her arms to herself.

"I don't know what to do," she says, any attitude from the start of this night gone, her voice small and unsure.

I know she's not playing or acting. It pisses me off a little because those things I can deal with. Those things are what I know.

This...her...it's foreign.

"Go to bed." I turn away.

"You didn't—"

"Go to bed, Melissa," I repeat.

"But you...the debt—"

I turn to her and when I take a step toward her, she takes one back. It makes me stop.

"Contrary to what you may think, rape doesn't get me off. Now go to bed."

4

MELISSA

I walk back into the bedroom and close the door.

I look around, take in the sophistication of the place and for all its beauty, it's sterile. Cold. Too clean and impersonal. Only the rumpled sheets and the smell of sex make it less clinical.

I walk into the bathroom, glancing at the lights of the strip as I go. The bathroom is big and it's the only room without windows for walls. I lock the door behind me although I don't think I need to. He won't come in.

It smells like his aftershave and I wonder if he ever has women here because everything is so masculine.

Switching on the shower, I step beneath the flow. Even his soap, when I lather it, smells like him. Like he's in here with me.

"You're safe."

For some reason, being here, in his shower, in his room, in his bed, I *feel* safe. Which just goes to tell you how screwy my radar is.

It's not that he's not dangerous. He is. But not to me. At least not right now.

Tonight, I don't have to double-check the locks. Test every window.

Liza's in town and she's hurt. I wonder how long she's been here. If she came looking for me. Why would she seek me out now?

But Liza isn't the problem. She's not the one who scares me.

I turn up the hot water. It's almost too hot, but I stand under it and close my eyes.

I'm tired.

When the steam is too thick to see through, I switch off the water and grab one of the towels on the rack. I wrap it around myself and take a second to make a turban for my hair.

I wipe steam from the mirror and look at myself. All I think when I do this is it's not me. It's like this woman, she's a stranger. Like I'm still that kid inside looking out of her eyes.

That's the only part I recognize of myself. My eyes. I peer into the mirror and there I am, same as always.

If I look closely, I see the fear.

I wonder if others see it too. I doubt it though. Most people never really look close enough to see much of anything that's real. That may make them uncomfortable.

I wipe the back of my hand across my nose and turn away, pull the towel from my hair wishing I had a hair tie, and walk into the bedroom to pick up his shirt. I slide it on.

It, too, smells like him. I don't mind it. Besides, I don't have anything else to put on.

I get into the bed and switch off the light because I don't know what else to do. I'm wide awake and turn onto my side, looking out at the city below through the smoky glass.

It's been a long while since I've had sex. This was the

first time in almost seven years, in fact. I didn't have any idea how I'd react to it, to someone touching me. I never thought I would let it happen again.

But what happened, I wouldn't have guessed it'd be like that. I expected to disappear. Just vanish.

Maybe it's because of what he said. That I was safe.

I guess I'm lucky that it was with him. Another man may have forced me. Held me down and did what he wanted to do.

Who am I kidding? Every other man would have done that.

"Rape doesn't get me off."

Then he's in the minority.

This loan shark, criminal, auctioneer of women, the one I would have expected to be a rapist, he's the opposite.

And then there's the fact that I came.

He made me come.

I haven't come with a man ever. Not once.

But what does the fact that he didn't exactly get what he paid for mean for Liza? Is our deal off?

That's what I'm thinking about when the bedroom door opens a little while later. I stiffen, close my eyes and hope he thinks I'm asleep.

He goes into the bathroom and I hear the shower go on. Ten minutes later, he's back in the bedroom and I'm glad my back is to him when I feel the blanket lifted and the bed depresses beneath his weight.

When he drapes his arm over me, my eyelids fly open.

"Relax," he whispers, like he can feel me tense up. I assume he can because he tucks my body into his, my back against his front. He's warm and his arm is heavy over me, but I don't mind it.

"Hawk—"

"Sleep."

"But—"

"Do as I say and sleep, Melissa. This is hard enough."

5

HAWK

She's asleep when I wake in the early morning.

It took her a long while to fall asleep but when she did, she slept heavy, not moving once as I held her. Her hair is still a little damp and I smell myself on her. My shampoo, the cologne still lingering on my T-shirt that she's wearing.

Even after my shower and while I dress, she remains a still form beneath the covers of the bed.

I leave instructions for her by the coffee machine. When she's ready, one of my men will drive her home. If she wants breakfast, she can go downstairs to the restaurant. They'll know to look after her.

On the elevator, I type a text to my attorney.

Find out what you can about the Boyd family, Senator Sean Boyd of Maine. I'm interested in the years Melissa Doe was fostered there. She was eleven years old so I'd guess twelve or thirteen years ago. Goes by alias Melissa Chase now. Photo to follow.

I send both the text and a photo of her fake driver's license and it seems as soon as I hit send, my phone rings. It's Axel.

"It's early," I answer. I've got a headache and jerking off in the shower didn't satisfy me nearly as much as sinking my cock into her tight pussy would have.

"We've got a problem."

"Where are you?"

"In the lobby."

"Be right there."

The elevator doors open and I spot him. "What is it?" I ask as we walk toward the exit. Axel isn't exactly a morning person and for him to be here like this, it's bad.

"Marcus. The girl, Calla. She's underage."

"Fuck. How underage?"

"Fifteen."

Fuck. Fuck. Fuck.

"How bad are we talking?" I ask, berating myself mentally for not insisting on seeing the paperwork myself. For not talking to the girl myself.

"We got lucky. Twice. She freaked out about having her ass fucked and blurted out the truth before it happened. And Ronny's the one who bought her. He doesn't need any trouble."

Ronny's on parole at the moment. If he gets caught with a minor, he's fucked.

"Fifteen, huh?" I thought she looked young but not that young.

"She's a friend of Marcus' daughter. Fucking sick prick. Marcus promised her a grand."

A single fucking grand while he kept about fifty times as much after paying off his debt to me.

"Where's the girl now?"

"Home."

"She okay?"

"Yeah. I mean, the auction may have been out of her league but this girl wasn't exactly inexperienced."

"Still, underage is underage. And at fifteen, she's a child." We climb into the back of the waiting sedan. "Where's Marcus?"

"At his house. I've got men there."

"Let's go."

"I can handle it," Axel says. "Just needed your go-ahead."

"I want to see his face."

When we pull up the driveway of Marcus' house, I see two of my men stationed at the door.

Axel and I step out. I take in the view, the wide expanse of land so opposite where I came from. I wonder if one day, I will call this place home. Although a part of me knows if it hasn't happened yet, it's probably not in the cards.

We walk up toward the pretentious entrance.

"Gentlemen," I greet the men when we reach the door and one of them opens it.

Axel and I step inside, and I pause to take in the house. It's been a while since I've been here. He seems to have done well for himself. With my money.

"Hawk."

I turn to find Marcus rising from the chair in which he was seated in the large, open kitchen. One of the men behind him puts a hand on his shoulder and encourages him to sit back down.

"Anyone else in the house?" I ask Axel.

"Cleared."

"It's not what you think. I really didn't know," Marcus whines.

I enter the kitchen, good choice of location. Tile floors are easier to clean than carpet.

Taking a chair from the table, I set it across from him

backwards and straddle it, resting my arms on the back. “Don’t talk to me like I’m fucking stupid, Marcus.”

“She wanted it. Was excited for it. You know how girls are. Little sluts.”

“Is your daughter a slut too? They’re friends, right? Would you put your daughter on the auction block?”

“What? No. That’s different. Calla’s different.”

“She’s fifteen. A child.”

“Not a child, trust me.”

The way he says it turns my stomach a little. “Yeah, still a child. We’re low on options and I have somewhere I need to be so we’re going to do this quick.”

His face pales a little. “Hawk, come on. You know me. I’ll get you another girl. You know I’m good for it.”

“Yeah, no thanks. So now I’m not only out my money but there’s the cost to my reputation. And you know how I feel about being fucking lied to. I’m going to give you a choice, Marcus, because we’re old friends.” I look around me. “House is nice, not my style but not bad. You can probably get half a million for it. I’d take it but then where are your wife and kid going to live?”

“You have a soft heart, Hawk,” Axel deadpans.

“Shut up, asshole,” I tell him.

He chuckles.

“Hawk, just give me—” Marcus starts.

“The matter of my reputation, that’s a whole other can of worms. Money can’t fix that, so you have a decision to make. Knee caps, both, or I’ll take your right hand.”

“No, please, Hawk, please, you can’t mean that. You know I’ve been loyal to you. I’ll do anything for you. I just fucked up. I fucked up big, I get that, but please. Please.”

“Crying is for girls, Marcus. Little girls like the child, Calla, who you stripped naked and sold in my fucking club!”

"I'm sorry! I'm sorry!"

I hear Axel snort behind me and check my watch. I'm hungry and I've got a lot to do today.

My phone vibrates with a message. I reach for it, swipe the screen to read the text.

Come by this evening and I'll have something for you.

It's Jack, my attorney. When I need shit like this, Jack takes care of it. When I need assholes like Marcus dealt with, it's Axel, unless I'm doing it myself.

"Where was I?" I ask, putting my phone away.

"You were giving him a choice," Axel reminds me.

"That's right. It was between knee caps or his right hand. Now, if it were me, well, fucking having my knee caps blown out, not sure I'd go for that. I hear it hurts like a mother fucker. But to lose my right hand. I mean, left, I could probably deal with that, but right?"

"Please, just give me one more chance. I'll have a girl for you tonight. Two. Ten!"

I get up, put the chair back at the table.

"Take care of this, Axel. Let me know what he decides. And hell, if he can't decide, just do it all."

"No!" Marcus is whimpering behind me.

I take two steps then turn back to look at him, shake my head and leave.

I don't mind making an example of an asshole like him. And examples do need to be made. One or two every year.

It's when you go soft that they fuck you. Swarm in like vultures with their hunger. Their greed. Always grasping at things they have no right to.

After a day full of visits similar to this one, I head to

Jack's office. It's early evening, the sun setting on the horizon. It's my favorite time of day.

I try to watch it alone when I can. There's a stillness that belongs only to the sunset and the sunrise. It's almost peaceful, even inside my head.

But tonight, my head's full.

I've known Jack for over a decade. Met him when I started to work for Lanigan.

Murray Lanigan was about eighty when I met him in an alley where two idiots were trying to rob him. I say idiots because the fools didn't realize who they were fucking with.

I knew. I knew from the minute I set foot on the strip.

What the old man thought he was doing without his bodyguard I have no idea. To this day, I'm certain he suffered from some sort of dementia.

The casino I own used to be his, but by the time I started working for him, he was old news. A legend, but old news.

I beat up the two-bit thugs trying to rob him, and he hired me on the spot. I still think it's because he mistook me for one of his sons, long dead by the time I came on the scene. It was partly my accent, heavier then since I'd just gotten into the country about a month earlier.

During one of his rare lucid moments, he changed his will, leaving the casino, hotel and the building itself to me. His children were pissed, but fuck them. I was the one who was with the old man the last years of his life. I was there when he was sick. When he was scared. I held his hand when he died.

And in some ways, he was like a father to me.

They contested the will, of course, but by that time I was eighteen, legally an adult, and thanks to him, a citizen of this country.

The will was iron-clad. They couldn't touch me.

It's because of me the casino's standing and profitable today at a level it never was when he was alive. At his request, I honor my promise to make sure his family is taken care of. Even the vultures.

Jack was Lanigan's attorney and I guess I inherited him, too.

His office is off the strip and by the time I arrive, he's waiting on me.

"Hawk, it's good to see you," Jack says, shaking my hand.

"Good to see you, Jack. I hope I'm not too late." I take a seat in his office and he tells the secretary to bring whiskey.

"No, you're right on time. And I've got some information for you." He takes his seat behind his desk and opens a file on his computer.

After the secretary brings the whiskey, she leaves and he begins.

"You know the Boyd family, I take it?" he asks as he pours and hands me my glass.

"Sean Boyd Sr. was a senator on the east coast. Maine. Lived in D.C. for a time. Had a wife and son. Had fostered another girl for a year before taking Melissa Doe in when she was eleven."

That's as far as I got but I want more.

He knows me well enough not to ask why I'm interested.

"Wife died a few years ago. Cancer," he says. "The senator just recently passed away of a heart attack. He was involved in multiple scandals throughout his political career but nothing seemed to stick. The son, Sean, is twenty-six, and Liza, the other girl they fostered was actually adopted by them."

"Where's the son?"

"Maine. He's following in his father's footsteps."

"Another dirty politician?"

Jack smiles. "Something like that. The girl, Liza Boyd, is in town. Has been for a few months. You may know her current whereabouts better than I."

I nod once.

He mimics my motion and goes on, not mentioning Liza's current state.

"Now the girl they fostered but didn't adopt, her name was Melissa Doe. Chase is new."

"Where does the Doe come from?"

"She was a Jane Doe—found when she was about a year old. Left in a public restroom, poor kid."

He hands me two print outs of a too-skinny baby. I know it's her the minute I see her face. It's the eyes. Almond-shaped, and whiskey-colored and already scared.

I feel my chest tighten.

"She was filthy and starved. Had a gold bracelet with the name Melissa on it wrapped around her wrist."

I remember the only piece of jewelry she wore last night was a thin gold bracelet. At least she had it on when she was first brought to me. They would have stripped her of everything before the auction. No personal effects.

"She kept Doe as her name."

"Did she legally change it to Chase at some point?"

"Not legally, no. Not as far as anything I found. And she's been off the grid for seven years. No social media accounts. No publicly listed number. Nothing. There was some talk about an accusation she made against the senator and his son some years back. Went to the police to report abuse."

"What kind of abuse?"

Jack looks through something on his computer, shakes his head. "There's no file. Just says it was disproved. This I'm getting from a gossip magazine. No police report to prove she ever even went to them. If there was ever a file, it's gone now. And then the girl disappeared. I'm guessing after what she did, she'd probably overstayed her welcome at the senator's house.

"Now as far as the name Melissa *Chase* goes..." he trails off, he turns his monitor around. "Three living in the state of Nevada, none in Las Vegas. A Melissa Chase did pass away some years ago. It's probably where the driver's license she's using comes from."

"Huh." I study the screen. *What are you hiding from, Melissa Doe?*

Doe.

Like she doesn't exist.

"All right. Thank you, Jack." I stand. "Let me know if you find out anything else. Dig for that police report. And find more gossip if you can."

He stands too, extends his hand to shake mine. "I will. You take care now."

6

MELISSA

I blink my eyes open and wait for the room to come into focus. It's silent, a quiet I'm not used to, and bright with morning light.

And the instant I remember where I am, my heart rate picks up.

I roll onto my back, glance at the empty space beside me. I tug the comforter up, appreciating its weight. I wouldn't use one so thick at home. It's too hot in the summer, but it's cool in the penthouse. Hawk's got better air-conditioning.

The pillow still has its indent from where he slept, and I remember the feeling of his arms around me, his body like a solid wall at my back.

I sit up to take in the room. The bathroom door is ajar, the light out. He's not here. I know. Not in the bedroom and not in the apartment.

I get out of the bed. I'm still wearing his shirt and I catch the hint of aftershave clinging to it.

Barefoot, I pad across the hardwood floor and open the door to step into the hallway, putting a hand to my hair to tamp it down. It seems to grow to three times its size when I sleep.

My purse is on the couch. My clothes hung up neatly in a dry-cleaning bag on the back of a closet door.

I open my purse, take out my wallet and from the zippered coin pocket, find my bracelet. I didn't want to take it off last night, but I'd had to. Their stupid rules.

A quick peek tells me the twenty-dollar bill I had in there is still there. Although I suppose to people in this world, twenty dollars is like a nickel. No, a penny. Not even.

Holding my wrist against myself, I close the clasp and touch the gold plate. Melissa. And a date beside it which I've always assumed was my birthday. That's all I have of my life before I became a ward of the state.

I remember nothing about my mother or father. Not a single thing. But I was only a year old when I was found abandoned in a public restroom. I guess it's normal for kids not to have memories from that age anyway. I don't know. The kids I grew up with, the ones in the system, they didn't.

But maybe that's just us.

I was adopted before I turned two. Young kids are. Babies mostly, but toddlers too. And I lived with my adopted parents until I was seven when they died in a car crash. I then went back into the system.

Seven is older. You're not as cute anymore. Not so much an empty slate for a family to stamp their expectations on you. To make you match them.

From then on, I bounced around from house to house until the Boyd family took me in.

They were the last family I lived with.

I give a shake of my head and walk to the kitchen counter where a mug has been set out and a piece of paper is standing up against it.

Help yourself to coffee. If you want breakfast, call down for it.
One of my men will drive you home when you're ready.
Hawk

I read the note again. His handwriting is different than I think it should be. More old-fashioned. Maybe European, I guess.

I take the mug and walk to the high-tech coffee machine. I set it down beneath the nozzle and read the various options, then push the button to make a cappuccino. A moment later, it whirs to life, grinding coffee beans and steaming milk from somewhere I can't see.

When it's ready, I take the steaming coffee and walk to the wall of windows to look out over the strip which is already busy in the morning.

I'm more of a tea person, but I do drink a cup of coffee in the morning, and this is good. Better than my drip coffee at home.

After finishing the coffee, I return to the kitchen to wash my cup, then open the refrigerator, which is clean and organized, like the rest of the place. Although all that's in it is a carton of milk, two bottles of champagne, and some fruit in the drawer.

Opening it, I take an apple and bite into it. Crisp and cold and fresh.

I look around, peering up in the corners, wondering suddenly if he has cameras in here. Why did he leave me alone? Isn't he afraid I'll snoop or steal something? Although I guess he knows where I live. He has my driver's license, after all.

And he knew right away that it was a fake. But I guess a man in his line of work would know those things.

I pick up the hanger with my clothes and notice there's

even one with my cleaned underthings neatly pinned to it—do they dry-clean underwear?

On my way back to his bedroom, I try the doors, finding only empty bedrooms and one locked door. Probably a study.

After finishing my apple, I have a shower and get dressed. I smooth out the bed and take one last look at it before turning away, putting on my shoes and collecting my tote, to call the elevator.

I notice the key card in the slot and assume you need a key to unlock it. It arrives momentarily and when the doors open, I step inside and push the L for lobby.

As they slide shut, I feel a strange sense of loss. Last night wasn't what I expected. He wasn't what I expected. Not the kind of man I thought he would be at all.

And it didn't end the way it began.

Although what will this mean for Liza? A quarter-of-a-million-dollars is a lot of money to pay for a woman to scratch at you and turn into a whimpering mess when you try to get what you paid for.

I shake my head, turn to watch the city as the elevator descends. More glass. I wonder if he ever feels like he's living in a fish tank, exposed and vulnerable.

No, of course not.

There's nothing vulnerable about the man I met last night.

Digging into my tote, I find my phone and check the time. Almost ten in the morning.

The elevator doors open and I hear the sound of the casino, already alive with gamblers at the slot machines, a lot of whom have probably been here all night.

It's too much, after all that silence of upstairs. A rude re-entry into the real world.

That sense of loss is back again as I take a step forward, but then a man steps toward me.

"Miss, your car is ready."

"My car?" I remember how rudely I was brought here.

"Hawk—"

That's right. Hawk.

I shake my head. "No, thank you." Best to get back into my world as soon as possible. "I'm fine. I don't need a ride."

"But I was told—"

"I'm fine," I repeat and walk out of the casino and into the summer heat. I walk down the street for a moment feeling like people I pass know what I did last night. My walk of shame.

Around the corner, I have to sprint to make the bus. I only look back once at the building as we pull away from the stop. Only crane my neck to look at the penthouse level for a moment before I dig out my phone and call the shop. I leave a message for Deirdre to let her know that I'll be late today. I don't tell her why. I then read the text from Jim, my mechanic, telling me my car is ready.

At least that's one thing going my way.

From the bus stop, I walk three blocks to the garage and when I get there, I see the old model VW Golf in the lot. I walk into the office, glancing at the lone car in the shade of the garage.

Jim is inside on a call and nods in greeting when I enter. It takes him a few minutes to wrap up the call before he looks up at me.

"Out-of-towners," he says, shaking his head. "They expect everything for free these days." He looks down over his reading glasses at the ancient computer screen and pushes a button. The old printer starts chugging. "And you, miss, you can't keep driving that thing like you are," he says to me, setting a printout on the counter. "Duct tape cannot hold a car together."

I've been known to do my own repairs now and again, but this car just needs to get me from point A to point B. House to shop and back. I can't afford expensive repairs.

"It's fine for now, Jim. What's the damage?"

He hands the printout to me and explains what he did, which I don't follow, but I trust Jim. I bought the car from him years ago and I've been coming to him for repairs since.

"Okay," I say, digging my credit card out of my wallet and handing it over to him. "Here you go."

Eight-hundred dollars is still more than I want to spend, but I have no choice. Besides, any other garage would charge me double that.

When he runs it through the little machine, I keep my fingers crossed it'll go through.

I think about last night again. At the sound of Hawk's voice calling out the quarter-of-a-million-dollars like it's nothing. Spare change.

Jim puts the receipt in front of me. I sign it, then take my keys but before I go, and for reasons I don't quite understand myself, I lean over the counter and hug him.

He's obviously caught off guard, but he pats my back.

"Thanks for everything, Jim. I really appreciate it."

"Anytime, kiddo," he says, his old eyes worried when I give him a sad smile.

No, I do know why I do it. I've tried not to think of Liza for years. Anytime guilt crept in, I pushed it away, going back to what happened. To the fact that she lied.

We were in this together. We had a plan. But she betrayed me and when I got the chance to run, I took it.

But leaving her there, that was my betrayal of her, wasn't it? And a more dangerous one?

I drop my tote in the passenger seat and start the car. The reality of Liza being here and what that could mean settles like a brick in my belly.

I need to go to the hospital. I need to see Liza, make sure she's okay. Make sure she hasn't told Sean I'm here. But first I need to go home and change my clothes.

Once I arrive at the little yellow house, I go up to my room and put on a pair of jeans and a T-shirt. Then, before I leave the bedroom, I think of something.

What if she's called Sean? Or if she was unconscious, maybe the hospital staff would have found her identification and contacted next of kin. They did adopt her once I was out of the picture and it makes sense that they'd call him if she was unable to.

Would she tell him about me being here? I want to believe she wouldn't.

Just in case, I take a duffel bag out of the closet and throw some clothes in.

From the bathroom, I gather my toothbrush and few toiletries, putting them in too. It's just a precaution, I tell myself. I don't want to leave. It's just in case I have to.

Things are different now, though. With the shop and so many people depending on me.

And maybe I'm overreacting.

Liza's not my enemy. She'd know not to let Sean know where I am. And besides, she didn't know exactly where to find me. If she had known, I'm sure she'd have come to the house or the shop by now.

Leaving the half-packed duffel, I get back into my car outside to head to the hospital, my anxiety growing as I do. I'm not sure what I'm going to do. I have no plan.

Once I arrive, I park my car and head inside. I walk up to

the reception desk and think maybe I should have called instead of showing up here.

"Can I help you?" the middle-aged woman behind reception asks.

Too late now. "I'm looking for Liza Boyd's room?"

She looks down at her computer screen, punches some keys. "You just missed her," she says, looking up at me. "Discharged. She's being moved to a private facility."

"Oh. You said I *just* missed her?"

"Yes. Her brother signed her out not half an hour ago and the private—"

"Her brother?" I feel my face drain of color. Feel the weight of cement in the pit of my stomach.

The woman's smile fades. "Are you all right, hun?"

"You said her brother?"

She looks at her screen again. Nods. "Sean Boyd. I recognize him from TV. Nice guy."

No.

No, there's nothing nice about that guy.

I turn in a circle, look around the lobby half expecting him to be here lurking in a corner.

"Miss, are you all right?"

I force my legs to move. Force my knees not to buckle. To hold me upright just a little while longer. Just until I get to my car.

Then I can panic.

There I can collapse.

I'm in a daze as I make my way through the parking lot. Twice cars have to screech their brakes to stop before hitting me.

The button entry doesn't work on the old Golf anymore and it takes me three tries to get the key into the lock. Three tries before I'm in my car and my hands are on the steering wheel. The lingering garage smell fills my nose. Gasoline and sweat. I should roll down my window.

I force the key into the ignition and start the car, taking a deep breath in before backing out of my spot and getting on the road.

This doesn't mean he knows about me. Sean being here, it's not about me. She is his sister. And if she's involved with people who beat her up, if she's involved with men like Hawk, I can't imagine that's good for Sean. His political ambitions rival his father's.

Him being here is about that. It's not about me. This is just damage control.

It's only when I'm driving away that I think I should have asked which facility Liza was transferred to. I can call and ask, although I doubt they'll give me that information.

The car behind mine honks their horn and I look up to find the light is green. I drive through the intersection.

It's fine. I'm fine.

And I need to get to the shop. Deirdre has to leave by one. She babysits her granddaughter almost every afternoon until her daughter, who's a single mom, gets home.

It's one of those drives that you have no idea how you got to where you were going but about half an hour later, I'm parked down the street from the shop. I look around when I climb out.

Wrinkles in Time is a second-hand clothing store several blocks off the strip. I inherited it when the owner, Marjorie Adams, an old woman I met when I first moved here, passed away after a long illness.

She asked me to keep it going, explaining it was important work. I had no idea she owned the shop outright or that she gave fifty-percent of any earnings to the homeless shelter. I knew she donated some of it, but I didn't realize it was half.

I also learned that the other half went to pay me.

Mrs. Adams owned the building, which passed on to her children upon her death, and they were bound by her will to only charge me minimal rent as long as I kept the shop up. I've done exactly that for two years.

The bell rings over the door when I enter, and Deirdre is standing behind the counter reading a tattered book. I recognize the title. A dark romance. I think she's read it about eight times.

"There you are," she exclaims, checking her watch. "They called from the school and the little munchkin has pinkeye. Can you believe it? Poor kid."

"Oh, no, that's lousy. I'd have gotten here sooner if I'd known. I'm sorry."

"It's all right. Pinkeye isn't the end of the world, but I may not be able to come in tomorrow at all if I have to keep her at home."

"That's okay. Just let me know."

She nods as she collects her purse. "I'll call you later."

"Thanks."

"Oh, sold that fancy jacket this morning," she says on her way out.

"That's great." It was an old and rare designer item I had in the window.

"Fifty bucks."

I smile, nodding as I look out onto the street through the glass storefront windows only half hearing what she's saying as she hurries outside.

Before I can lock the door and turn the sign around, two women walk in. I head behind the counter after greeting them. I pick up the phone, then put it back down again.

I need to think this through. I need to go see Liza to find out what happened, and make sure she's okay.

I've reached out to her before, a little while after she'd left the Boyd house. I'd wanted to check in on her. Make sure she was okay.

That had been a mistake, though. And the other times she contacted me, she was looking for money. More than once, I gave her all I'd managed to save up. I suspected it wasn't to pay the rent like she claimed but I couldn't say no. And each time, I'd felt a vague threat when she'd mention Sean.

I changed my number after that last time.

But there's a part of me that can't just ignore the fact that she's in a hospital after being beaten. No matter what, she and I were close once. What happened to us, it did this to her. It made her the addict Hawk claims she is.

I got lucky—if you can call it that. She didn't. And I will always know this.

It's a risk though. I've managed to stay hidden for years. I know what will happen if Sean finds me. I know what he'll do.

I busy myself tagging new items, the day passing in a blur, my thoughts a whirl with everything.

In my mind, I'm weighing options. If I leave here, I'll need to get a new car. One that won't break down on the side of the road. The Golf is fine for short trips in town where Jim is available if I run into trouble. It won't make a long-distance trip.

But what will happen to the shop?

Deirdre could take it over. She'd like that, I think. Right? But there's her granddaughter to consider. This is just a part-time job for her.

And I don't want to leave. I don't want to start again.

I don't want to be afraid.

I go back and forth all afternoon, deciding and changing my mind about everything again and again. All the while, thoughts of Hawk last night, of how he was, how gentle he became. How almost careful with me.

But I will never see him again. Best to get him out of my mind. He's not my prince charming and there won't be a fairy-tale ending. Not for me.

As much as I want to close up shop, it's Saturday, my busiest day, and I need the money. By the time I leave, it's half-past nine.

I drive home remembering how the last time I'd walked into my house, Hawk's men had been there waiting for me. That was just last night. It seems like so much has happened since.

I think about Hawk and I wonder if I could go to him. If Sean were here, could I go to him and ask for help?

But that's ridiculous. He's a criminal. A loan shark. That's the reason I was in that situation at all. What happened after the auction, well, I should just keep my head down before he decides he'd like his money's worth after all.

Besides, for a man like him, that sort of transaction we had, it's business. I wonder if he has someone else paying off their debt tonight.

The thought makes me feel a little sick and I distract myself by switching radio stations.

I pull onto my street and do a quick scan. Nothing looks out of the ordinary.

At least not until I get near enough to my house to see the black sedan parked high on my driveway.

My heart skips a beat and my hands grow sweaty on the steering wheel.

It's the same car as the other night. I think. Although it's not like I saw the license plate. But I do recognize the man smoking his cigarette out on my porch.

I park my car on the street and take a breath that should be calming but my heart is still thundering against my chest as I step out.

The man takes a deep drag as he watches me walk up the cracked walkway to the front steps. My heels click as I go and although it's not a quiet neighborhood, the sound seems too loud tonight.

When I climb the stairs, he nods, reaches to open my front door for me.

The lights are on and I step into the living room. I can see the small kitchen and find another man looking in my refrigerator. He'll be disappointed, I think.

The door closes behind me just as I hear Hawk's voice.

"Mother fucker," he says. "Just make sure the family's taken care of."

He ducks his head as he descends the stairs and when his strange eyes meet mine it feels like a thousand butterflies take flight in my stomach.

"I'll talk to you later," he says, eyes on me as he disconnects the call and tucks his phone into the pocket of his suit jacket.

The house looks tiny with him in it. Not to mention old and dusty.

"How did you get in here?" I ask, taking a step back when he comes to stand just a few feet from me.

He shrugs a shoulder. "That lock wasn't keeping anyone out."

I look at the door and remember I'd only used the lock on the doorknob the other night.

"Don't worry, I'll fix what I broke."

There's that accent again. And it's so subtle, I imagine most people don't notice it at all.

I turn back to find he's moved closer. His gaze roams over my face, travels down to my chest, then back up to my eyes.

"Get out," he says.

"What?" I ask.

But then his men leave. He was talking to them.

"Why did you refuse the ride this morning?"

I step backward to give myself space. Room to breathe. I turn my attention to putting my keys and tote down on the table by the door.

"I didn't need it."

"You took a bus."

When I turn, it's to find him in the same place still watching me. "What's wrong with the bus? Men like you don't ride it, I guess? Too good for public transportation?"

He chuckles, shifts his weight to one leg. "Men like me?"

I shrug a shoulder, hoping I look calmer than I feel because my heart is racing and in my mind are images of the way he looked last night. The way he looks under those clothes.

Images of the way he looked at me.

"I don't mind public transportation," I say, my voice coming out strange.

"No, please, explain the *men like you* part?" he says, stepping forward.

It takes all I have not to back up. "Don't you have a stable of women available to you at any moment of the day?"

He cocks his head to the side. "What does that have to do with public transportation?"

I flounder. Why did I even say that?

"Or are you jealous?" he asks.

"Jealous?"

"Of those women. My *stable*. Maybe you'd like to join—"

"No. I…of course not. Just forget it. What do you want? Why are you here?"

I swear he comes even closer if that's possible. "Take better care with your words, Melissa *Chase*."

I note the emphasis on my borrowed last name. I wonder what he knows and why he'd care to know anything at all.

"Where are you going?" He breaks away and I can breathe again.

"What?"

"Half-packed bag upstairs."

Shit. "You had no business going through my house."

"I wanted to see where you live. And by the way, you're messy."

"Why did you want to see where I live?"

He shrugs his shoulder now. "Curious." He looks at my wrist, at the bracelet there.

I cover it with my other hand.

"You didn't answer my question," he says.

"I was unpacking, actually," I lie.

He studies me like he doesn't quite believe me but then he drops it.

"Do you have whiskey?" he asks, turning to walk into the small living room. I'm pretty sure this entire house fits inside one room of his penthouse

I shake my head when he looks at me. "I have vodka."

"That'll do."

I exhale and walk into the kitchen to get the bottle of Absolut out of the freezer. I take out two water glasses, not wanting to feel embarrassed but feeling it anyway.

I don't have a lot of nice things. No crystal tumblers. My

furniture is second-hand. Most of my clothes too. I've never been embarrassed by it before.

"Ice?" I ask, not turning around.

"No. Dilutes it."

Of course, it does. He wouldn't want that.

I pour the vodka and go back into the living room. I hand him his and when his fingertips brush mine, it makes my breath catch. It's like electricity, that spark, and all I can think when I'm around him, when I smell his aftershave, is how he looked at me. How he touched me. Held me.

How he had his mouth on me.

I swallow my vodka in one go.

He chuckles. "Do I make you nervous?"

I try to chuckle too, but it just comes out weird. "Yeah, actually, you do." I don't lie. What's the point of lying to him about this?

He takes this in. Drinks a sip of his vodka.

He looks around again. "No photos, Melissa. Not anywhere in the house."

"I haven't had a chance to unpack them," I lie.

He turns back to me, swallows the rest of his drink. "You've lived here for years."

"What are you doing here?" I ask.

"Why did you lie to me just now?"

"Why do you care?"

"Like I said, I'm curious."

"Are you here because you changed your mind?"

"Changed my mind?"

"Last night. You didn't exactly get what you...paid for."

"No, I didn't. But that's on me. The debt's cleared."

I have trouble holding his gaze. "Thank you. I guess."

"You didn't expect that."

"I don't know what I expected. You're not really who I thought at all, to be honest."

He studies me. "Why are you like that?" he asks.

"Like what?"

"Twitchy. You were terrified when I touched you last night."

I turn my back, go to the kitchen and pour myself more vodka. I drink it before I answer. "I don't know you and I was naked in your bed."

I face him, lean my back against the counter, force a blank expression.

Evade.

I know how to do that.

He raises an eyebrow. He's waiting for more.

"And I'm not used to being naked in strangers' beds. Maybe the women *from your stable* are but not me. I think fear is pretty natural."

I don't know if he's offended by the insult. But I do know he doesn't deserve it.

He just stands there watching me, though, his expression closed off as he sips his drink. The way he looks at me, it's so focused, so intent, that I wonder if he can read my mind.

"I wasn't going to hurt you. You knew that."

"How would I know that? Because you said so? You're a loan shark. A man who'd had me stripped and put up on an auction block. You can understand—"

"I told you you were safe. I'm a man of my word. But fair enough."

Again, something I don't expect.

"I know most men in your situation wouldn't have handled last night the way you did and I'm grateful to you for that."

"Any man who gets off forcing a woman is an animal, Melissa."

Then even in my limited scope, animals are all I've known.

He walks into the kitchen, stands too close as he reaches over me to refill his glass. He remains there drinking, studying me.

He's so much taller than me and I have to crane my neck to look up at him, but holding his gaze is a struggle so I look at his chest instead and think how much stronger than me he is. How power seems to throb around him.

I wonder what it's like to be so powerful. So unafraid.

But it's taking all I have to remember that he's a very dangerous man. That any attraction I feel I need to quash.

"What are you really doing here?" I finally ask, the words somehow coming out sounding normal.

His sips his vodka and I don't know if he's comfortable with this strange, heavy silence but my ears are drumming with the adrenaline pumping through my veins and I need for him not to be here.

He makes me feel strange. Like he takes up the whole world when he's in the room. Being this close to him is hard, harder than I like to admit. Everything about him from the way he looks to the way he speaks to the way he smells makes me want.

He takes his time to answer me, as if he's collecting his thoughts. When he gets a strange glint in his eye, I know what he's going to say next will change everything.

"I have a proposition for you, Melissa."

I feel like my heart is going to beat its way out of my chest. "What sort of proposition, Hawk?"

"I want one month."

7

HAWK

"What?"

She's staring up at me, eyes huge. There's something inside those yes. A child-like quality.

A child's hope.

A child's fear.

I wonder if it's me she's afraid of or something else. Because I got a call from Jack about an hour after leaving his office and I'm going to bet it's that something else. Especially considering the half-packed duffel upstairs because I know for a fact she wasn't unpacking.

"One month. With me. Like last night."

"I don't understand."

"One million dollars."

Her mouth falls open.

I wait for her to process.

"One million...That's..." her voice trails off and she looks away like she's trying to count it.

She gives a shake of her head and scoots under my arm. She walks into the living room and sits down on the couch to swallow the rest of her vodka. She sets her glass on the coffee table before returning her gaze to mine and when she does, it's steelier than I expect.

"I am not a prostitute. What I did last night, I did because I had to. Because of Liza. This isn't something I just do."

"I didn't mean to infer it was," I say, going toward her. "I'm well aware of your...inexperience."

"Inexperience or not, money for sex, it's—"

"A business transaction. An equally beneficial transaction."

"Business," she snorts. "I don't even understand why you'd want this knowing full well...I mean...after what happened last night."

I move closer to her. She has to crane her neck to look up at me.

"You make me curious, Melissa. I haven't felt curious about a woman in...well, ever."

"Is it just that you're not used to a woman turning you down? Did I damage your ego last night?"

I smile, give her a wink. If this is how she wants to play it, I'll play.

"Maybe I just want to lick your pretty little pussy so I can hear you come again."

She slaps both hands against my chest. "Get out."

"So no, no damaged ego," I continue, ignoring her.

"I said get out."

I take her wrists, circle her arms down to her sides and keep her close. "No."

"This isn't your club. You're in my house. No auction blocks to humiliate me on!" She struggles to free herself, but I hold tight.

"No block. No auction. I don't intend on selling you."

"Do you even hear what you sound like?"

"I want what I want and what I want is you."

"And I bet you're used to getting everything you want exactly how you want it."

I move her arms behind her back and pull her close enough that our bodies are touching. Her pupils dilate and I wonder if it's fear or arousal. Probably a combination of both. Although the hardening of her nipples through the thin fabric of her T-shirt tells me it may be the latter.

I put my nose to her hair, inhale. She smells like me, like my shampoo. I like my smell on her.

"Don't be so quick to turn it down. Like I said, this will be beneficial to both of us and I don't just mean the financial benefit to you."

"What does that even mean?" She shakes her head. "No, it doesn't matter. I don't...This is crazy. Just...get out." She twists her wrists, but I transfer both into one of my hands and with the other, I tilt her face upward.

"I want you in my bed and I think you want to be there."

"Has this approach ever worked on any woman ever?"

"I've never tried it before."

Her eyes search mine.

"I'm not a whore." Her face crumples and I see tears well in those unbelievable eyes.

"You're the farthest thing from a whore, Melissa."

"I don't even know your last name."

"MacLeod."

"That's not...what I meant is—"

My phone vibrates with a message. Without releasing her, I reach into my pocket and take it out to read the text on the screen:

"One share left, then you'll have control."

I want to smile, but what I'm doing, it doesn't make me happy. It never has.

"What happened to dinner and a movie?" Melissa asks as I tuck my phone back into my pocket without replying.

"I don't do relationships," I say, hearing the coldness in my voice as I release her.

"I didn't mean to infer I wanted a date," she says, rubbing her wrists. The blush on her face tells me she's embarrassed.

"I just want to be clear. This will be a business transaction. That's all."

"I haven't even said yes."

"You also haven't said no and I'm a cup-half-full kind of guy. I'll be back for your answer tomorrow night, Melissa."

I walk to the door.

"You're assuming I'm going to agree to this insane proposal."

I just give her a wide, confident smile. "I know you are. These next twenty-four hours are a courtesy so you can wrap your brain around the fact that you will say yes."

Her mouth falls open but she has no reply.

"Pack essentials," I tell her. "You'll be staying at the penthouse."

"You're wrong. You don't know me."

"I'm rarely wrong about people." I open the door. "Good night, Melissa."

I walk outside, take three steps toward the waiting sedan before she calls my name. I stop, turn back to her.

She pivots, bites her lip and the look on her face tells me she's considering whether or not to speak.

"Liza," she finally says. "Do you know where they moved her?"

I'm surprised by her question and he fact that she can't hold eye contact tells me she's hiding something.

Or hiding *from* something.

I give her a long look. "Are you going to pay her a visit? I didn't think you two had contact anymore."

I remain silent, keep my gaze level.

She doesn't reply.

"Brewster Clinic. Sean Boyd took her this morning."

Panic flashes across her eyes, just momentarily, just long enough for me to catch it before she schools her features.

"Anything else?" I ask.

She shakes her head.

I give her one more long look before resuming my walk to the car, taking my phone out of my pocket to get the details on that text.

8

MELISSA

I watch him from behind the curtains of the window.

Is this even real? Did he just offer me a million dollars to sleep with him? To be his for one month?

No. This makes no sense. Not after last night.

I wonder if this is some sort of personal challenge. Maybe his ego can't take a woman not panting for him in his bed.

The sedan disappears and I flip the single lock that still works on the front door. I go upstairs and look at my room, at the half-packed duffel, the clothes strewn here and there.

He's right. I am messy. The opposite of him.

I pick up the clothes and hang them up or put them away in the dresser drawers, all the while my mind working.

Can I do it? Would I?

I want to tell myself I wouldn't say yes just for the money. Although that's a lot of money.

But there's something about Hawk MacLeod. A thing that makes me want to be near him.

Which is ridiculous because he is who he is.

Everything set aside, though, there is one thing that will take this decision out of my hands.

I go back downstairs and pickup my cell phone. I look up the Brewster Clinic and, taking a deep breath in, hit 'call'.

A woman answers on the second ring. "Brewster Clinic, how can I help you?"

"Hello, I'm calling for patient Liza Boyd."

"Who's calling?"

I assumed they'd just transfer me to her room, but this is a private clinic, I have to remember. "This is her sister," I lie, "Josie." I make up the name on the fly. "Can you transfer me to her room?"

"I'm afraid patients don't have telephones in their rooms, ma'am. Visiting hours are in the afternoon between two and four and then again in the evening between six and eight. You're welcome to come visit her then."

"How is she doing?"

"That's private information, ma'am."

"Do you know if she'll have other visitors tomorrow? So I can plan mine, I mean." I add on.

"Well, I know your brother said he'd be back tomorrow evening but I'm not sure of the exact time."

My throat tightens.

My brother.

No, not my brother.

Sean.

"Okay, thank you very much."

"Have a good evening."

We hang up and I wipe my sweaty palms on my jeans. I go upstairs to have a shower, knowing it will be a long night.

I GO TO WORK THE NEXT MORNING AND CLOSE UP SHOP IN THE afternoon when I leave for the clinic. I arrive a little before visiting hours commence. At two o'clock on the dot, I walk to the entrance where the glass doors slide quietly open and I enter what looks more like the lobby of an expensive hotel than a clinic.

Two women sit at the front desk taking calls. I walk up to them.

"I'm here to visit Liza Boyd," I say, trying to sound confident.

"If you'll sign that log there, she's in room 218."

That's easier than I think it should be, but I nod and enter the name Josie Boyd in illegible handwriting in the guest log. I also scan for Sean's name. I don't see it, but maybe he didn't have to register since he's the one who brought her in.

"Is Sean here?" I ask, taking a chance.

"No ma'am, not yet. We're not expecting him until later."

Relief. "Thank you." I take the stairs up rather than waiting for the elevator.

I'm anxious. What if they're wrong and Sean shows up early? I don't know what I'll do if I run into him. But we'll be in public. He can't hurt me if we're in public.

And if he does see me, I will go directly to the casino after leaving here and accept Hawk's offer. Sean will not be able to touch me there.

Liza's room is half-way down the hall on the second floor. When I get to it, I don't knock. Instead, I listen first, then push it open a little, as quietly as I can.

She's turned away looking out the window at the sunny day.

I push the door wider and step inside, clearing my throat.

She turns, and even with her face like it is, one of her eyes swollen and sealed shut, I see the surprise on her face.

"Missy!"

It's strange to hear her call me that. First time anyone has since I left the Boyd house. The name and the tone of her voice remind me she's a few years younger than me. Remind me that once upon a time, I took care of her.

I close the door behind me and go to her, take in the damage. One arm is cast, her face brutalized, and I'm sure there's more I can't see.

"Are you okay?" I ask her.

She smiles and I can see it's painful, but she tries to reach her arms out to me anyway. I lean down to hug her and feel her tears on the side of my face.

"You came."

"I didn't know you were in town," I say, pulling back. "Hawk—"

"I knew he'd find you if I told him."

"Why did you tell him about me? What are you doing with men like that anyway? And how did you find me?"

She stares up at me like she can't believe I'm standing there. "Do you remember Julia?"

I shake my head.

"From school. She was in my grade so maybe you didn't know her. She asked if you were out here. Said she thought she saw you."

I don't remember any Julia and am surprised someone remembered me at all.

"Who did this to you, Liza?" I ask, changing the subject.

Her smile vanishes. "Doesn't matter."

"Was it Hawk?" I hate asking it, but I have to. I hope she answers no and when she shakes her head, I'm relieved.

"I missed you, Missy. You just left."

I think back to the last time I saw Liza all those years ago.

"You know I can't take a chance on Sean finding me."

Liza's face hardens. "He found me."

"It's not you he'll hurt."

"He did hurt me. When you left me there."

Shame leaves me mute.

"But that's past," she says, although the tone of her voice tells me something else.

"Does he know why you're in town?" I ask.

"You mean does he know about you being here?" she asks, answering my question with her own.

I nod.

"I didn't tell him."

I listen to how she says it, how she doesn't quite look at me when she does.

"But does he know?"

She meets my eyes. "If I can just get a little money, I can get out of this place."

She wants money. That's all.

I feel the sudden shift, the coolness of her gaze, and wonder if she read the change in my expression.

"The sooner I'm away from Sean, the better. Now that you're here, I can stay with you," she says.

"No. I'm sorry. I'm leaving town for a while." I reach into my tote, take out the envelope with half of the money I had saved to donate to the shelter this month. I hold it out to her. "It's not much, but it'll help you when you're out." She reaches for it, but I pull it away. "You can't tell him about me, understand? He can't know I was here. He'll hurt me, Liza. Really hurt me. And you know it."

"He already hurt me, Melissa," she spits, using my full name. "When you left."

"I had no choice. He would have killed me after what I did."

"We were supposed to go together."

I lower my gaze. We had a plan, yes. We would go to the police. Tell them everything. But then she lied. Changed her story.

"I need to go." Because every minute I'm here, I'm in danger. I set the envelope of cash in the drawer of the nightstand by her bed.

"Can I call you at least?" she asks.

"That's not a good idea. I told you that the last time. I can't see you again, Liza. It's too dangerous."

I walk to the door.

"So that's it?"

I stop. "I'm sorry, I—"

"You just walk away? Again?"

I turn to face her. "Do you know Hawk's men came to my house?" I ask, remembering how scared I'd been. Letting myself get angry. "Do you know they were waiting there for me when I got home? Do you know what I did for you last night?"

This time, it's her to shift her one good eye away.

"I think we're even, Liza."

I walk out the door then, feelings of guilt and anger warring inside me. I believe her when she says he hurt her after I left, but the family adopted her months after I was gone. She's officially Sean's sister. And he won't hurt her now if only because it won't look good if he does. He's like his father, image is everything. I guess if you're a politician, it matters more than the truth.

I don't feel easy when I walk away and as if on cue, when I get into my car, my phone vibrates with a message. I take it out and see a text from an unknown number.

"I'm having a dress sent over. Car will pick you up for dinner. Hawk."

"How did you get this number?" I text back.

"He'll be at your house at seven." I'm not surprised he doesn't answer my question, am I?

The timing is serendipitous.

If I accept, I will be safe. Safe from Sean, at least. Maybe I'll be jumping out of the frying pan and into the fire, but the only thing I know for sure is Sean will come after me if —*when*—Liza tells him I'm here. Because she will tell him.

She may say she misses me, and maybe she even believes it, but I think she hates me. Hates me for leaving her behind even if she knows it was the only choice I had.

And now, I make another choice.

I type a text to Hawk: *"I have terms."*

9

HAWK

I see her before she sees me.

I'm in the restaurant at my usual table. Here on the floor above the casino, the constant ringing of slot machines is absent. Instead, a pianist plays softly in the background and given the prices of this particular establishment, it's only the cream of the crop who can afford it.

The hostess gestures to me and Melissa turns. She looks stunning in the long, tight-fitting black gown I sent for her to wear. A look through her closet yesterday told me she wouldn't have anything appropriate. The dress is slit almost all the way to her hip and the deep V between her breasts displays the curves of those heavy mounds.

Her hair is up but for one tendril that she tucks behind her ear. Although she's wearing more makeup than she was when my men picked her up the other night, it's still minimal compared to the women in here.

I don't miss the eyes that follow her as the hostess leads her to me.

I stand as she nears the table. I don't hear what the hostess says and I don't care about the people watching us. I walk around, pull out her chair and get a look at the expanse of skin the low cut back of the dress leaves exposed. Right down to the two dimples on her lower back that I plan on licking later.

"You're stunning," I tell her.

"I feel naked."

"I'm sure the men in here wish you were."

She sits down and I push her chair in, then resume my own seat.

"I have my own clothes, you know."

"You'll wear the clothes I choose for you," I say. "Term number 1."

"I thought terms were things people discussed, not something one dictated."

I signal for the waiter who walks over and pours her a glass of wine.

"Besides, I'm not used to this kind of dress," she says.

"Well get used to it. I take care of what's mine."

"I haven't agreed yet."

"Haven't you?"

She doesn't reply, just shifts her gaze away.

I smile because yes, she has agreed. Even if she doesn't realize it yet.

"Are you hungry?" I ask.

She nods, opens her menu. The waiter hovers nearby to take our order.

Melissa studies the menu for longer than I'd say is normal, closes it and looks up at me. She's not used to this either, I can see it in her flustered expression.

"I don't know what to order," she says.

"Then I'll get you my favorite. Two of the special," I tell the waiter.

"Yes, sir." He takes our menus.

She picks up her glass and looks around, drinks a sip then sets it down.

"Name your terms," I say.

"I will be free to work during the days. I have a shop."

"I know about the shop and that's fine. You'll be driven back and forth to work."

"I have my own car."

"That thing is a death trap."

"It's not a death trap."

"It's duct taped together."

"It runs fine."

"Is this worth a battle? Really? Like I said, I take care of what's mine, Melissa."

"You realize I'm a person, not a thing, right?"

"I never said you were a thing. You're very quick to attack."

"I told you last night that I won't be bullied."

"Did I bully you into putting on a beautiful dress? Did I bully you into having dinner with me? Am I not here listening to your terms?"

She exhales, shifts her gaze to her wine glass and picks it up to drink another sip.

"You won't put me on those blocks again."

"I wasn't going to. I already told you that. Next."

She looks around. "I wish we could discuss this somewhere private."

"It's none of anyone's business."

"If there's anything…I don't want to do…" she starts, lowering her voice. Her eyes dart around the room and I can see the effort it takes for her to meet my gaze again, to say the words. "If you force me—"

"Doesn't need to be said, Melissa." I choose my words

carefully, but I want to be clear. "You insult me by suggesting otherwise."

"That's not—"

"Besides, you already know that, or you wouldn't be here."

She studies me, and I see that child inside her eyes again, cautious and fearful.

"And since you bring it up, after dinner you have an appointment for a check-up."

"Check-up?"

I lean in close. "I need to be sure you're clean."

"I am."

"Regardless, you'll submit to the examination."

"I have a doctor."

"So do I. She'll be waiting for you in an hour. Non-negotiable."

"What about you?"

"I'm clean." I give her a wink.

"You're a jerk, you know that?"

"Yeah, I do."

"Are you going to be sleeping with anyone else during this time?" she asks.

"Anyone from my stable, you mean?"

"Your stable or anywhere else."

"I don't plan on it, no. Do I need to ask the same question to you? If there's a stable of men…"

"Don't make fun of me, Hawk. If we're having sex, I need to be sure."

"You can be sure. This is an exclusive arrangement."

"Have you done this before?"

"A contract like this?"

She nods.

"No, I've never had the need or desire to. You're the first."

"Like a test-run?"

I take a breath in. She's trying my patience and I understand why.

"You're free to say no, Melissa. Money hasn't yet been transferred. But if you agree, you own your part in this. You own the fact that I gave you a choice and that *you* chose. That *you* said yes."

She purses her lips in irritation. That's fine. I continue.

"I will know where you are at all times. If you want to go somewhere, that's fine, but I will know, and my driver will take you. If you need anything, you ask me, and I'll take care of it."

"I won't be a prisoner."

"I don't want a prisoner."

"Why do you need to know where I am all the time?"

"I don't need to. I just want to." I lean in toward her. I want to be sure she understands what I say next. "I won't put many restrictions on you. I'm a reasonable man. But if you say yes then we have an agreement, and these are my terms. Your acceptance means your compliance to said terms."

"Your rules you mean?"

"Whatever language you're comfortable with."

"I want to talk—"

"And know that there will be consequences if you break those rules."

"What does that mean?"

I relax back and give her a wide grin. "It means don't break them. Did you visit Liza today?"

"No personal questions. Like your 'no personal effects' rule during the auction."

"Touché."

The food comes then, filet mignon with roasted potatoes and asparagus. She puts her wine down and picks up her knife and fork. I'm surprised at the zeal with which she eats. She's half-way through her steak before I take my first bite.

When she notices me watching, she sets her utensils down and wipes her mouth.

"Have you eaten today?" I ask.

She shakes her head. "Just coffee this morning. I was busy."

"Another term then. You'll eat regular meals. I need you healthy. I don't want you passing out."

"I don't typically starve myself. I've just had a lot on my mind."

"Like Liza?"

"No personal questions. We just agreed."

"Testing."

"Don't test."

"Eat, Melissa."

She picks up her knife and fork and resumes eating. "Is Hawk your real name?"

She's breaking her own rule, but I answer with a nod. "Family name. Always the first-born son's name."

"Is that a Scottish tradition?"

"Not particularly. Just my family."

"Are they here too?"

I lean toward her and she meets my gaze. "No personal effects, remember?"

She shifts her gaze back to her meal, and we eat in silence. When we're finished, I pour the last of the wine into her glass and watch her sit back and drink.

"Why are you doing this?" she finally asks. "I'm pretty sure you can have any woman you want. Why me?"

I've been waiting for the question, asked it to myself more than once. But I don't have an answer.

"That's personal," I say, deflecting. "Would you like dessert?"

She studies me, shakes her head no and that lock of hair falls forward. I think how it would feel against my face, my chest, my cock. How her heavy breasts would feel hanging on me, all that hair tickling me as she takes me into her mouth.

"Are we agreed, then?" I ask. I want to get out of here.

She studies me, nods once.

"Good. I'll transfer funds tonight. Half now, half at the end of the thirty days." I stand, walk to her side of the table. "Let's go."

Again, she blushes as she sets her napkin on the table and rises.

I touch my hand to her naked back, running my knuckles over the curve of her spine. She stiffens, sucks in a breath at the touch, and when I lay the flat of my hand across her back, it spans almost the whole of it.

We exit the restaurant, walking to the elevator. I signal to one of my men.

"Take Melissa to the penthouse. She has an appointment."

"Yes, sir."

I turn back to Melissa who's watching me with a worried expression.

"Is this really necessary?" she asks when the elevator doors slide open.

I nod.

She glances at the man but if he's listening, he's smart enough not to show it.

"Thank you for dinner," she says.

"You're welcome."

She looks at me a moment longer like she has something to say, but then she steps onto the elevator and I watch her until the doors seal closed and carry her away from me.

10

MELISSA

Hawk left a few things out.

One, that the doctor would be administering a birth control shot and two, that directly following my appointment with her, I'd be getting waxed.

When I finally hear the ding of the elevator doors and watch them slide open, I'm fuming.

Hawk steps out, looking like a giant even here. His smile doesn't waver when he sees my face or my stance. I'm wearing a bathrobe, underneath which I'm naked, and standing with arms folded across my chest. I'm sure my face is red with anger.

He takes off his jacket casually, sets it over the arm of a chair and moves directly to the liquor cabinet to pour himself a whiskey.

"Vodka?"

"No, thank you. I didn't know I'd be getting a birth control shot."

He shrugs his shoulder. He does that a lot and it irritates me that something so important to me is a shrug of a shoulder to him.

He sits down on the couch and sips his drink. "No risk of pregnancy," he says.

"It's my body. You can't just decide on birth control for me."

"I just transferred a considerable amount of money into your bank account which says I can."

"Are you going to hold that over my head every time I don't go along with what you want?"

"Maybe."

"Well don't. We agreed. It's an even exchange." But is it? Even as I say the words, I know they're not true. He has the upper hand and we both know it.

He just swallows his drink and watches me looking somewhat amused.

"You had me waxed."

The hint of a grin I glimpsed now spreads wide. "That's right. Let's see."

"You have to ask me, Hawk."

"You could have said no, Melissa," he says, his tone matching mine.

I stop. It didn't even occur to me to say no. That it was a choice.

"I didn't—"

"I told you you're not a prisoner. I won't force you to do anything you don't want to do. Would it be easier for you if I did? Is that it? Relieve you of your responsibility in this?"

"That's not...I just didn't realize it was a choice. The birth control shot wasn't."

"Who says?"

"Are you serious?"

"Get the whiskey and come here," he says in reply, pointing to the space between his legs.

With a frustrated exhale, I go to the liquor cabinet but hesitate.

"It's the bottle without a label."

I pick up ornate bottle and go to him.

"Do you make it in your bathtub?" I ask, looking at it.

His face becomes serious momentarily. "I own stock in the company," he says, signaling for me to come closer.

I do, standing between him and the coffee table. He takes the whiskey and sets it down.

"Open the robe."

"Is this a choice too?"

He sips his drink. "Are you bored of this conversation yet? I am." He gestures to the belt holding the robe together.

I look over his shoulder, out at the lights of the strip.

"Open it," he orders.

Without returning my gaze to his, I undo the belt and let it fall open. I feel his hands on me, big and rough on my bare skin, his touch making my already racing heart beat faster. He opens the robe wider.

I look down at the thick dark hair on top of his head as he takes in my newly waxed pussy, only the thinnest strip of hair remaining there now. I think about yesterday or the day before or the week before. I think about how my life had been normal then. Now, this, him…it's about as far from my normal as it can get. I'm not really even sure how I got here. Or how I said yes to this deal. Or why.

Even given the situation with Liza and Sean, wasn't there an alternative? One that made more sense?

But then his fingers are on me again, touching the strip of hair and I can't think about Liza or Sean or anything anymore. Especially not when he looks at me with his strange now darker eyes.

"Sit."

I sit on the coffee table behind me.

"Lie back."

"I'm not a dog."

"Lie back, Melissa."

I do as he says and immediately, I feel his knees between mine, nudging my legs apart. I startle when a moment later, cool liquid spills on me and when I look at its source, I find him pouring the contents of his whiskey glass on my sex.

He meets my eyes and his are black now, only ringed in blue and green. I can't look away from them as liquid slides down between my lower lips, the sensation erotic.

Although maybe it's the way he's looking at me while doing it.

When he touches my knee, I gasp. But he just pushes it wider, eyes on me as he does. He shifts his gaze slowly down to my pussy, takes both ankles and sets my feet up on the coffee table so I'm completely open to him.

He stands, a giant looming over me. He picks up the bottle of whisky, brings it to my breasts, tilts it. It takes just a few cool drops on each nipple and they're hard.

When he sets the bottle down, he leans over me, places his hands on the table on either side of me, bracing his weight, caging me in, and, eyes locked on mine, he licks the whiskey off one breast, then the other.

I grip the edges of the coffee table to keep from grabbing hold of him. I'm not sure if I'd push him away or pull him closer.

He straightens, crouches between my legs and slides his tongue over my belly and down to my sex. I can't breathe. All I can do is watch him as he watches me. When I don't close my legs, he slides his tongue through my folds, and I hear the shudder of my breath as he licks the whiskey.

As he licks me.

His breath is warm, his tongue wet and tickling my clit while the scruff of his jaw scratches me. I close my eyes, grip the edges of the table and find myself arching my back, lifting into him. Wanting him.

But then he pulls away.

Sits back on the couch and refills his glass, eyes on me, his erection a steel rod in his pants.

"Whiskey and pussy are two of my favorite things in the world," he says.

I release my grip on the table, begin to close my knees, but he stops me.

"Stay. Just like this. Knees wide. I want to see."

11

MELISSA

The next hour is torture.

He drinks his whiskey and pushes buttons on his phone, and he could be playing a crossword puzzle for all I know while I lie here, whiskey sticky between my legs.

What he did, it was a tease. And I know he did it on purpose. Leaving me like that. And I want his mouth back on me, sucking my clit, dipping inside me. I want him to make me come.

He's still hard, but he won't touch me. Is this to prove some point? Because all it's doing is pissing me off.

But I can't admit that. I won't.

Is that what he wants? For me to ask for it? Beg him for it? Because he seems perfectly content to just look at me every now and then between whatever's got his attention on his phone.

It feels like an eternity when the thing finally rings and, after a quick glance at it, he stands, his expression darkening.

"Go have a shower," he tells me, the phone still ringing

in his hand. Without a backward glance, he walks into another room. I hear him talking just before he closes the door and I sit up, feeling ignored and annoyed.

Is this all I'm here for? For him to play with me?

But what do I expect? He owns me. He just paid me a deposit.

I shake the thought away, stand up, walk to the bedroom and when I switch on the lights, the windows tint. I'm glad because even though we're on the top floor of the building, I feel like everyone can see me.

I have a shower and towel-dry my hair, then walk back to the living room but when I pass the door he disappeared into, I hear his raised voice. He's pissed.

"What do you mean, *small* setback? This is going to cost me months!"

Silence, as I guess whoever is on the other end says something. When that silence is followed by the sound of a fist being slammed into a wall, I quickly retreat to the bedroom and climb into the bed.

I wonder who he's talking to and why he's so pissed off. I think I don't ever want to see that side of him. Not directed at me, at least.

I consider switching out the lights and trying to sleep, but I won't be able to. I'm too wound up. I get up, grab my phone out of my tote and check for messages. There aren't any.

When I'm walking back to the bed, I notice a book lying open and face down on the dresser.

I pick it up, read the title. I don't recognize it. I open it, meaning to flip through to read the first few pages when a photograph falls out.

I bend to pick it up. It's a photo of an older man with his arm around a younger woman and beside them stands a man who resembles Hawk. He's got a baby in his arms and the woman, I assume the baby's mother, has her face turned to the baby. A little hand has got a fistful of her hair and she's trying to loosen it.

I turn it over to look to see if it has a date, but there isn't one and when I look at it again, I have to smile at the woman's expression.

I'm so engrossed that I don't hear him come in.

"Are you going through my private things?"

I'm so startled when he snatches the photo out of my hands that I almost don't understand what he says. I don't know if it's the anger in his tone or something else that makes his accent suddenly so much heavier and his voice so much deeper. Like a roar. Like he sounded when he was talking on the phone.

"I wasn't going through your things," I quickly defend. Was I? No. It was right there. On top of the dresser.

He looks at the photo, his face darkening a little.

I stare up at him. When he shifts his gaze to me, glaring down at me, I find myself stepping backward, not realizing the bed is at my back until my knees it it.

"Did this just jump out of the drawer at you, then?"

I shake my head, confused, taken aback. And scared. "The book was on the dresser. It fell out. I wouldn't—"

But before I can finish, he leans down, takes me by the throat and hauls me up to tip-toe.

"Hawk!" I grip his forearm but he's too big. Too strong. And his fingers, they're squeezing too tight.

"You will respect my privacy."

I slap at his arm, his chest. God. Does he know how hard he's squeezing? Does he know I can't breathe? Can't make a sound.

It feels like an eternity passes and the edges of my vision

begin to darken like an old-fashioned photograph before he finally releases me.

I drop onto the bed.

I gasp for breath, clutching my neck, knowing I'll have bruises in the shape of his giant hand.

He stares down at me and I stare back, mute.

The rage on his face, it's a terrifying thing. Like the beast has been let out of the cage. No. Like it's chewed through the bars in its rage and is on a rampage now. A murderous rampage.

Then, just as quickly as it came, it's gone.

His expression changes and for a moment, I swear it's like it wasn't him just then. Because that man I just saw, I'd never have made a deal with him.

I'd never get in his bed.

No, I'd run like hell from that man.

But then, without a word, he turns his back and stalks away, into the bathroom, locking the door, leaving me trembling on his bed.

12

HAWK

I stand under the shower letting the spray hit me in the face, the water cold as ice.

The look in her eyes. That terrified look. The feel of her delicate neck in my hand. Her hands falling away as I strangled her.

Christ.

What the fuck is wrong with me?

I shake my head, try to clear away the image, but it's impossible.

No personal effects.

That photo is a personal effect. Am I going to have to lock every drawer?

I switch off the water. I'm fucking freezing now.

I dry off, my mind wandering back to the phone call. Jack telling me the deal didn't go through. Jack telling me to be careful.

I'm close.

Too close for it all to get fucked up.

I walk back into the bedroom to find her sitting on the bed much like she was yesterday. Like a terrified little girl.

Fuck.

This night has gone straight to hell.

Her gaze is locked on me and she pulls away when I sit on the bed. Bruises are already darkening her neck.

When I reach out to touch her, she flinches.

"I'm not going to hurt you."

"You already did."

I grit my teeth, but I accept that. I own it.

"I can't fight you," she says. "You're stronger than me even without trying."

"Don't look through my things and you won't have to worry about it."

"I wasn't looking through your things. I wouldn't. It fell out of the book that was on top of the dresser."

I switch out the light. Was it? I'm usually more careful with things.

"Lie down and go to sleep."

She switches the light back on on her side. "What happened? Why did you get so angry?"

This is unexpected.

I give a little snort. "No personal effects, remember?"

"It was a photograph."

"Shut off the light and go to sleep." I lie down and turn my back to her.

"Was it the phone call?"

I roll to face her. "Were you eavesdropping too?"

"No. I just came out into the hall after my shower and you sounded pissed. I came right back in here."

"Good. Don't eavesdrop." I roll away again.

"I can't do this if you turn into this...this...monster when I do something I don't even know will piss you off!"

I get up, reach over her, eyes boring in to her and switch off the light. "Go. To. Sleep."

It's on again before my head hits the pillow.

"No."

I ignore her, close my eyes. But then she shoves at my shoulder.

"Get up!"

"You're getting on my nerves, Melissa."

"I'm sorry to get on your nerves but you scared the crap out of me. You almost killed me, Hawk!"

"I didn't almost kill you."

"I couldn't breathe!"

"It won't happen again."

"You're right about that," she says with an attempt at putting steel into those words. "Get up."

I chuckle. It's funny, this. Her trying to command me.

"I mean it." She shoves again, harder this time.

"Christ," I say, turning, grabbing her wrist. "You want me up? I'm up. Now what?"

She tries to pull away but when I don't let her, she shoves at me with her free arm.

"I thought you said you couldn't fight me," I say, taking her other wrist and just catching her knee between my thighs when she goes for my balls.

"You're used to people jumping when you say jump, but I'm not one of those people."

"Like hell you're not. Let me explain something to you." I rise up, pin her to the bed and loom over her. I watch her eyes as she takes me in. "I own you. For the next thirty days, you are mine. *You* belong to *me*."

"Get off me."

"The balance of power is tipped in my favor, Melissa. That's what this is about. That's what that hefty deposit into your account ensures. *You* do as *I* say, not the other way around and you know it."

"Fuck you."

She tries again to knee me, but I'm faster than her.

"And you're right, I am a man used to getting what I want. Exactly what I want. And you will learn to jump when I say jump. Hell, when it even looks like I'm about to utter the word jump."

"You're dreaming."

"I don't think so. And just to be clear, I want you to fight back. You should always fight back. But don't ever knee me in the balls. That's dirty fighting and I won't forgive it."

"What happened, Hawk? Why did you get so angry?"

I loosen my grip on her, let her free, let her push against me so I'm on my back and she's on top of me. "Leave it alone, Melissa."

She shifts her weight and I wonder if she realizes her pussy's rubbing against my abs. And lower. Does she have any idea what that's doing to me?

"What are you scared I'll see?" she asks, straddling me, hands on my chest.

I don't know if she thinks she's keeping me down or what, but she's leaning her full weight into her hands.

What I do know is that one little shift from me and she gasps, her eyes growing huge in the precise moment she feels my dick between her ass cheeks. It takes all I have not to laugh at her surprised, almost comical expression.

She's quick to roll off me, but we just tumble again, me taking her arms, stretching them wide, her twisting this way and that, me letting her get free. Back and forth and back and forth and for as little as she is, she's got some fight in her.

"Tell me. What are you afraid I'll see," she asks when I've got her pinned, her energy finally spent so she's left panting for breath.

I look down at her, at her pretty little mouth, her perfect breasts. I slip one knee between hers and spread her thighs.

She twists, pulling at her arms, but I keep her pinned.

"Take my advice, Melissa," I start, rubbing my cock between her folds. "Leave it alone."

Her pupils are dilated and she's wet, but she's gone quiet.

I watch her mouth open when I test. When I push inside her slowly, just the head of my cock and fuck she's warm and tight. Like a snug glove perfectly made just for me. One I'm desperate to slide into.

I should wait. I should wait until I have the results. This could be a big mistake. But I can't. No way.

It's just a little taste. Just a dip into that wet heat.

Fuck.

She stares up at me and bites her lip. I switch my grip and intertwine my fingers with hers. I feel her hold tight to me, nails digging into me.

"I want you," I say through gritted teeth.

I push deeper, slow and deliberate and we're so close, our faces not an inch apart, our bodies touching, connected. I start to move inside her and she arches her back—at least momentarily.

I let go of one of her hands, cradle her head instead. Gentle still. I don't want to scare her off.

"Melissa," I'm half way in and she's so fucking tight, and all I want to do is ram into her. I won't be able to stop soon. Fuck. I don't think I can stop now.

Her free hand is on my shoulder but she's not tearing skin tonight. Just a few more inches, just a few more and her whimper makes me harder. When she licks her lips, fuck, I can't take it.

I thrust the last inches and she cries out, but I set my elbow at her shoulder and draw back a little to thrust again.

One hard, short thrust and she exhales with it, with the force of it.

When I find my rhythm and I'm fucking her, she clings to me, as if on a sheer rock face clinging for dear life. When I feel the walls of her pussy tremble and pulse. I watch her face, her eyes gleaming, mouth open, head thrown back, the softest sound coming from her.

I pull out then, trap my cock between us and I come. My cock pulses ropes of it wet on her, on me, pleasure throbbing through me as she watches me, and I watch her, unable to drag my gaze from hers.

13

MELISSA

It's suddenly cold when he slides off me and goes into the bathroom. I hear water running and a few minutes later, he returns. He's cleaned himself and now cleans me with a warm washcloth.

"I can do that." I try to take the cloth from him.

"Stay," he says like a caveman.

When he's finished cleaning me, he goes back into the bathroom to get rid of the towel before returning and switching out the light. He lies down beside me.

I turn my back to him, meaning to slide to the other side of the bed, but he wraps his big arm around me and pulls me to him. He holds me there, tight against his chest.

He doesn't say a word, he doesn't let me go, not for a second and all I can think is how warm his is. How soft his skin is over all that muscle and I find myself melting into him. Again, this feeling of something solid at my back. Something safe.

I should pull away. This is too close. But when I try, he just tightens his grip.

"Sleep," he says as if he hears my thoughts, hears the chaos in my mind.

And I do as he says because in a way, it's nice, this. Someone to look after me, even in the context of this strange arrangement. Even if he doesn't know it or realize it.

But am I safe here? His temper, I got a glimpse of it tonight. It's fierce, like him. He's volatile and I can't forget for a moment how dangerous he is.

And then there's this. Him like this, his arm around me, his body curled around mine, holding me. Is it stupid to say protecting me? I know it's just in my head. I have to remember that I am a warm body to him. One he paid to have in his bed.

His comment about the imbalance, the inequality of our relationship, he's right. I can try to deny it all I want. I can try to hide from it, but it's the truth.

He bought me.

He owns me.

I push that thought aside and just let myself feel this, feel safe, just for a little while. Just for one month.

Because as long as I'm his, I'm safe from Sean. And I have to remember that's the reason I'm doing this.

What happens after the month is over?

I force that thought away too. I just want to sleep. I want to forget and sleep and feel safe.

Safe in the bed of this beast.

I'M ALONE WHEN I WAKE THE NEXT MORNING, JUST LIKE THE last time I woke up here. And I'm tired. Heavy with sleep and maybe the wine or just Hawk's sudden and immense presence in my life.

I get out of the bed and go into the bathroom, splash cold water on my face. I look at my neck, at the bluish marks there. The big print of his hand.

Strange that I sleep so heavily here. Safe in his arms even though it's his hands that left these bruises.

I switch on the shower and step beneath the flow, making a note to buy conditioner because he doesn't have any. I use his shampoo, inhaling the scent of him, and scrub my body .When I'm finished, I switch off the shower and wrap a thick towel around myself.

Digging my wide-tooth comb out of my bag, I sit on the edge of the tub to comb through the tangles of my hair. Dark strands fall to the floor as I pull the comb through.

That's going to bother him. I lose a lot of hair every day. I also leave clothes lying around and don't always put the cap back on the toothpaste.

The order and almost clinical sparseness of his penthouse will be marred.

Messy.

When I can pull the comb through my hair without it catching, I get up, find my toothbrush on the counter—note that his electric one is in its holder. I pick mine up, smear his toothpaste on my brush and brush my teeth as I pad barefoot through the bedroom.

But as soon as I walk out into the hallway, I stop because I'm not alone.

There's a man at the elevator.

I'm at the far end of the hall and his only acknowledgement to me is a nod. He quickly shifts his gaze away maybe because I'm wrapped in a towel.

I swallow the toothpaste and steel my spine, holding my towel tight to me as I make my way inside.

"Where's Hawk?" I ask.

The man looks at me and he's the same one from yesterday, the one who stood outside my house. The one who'd offered me the ride yesterday morning that I'd refused.

"I'm to look after you. I'll take you where you need to go."

"I don't need that. I have a car."

He doesn't budge.

"You can go," I try again.

He looks me square in the eyes and there's a hardness to him. I wonder if he got in trouble last time. "I'm to look after you, Miss."

"Where's Hawk?"

"He had business to take care of."

I wonder if that business had to do with what I overheard last night. Back into the bedroom, I grab my phone type a text to Hawk.

"I don't need a babysitter."

I get a reply right away. *"Brian will drive you anywhere you need to go. My terms, remember?"*

Yes, I remember.

I log into my banking app and it takes me a minute to read the number there. I've never had this much money in my bank account. Ever.

Fifty percent up front. Fifty afterward. That was the agreement and he's kept his end of it. Maybe that's why Brian's here. To keep me from taking this money and running out on him.

I have a feeling I wouldn't get very far if I tried that. Besides, I need this time. This month.

Is it naïve to think that if I stay here, in this penthouse, that if or when Liza tells Sean about me, maybe he'll think I'm gone—that I took off—and I can slip back into my life once the month is up?

And with Hawk, I think I'm safe even as that image of him last night, that of the raging beast, flashes in my memory.

Who's going to keep you safe from Hawk?

I'm about to go back into the bedroom to get dressed, thinking I'll wear the jeans and top I'd quickly shoved into my tote last night when the elevator dings, announcing someone's arrival.

The doors slide open and a woman steps out, giving me a once over. Two men follow her, each pushing a rack into the penthouse.

"Put them there," she tells them.

"What's this?" I ask when she introduces herself as she tugs the cloth covering the first rack off.

I forget her name as soon as she says it when I get a look at what's on those racks.

Clothes. Not just any clothes.

Two racks full of designer clothes.

Casual and formal wear, dresses and jeans and tops and boxes and boxes of shoes.

"I think he got your size right. A four?"

"What?" I ask.

"Mr. MacLeod ordered the clothes. He said if you don't like something, you're to send it back."

What did he do?

She must think I'm an idiot when I stand there staring at the racks.

"I can help you get dressed if you like," she says.

"I don't need help getting dressed, thank you." I look at the clothes. "These are for me?"

She nods.

I walk to one of the racks and run my fingers along the fine fabrics, and gawk and a price tags that I can see.

"I don't...Are you sure?"

"Yes, Miss. Take your time. Look through everything. If anything doesn't fit, or you don't like something, let me know. And if there's anything else you require, let me know that too."

She hands me a business card.

I take it absently.

"I don't need all these clothes," I say, confirming what I'm sure is her opinion of my idiocy.

"I'm here all day and when I'm not, there will be someone in the shop to help you. We'll be back later to put the things you want to keep in the closet. Two more racks will be brought up later today. Take your time deciding."

She doesn't wait for me to say anything else before, with a wave of her hand, the men march back onto the elevator and she follows. They're gone and I'm left staring at the racks, with Brian, my babysitter, hovering in my periphery.

I walk back into the bedroom and close the door.

I feel like a whore. A prostitute.

The money's in my bank account and another sort of payment is out in the living. Racks of designer clothes I'd never buy even if I could afford them.

My cell phone rings, interrupting my thoughts. Deirdre's name pops up and I swipe the screen to answer.

"Hello?"

"Hi honey," comes her warm, grandmotherly voice. "I'm sorry to call so early."

"No, it's fine. What's up?"

"Well, the little munchkin's pinkeye has cleared up but as with everything else with the germ-magnet, guess who's got pinkeye now?" She doesn't wait for me to answer. "You guessed it. Me. Except that mine's come with a full on cold, too. I don't think I'll be able to come in this morning, hon. That's why I was calling so early."

"Oh, it's all right, Deirdre. Don't even worry about it. I was planning on going in today anyway," I say, even though I wasn't. "You just stay home and get better."

"Thank you so much, honey. I really appreciate that."

"It's no problem, Deirdre. Feel better."

We hang up and I think about those racks of clothes out there and the fact that I run a second-hand clothing shop where fifty-percent of the profits are donated to the local shelter. How would it look if I walked in there in brand new D&G dress and Jimmy Choo heels?

That's not even me.

I give a shake of my head, find my jeans and top that I'd stuck into my tote yesterday and put them on. I then towel dry my hair, braiding it into a fishtail down one side.

When I'm back in the living room, my babysitter's eyebrows go up. I'm sure he's wondering who'd be stupid enough to put on these old things when they have access to what's on those racks.

"I need to go to work," I tell him.

He nods and turns to insert a key into a slot on the panel beside the elevator and soon, the numbers on the display start climbing as it comes to the top floor.

I hold my tote on my shoulder and look straight ahead.

I just have to remember whatever Hawk is doing, it's for him, not me. This is his norm, and this is how he wants his women to look because whether I like it or not, I am a part of his stable now.

I think about the money again. About why I'm doing this. I think about the possibility that I may need to disappear again.

But how long will I run from Sean Boyd?

Forever, I think. He told me as much on the last night I saw him. I'll never forget his words.

"Keep one eye over your shoulder, Little Bitch Whore, because I will hunt you for the rest of your life. Again and again, I will come after you. Just when you think you're safe, I'll be there to remind you that you're not. That you never will be safe. I'll remind you again and again and..."

He'd trailed off then. Or I didn't hear any more because it hurt too much, what he was doing.

Pain overrides everything. It blocks out even your own thoughts. In a way, it's a blessing.

When we get to the lobby, I ask the man to wait when I see a coffee shop and stop for a to-go cup. I take out my wallet to pay but an older woman, I guess the manager, steps between me and the girl and pushes my money away.

"It's taken care of, Miss," she says. "Anything you need."

Of course, it is.

I'm his whore. And they all know it. The woman with the designer clothes. The man who is standing a few feet from me. This woman.

"Thank you," I say awkwardly, knowing it's no use arguing.

I put my money back in my wallet and take the cup, too distracted to even add cream or sugar before heading outside where the sedan that once brought me here carries me to the shop.

Sundays aren't usually that busy at the shop so being there today will give me a chance to take inventory.

On Monday I'll walk over to the homeless shelter a few blocks away and hand them a check for fifty-percent of what the shop took in minus what I'd given Liza. It's not usually that much, but people don't realize how little you need to live if you really are using it just to live. To eat. To have a warm, and hopefully safe, bed.

Although now, I can give them the whole of it. I will have a million dollars by the end of this month. The little bit the shop takes in monthly won't be as necessary.

When I arrive at the shop, I take one of the silk scarves in the window and tie it around my neck. The bruises aren't bad, but I don't want anyone seeing them.

The driver spends the morning sitting in the car or climbing out for a smoke. He's just out on the street like that. He must be bored to tears.

When I walk down to a small sandwich shop, he follows me.

"I'm just getting a sandwich," I tell him. "I'm not going to run away."

"Just doing my job."

"Fine. Suit yourself." I order my sandwich but when I try to pay, he steps forward and hands the woman a credit card.

"I can buy my own sandwich."

He ignores me and the woman who has always taken my order looks at me uncertainly.

"Anything she wants goes on this card," he says to her.

"That's not—" I start.

"This card," he interrupts.

The woman takes it, looks at the name and runs it, stealing glances at me. The two working in the back making the sandwiches are also there, peering out at me, at the commotion.

I've lost my appetite by the time I get the sandwich and walk back to the shop. I take out my phone and instead of calling Hawk, I send him a text:

"I can buy my own sandwich. Not everyone needs to know I'm your whore."

I hit send.

Not a moment later, I get one back.

"I like to take care of what's mine."

He likes saying that. Reminding me.

"You'd never know it from looking at my throat."

The phone rings not an instant later. It's him.

I decline the call and when I do, a text flashes across the screen: *"Pick up."*

"No."

"I said pick up."

It rings again and I decline again.

"Store's busy." I text and before he sends another message, I switch off my phone and walk back to the shop. I unlock it and try to smile at the customers who enter a few minutes later.

My babysitter lights up a cigarette and leans against the door of the car, scrolling through his phone.

I watch the women absently as they chat and look through the rack of Halloween costumes for kids. They're some of our biggest selling items. After a while, one of them comes to the register carrying an Ariel costume. She sets it on the counter.

"I called the other day and Deirdre put a dress aside for me," she says. "My name is Carol."

"Carol, that's right. A princess dress for your daughter, right?"

"Yes."

"I'll go get it. It's in the back." I walk away from the counter and go into the back room to look through the things we're holding for people. I find the dress, and I carry it into the shop, feeling the shift in the air the instant I open the door between the back room and the shop itself.

The women are still at the counter and standing beside

the door is Hawk. Beyond him, outside, a sedan is parked beside the one that brought me. It's still running.

My mouth goes dry when I meet his hard eyes.

He folds his arms across his chest and raises his eyebrows.

I clear my throat and walk to the counter.

"Here it is," I say.

The woman picks it up. "It's gorgeous. And I can sew this right up," she says, touching the slight tear at the hem.

"Oh, I didn't see it. I'll discount—"

"No, it's a few minutes work. Besides, I know how much you donate to the shelter," she says with a warm smile. She takes out her wallet. "I used to come here back when Marjorie opened the shop. I know she'd be proud you're keeping up her legacy."

"She was an amazing woman."

"So are you," she says.

Embarrassed, I turn to ring her up, make change and bag the items, not sure if Hawk heard any of that.

When the women leave, he steps to the counter.

"Where's your bluster when I'm standing in front of you."

"I'm not a thing."

"You are mine to care for during these thirty days. Period. End of fucking story."

"I'm not a whore." I feel my eyes fill up.

"The only person throwing that word whore around is you."

"I can pay for my own coffee and my own sandwich and my own clothes."

"You switched off your phone," he says.

"I told you it was busy."

"That was busy?"

"What do you want from me?"

"Why aren't you wearing the clothes I had delivered?"

"Look around you, Hawk."

He studies me.

"I'll wear what you want me to wear at the casino or when we're out together, but I'm not wearing those things here. I have my own clothes."

"I've seen your clothes."

"Money and material things, they're not everything, you know."

"I know how much I transferred into your bank account this morning."

"There are reasons people do things and you don't know anything about mine."

"I may not know everything but I'm willing to bet your reasons have something to do with the fake driver's license."

Shit. Why did I say that?

"I'll have the clothes swapped out for more appropriate ones," he says.

"I told you, I have my own."

"Is it that hard to let someone do something nice for you?"

I stop at that, but then shake my head. "You're doing it for you, not me. Let's just be really honest about that."

"There are reasons people do things and you don't know anything about mine," he says, repeating my own sentence word for word.

I bite the inside of my lip.

"Let me see." He gestures to the scarf.

"It's fine."

"Let me see."

He reaches over the counter this time and pulls the knot of the scarf loose. The silk falls away in his hand and he lifts my chin, turns it slightly, touches the marks. He turns my face back and looks at me.

"It won't happen again," he says.

"So you've said." I pull out of his grasp.

"Are you afraid of me?"

His question surprises me and it takes me a long time to answer. "I don't know what I am. I just know there are men worse than you out there."

His gaze on me is so intense I shift mine to the counter.

I don't know why I just said that. I mean, it's true. As ridiculous as it sounds, I do feel safe with him. And some part of me wants to tell him why I took the deal. Wants to tell him why I use a fake name. Why Liza knowing I'm here scares the shit out of me.

But I can't do that.

I can't ever do that.

When I look back up at him, he's studying me curiously. I have to get better at hiding what I'm thinking.

"That photograph you found, it's old. Old things carry memories," he says, surprising me.

I don't have a reply and we just stand there in an almost comfortable silence. But then the shop door opens and Axel walks in.

Hawk straightens, turns to him.

"We gotta go," Axel says, giving me one glance.

"Be right there. Wait for me outside."

Hawk shifts his gaze back to me and takes my jaw into his hand again. He draws me forward.

"When I call, you pick up, understood?"

"Understood."

14

HAWK

"*There are reasons people do things and you don't know anything about mine.*"

These are the words that go around and around in my head as I watch Melissa look through the new clothes on the racks in one of the spare bedrooms.

I had all the designer stuff taken away, well, most of it. She still needs some evening dresses. In their place, the racks are stuffed with more casual clothes, still good brands, but not the best designer labels money can buy.

"Better. Thank you," Melissa says, picking out every pink item and shoving each into my arms. "No pink though."

I take the hangers, curious about this peculiarity, but she turns away, her attention back on the clothes.

"You're welcome." My phone buzzes. I drop the clothes she handed me on the bed and step out to take it. It's a file from Jack with more details on Sean Boyd and I'm starting to figure out why Melissa accepted my offer. What some of those reasons are that she thinks I know nothing about.

She's been leaving breadcrumbs almost like she wants me to figure it out and I can't shake one comment in particular. The one that there are worse men than me out there.

I leave her there to get dressed and pour myself a whiskey in the living room. I read the file and it's not specifically about Melissa, this one. More about what a dick Sean Boyd is.

"Get me financials on the shop too. Wrinkles in Time," I text. I heard what the woman said about donations to the shelter. That shop can't be taking in enough for her to live on and donate regularly.

"I'll have that for you tomorrow," Jack replies.

I'm just tucking my phone back into my pocket when I see a message pop up about a voice mail. I check my missed calls. When I see the number and realize who it is, I ignore the voice mail.

My brother can fucking wait.

Fifteen minutes later, Melissa appears wearing the deep crimson dress I laid out for her. The silk hugs her close displaying just enough skin to leave you wanting. The color is perfect with her olive coloring and tonight, with her long hair loose down her back, she's magnificent.

She's slipping on the matching four-inch sandals and has a small clutch tucked under one arm.

"How do women wear these?" she asks as she gets the second one on and walks toward me.

I don't think she has any idea how she looks.

"You're beautiful," I tell her, unable to drag my eyes from her.

She stands in front of me. "Thanks," she says. "Again, I feel mostly naked."

I finish my drink and put the glass down before pushing the button for the elevator. "And like last time, everyone will be wishing you were when they see you. One thing," I say, and reach into my pocket to take out her driver's license. A better forgery.

"You made me a new one?"

I nod. "Yours was crap."

She looks at it, reaches out her hand to take it, but I snatch it away.

"I want to know why you need this," I tell her.

She looks suspiciously at me. "No personal effects. Terms, remember?"

She's using my own rule against me.

I concede, holding out the fake license to her. I'll find out. I always do.

Cautiously, she takes it and slips it into her clutch.

"One day you'll tell me, Melissa."

"Why are you so curious?"

"Because you make me curious."

"I'm not that interesting," she says.

"I think there's more to you than you let on."

She studies me, her eyes searching mine as if trying to glean what I know. But just as she won't tell, neither will I.

The elevator arrives and, with a hand at her lower back, I guide her inside, take my key out of the slot and tuck it into my pocket then push the button for the lobby.

"Why are you taking me with you?" she asks as she watches the city and I watch her.

"It's more fun than going alone."

"Why go at all?" She turns to me. "I don't get the feeling you're looking forward to it."

"I'm not. But I need to talk to a couple of people."

We get to the lobby where Axel is waiting beside the elevator. He's on a call but when he sees us, he nods, and disconnects.

We walk out to the waiting sedan and I open the back

door for Melissa. Once she's in, I sit in the passenger seat beside Axel.

"How's your brother?" I ask him.

Ever since the other night when one of the men at the quarterly draw caught his attention, he's been talking to his brother almost daily and I want to know what's up. Axel is my most trusted man. With Hugo living on the east coast, I don't want to take a chance on losing him.

"Good. Same." He looks over his shoulder as we head out of the parking lot and merge with traffic. "I may need to head east in a few weeks."

"How long?"

"A month at most." He keeps his eyes on the road.

I see the red of a new tattoo creeping up along the collar of his shirt.

"This have to do with that errand you ran the other night?"

He nods once.

I look ahead at the blinking lights of cars as we slow for a traffic light.

"Let me know when your plans are confirmed. And if you need my help..." I let that drop.

He glances at me. "Appreciate that, but Hugo and I will handle this one. Looking forward to it, in fact."

I see how his jaw tightens, how his eyes narrow as he says it.

"I pity the man," I say.

He gives a short smile.

Twenty minutes later we're at the house where the party is being held. I climb out, open the back door for Melissa.

Axel lights up a cigarette and leans against the hood of the car.

Melissa eyes the cars parked along the drive as we walk

to the front door. The men nod when they recognize me and noise swells when they open the front doors.

There must be two-hundred people in here.

We stand in the foyer for a moment and I take it in, scanning everyone on this floor and those I can see upstairs. I check my watch just as a man I recognize comes to my side. I don't know his name, but his boss is the one I'm here for.

"Mr. MacLeod," he says. "I'll show you to the study."

"I know where it is. Give me a minute," I tell him, and turn to Melissa.

She looks so completely out of place here. Maybe not to the casual observer because it's not that she doesn't fit in physically. It's in her eyes, they've taken on the same look they sometimes do with me when she's creeping into her shell.

"Let's get you a drink," I say, walking her to one of the bars. "What would you like?"

"Vodka tonic, please," she says.

I order and tip the bartender as she takes her drink. We walk to a quieter corner.

"I need ten minutes. Then we can leave."

She looks up at me. "I'm fine," she says. "You don't have to babysit me."

"Axel will be in any minute."

She smiles. "I think I'd rather be alone than make small talk with Axel, but thanks."

I nod and walk through the crowded room to the study which is at the far end of the last hallway. Scanning the room as I do, I note the man who's already got his eye on Melissa.

"Hawk," comes the gruff voice of James Douglas as one of the men guarding the office door opens it and the smell of freshly lit cigars pours into the hallway.

I enter, take in the older man behind his enormous desk. He's my father's age. And my father's enemy. Which in a right world, would make him my enemy. But in my world, he is my ally. Not friend. No. I don't make that mistake. But at this moment, our goals are aligned. They won't be for long, but right now, I need this bastard.

"What happened on the vote?" I ask as the door is closed behind me. "How the fuck did we lose our advantage?"

15

MELISSA

I hate parties. I always have.

I pretty much always feel awkward and can never figure out how people stand there and make small talk for hours.

There are easily two-hundred people here. Men and women and enough perfume and hair spray to smother you.

I notice how when Hawk walks away, people seem to part to clear his path. The way they look at him, men and women both, I know everyone knows who he is. I wonder if he notices how watched he is. If he cares.

As soon as he's gone, I find eyes turn to me. The men appear curious. The women, something else.

I drink my vodka and try not to make eye contact with anyone as I walk along the perimeter of the room, looking for a bathroom or someplace to disappear into for the next ten minutes.

When Axel walks inside, I'm at the far end and I don't think he sees me when he scans the room. He stands off to the side, his face impassive and closed. I'm guessing he'd like to make small talk with me about as much as I'd like to make it with him.

The thought makes me smile and when I get to the next drink station, I put my empty glass down and order another.

The bartender hands it to me and I slip backward into a shadowy part of the room where I can watch but not feel so exposed.

Although I'm not wearing a watch, I know it's past the ten minutes Hawk said he'd be gone when I order my third drink, this time just the tonic. We haven't eaten yet and I'm already feeling the two I've had.

I slip back into my corner but I'm not alone for long. A few moments later, a man, young, maybe just a year or two older than me, comes to stand beside me.

I look at him because he's standing closer than would be acceptable and when I do, I find him watching me with a strange look in his eyes. Like a boy who's excited about something. And I say boy because when I look at his face, I'm not sure he can grow a beard yet. He looks almost pubescent.

He's tall too, tall and lanky, like a skeleton in a suit, with blue eyes and black hair.

Something about him makes me shudder in repulsion. Makes me want to slip away.

He nods to me and I turn back to the crowd. All I can think is out of all these men—who look much more threatening than this kid beside me—he's the one that's got me creeped out.

"Big party, huh?" he asks.

"I guess." I don't look at him but keep my eyes on the hallway down which Hawk disappeared.

"Didn't know you were in town," he says.

"Excuse me?" I ask, turning to him. "Do I know you?"

His face takes on a flush. Or maybe it's just his coloring.

I think if he held out his hand to introduce himself and shake mine, I'd have to find some way to avoid having to touch him He's making the hair on the back of my neck stand on end.

But when he next speaks, that nervous expression is gone. He's serious. He swallows his drink loudly, never taking his eyes off me. What I see in them, it makes my stomach turn.

"You wouldn't know me, but I know you," he says.

There's a sudden chill in the room. The moisture on my glass, I'm not sure if its condensation or sweat from my palm. Because I understand what he means. I understand how he knows me. If I look hard enough, I may even see a resemblance.

Does this run in families? Do predators breed predators?

"Older now, but still pretty. I'd never forget those eyes."

I'm going to be sick.

"I didn't realize..." he's still talking but all I hear is noise. I can't make out the words. It's like my ears can't take them or my brain can't or won't process them.

The boy-man leans toward me, licks his already wet lips, then touches the back of one knuckle to my shoulder.

But in the instant his skin makes contact with mine, I swear in that same split second in time, Hawk appears out of nowhere. His hand clamps over the man's wrist and the sound the man makes is a feminine-sounding scream.

"What the fuck do you think you're doing?"

Instinctively I step backward, letting Hawk's body come between myself and the man. Letting him shield me from the awful boy-man who stares at Hawk.

He's as tall except that Hawk is huge compared to this almost awkwardly skinny boy-man with the look of terror on his face. I notice the spot on his suit jacket. His drink. It must have spilled when Hawk grabbed his arm.

Axel's at our side, too, now.

"I asked you a question," Hawk says.

The boy-man looks beyond Hawk to me, then back. "I'm sorry. I didn't know she was with you. I'm so sorry. I just...I thought..."

Oh God. Oh my God. Please don't say it. Please don't.

Hawk thrusts him backward. "You thought wrong. Step the fuck back."

I realize how much quieter it suddenly is. Realize those nearest us are watching.

The boy-man apologizes once more, or tries to, before turning and almost running away.

Hawk turns to me, looks me over. "All right?"

I nod quickly. "Can we go?" I want to leave. I want to get out of here. Get away from these people. From all these eyes on us.

Because if that boy-man knows, if he recognizes me, who else will? Who will ask questions and find out?

And how long until Hawk finds out?

"Do you know him?" Hawk asks.

I shake my head. "Please can we go?" I ask again. "Everyone's looking."

He turns to Axel. "Take her back. I need to stay and handle a few things."

Axel nods.

Hawk turns to me. "Have dinner sent up. Just call the restaurant. They'll make anything you want."

I just nod, knowing I won't do that. Knowing I won't be able to eat at all. I'm grateful he won't be with me. Grateful I'll have a reprieve from questions, even though that reprieve will be a brief one.

What I should have done was slapped that boy-man's hand away myself. Told him he was mistaken. Walked away before the spectacle occurred. But I was wholly unprepared.

Axel walks me outside and I sit in the back of the sedan to stare out the window. I need to keep it together for a little bit longer. Just until I'm alone. Back at the penthouse. Then I can freak out.

Then I can fall apart.

16

HAWK

The meeting that should have taken ten minutes takes almost two hours and my attention is split.

And on top of that, there's the voicemail from my brother that I should never have listened to. My bastard brother telling me to go to hell. Brandishing his victory.

He should be more careful. He won a battle. I will win the fucking war.

When I walked out to tell Melissa that Axel would take her home and found that man beside her, having almost cornered her, when I saw his hand on her, I lost my shit. All I saw was red.

Rage.

That idiot boy was touching her.

And she looked scared shitless. Pale as a ghost. Eyes huge. And fucking terrified.

The elevator seems to be crawling tonight as it climbs to the penthouse. I wonder if she's figured out that she can't leave it without a key yet. That's why I don't keep a man on her in the apartment.

When the doors finally slide open, it's dark.

I hit the switch and soft light bathes the large, open room.

"Melissa?" I call out, glancing around to find her outside on the balcony. She's sitting with her feet up against the railing, a bottle of vodka by her side, the glass in her hand. The sliding door is closed which explains why she doesn't hear me.

I take off my jacket, toss it over the arm of a chair and open the glass door.

She startles, turns to me.

I look at her, see the smeared mascara under her eyes, see how her skin is blotchy from crying.

"What are you doing out here?"

"Getting fresh air," she says. I hear the slur of her words. "I couldn't go downstairs. You should give me a key to the elevator. I'm a prisoner."

"You're not a prisoner. You just have to call down if you need something."

I go out there and pick up the bottle, notice how much she's emptied. I look down at the city, the people like ants on the street, the constant lights, the sounds muffled a little at this height.

And I think about the drop and the fact that she's drunk and shouldn't be out here.

"Come inside," I tell her.

"I like it out here," she says, only glancing at me momentarily before returning her gaze to something in the distance.

"You shouldn't be out here when you're drunk."

She smiles, looks up at me. "Afraid I'll hurl myself over?"

That wasn't exactly what I was thinking. "Would you?"

Sadness in her eyes again. That child again. Just for a moment.

Then she shakes her head. "I'm too chicken for that."

Too chicken to do it.

Not no, she'd never think of jumping.

"Come inside now, Melissa."

She brings her glass to her mouth, notices it's empty and looks for the bottle on the table, then realizes I have it. She holds her glass out to me.

"Inside. Then you can get some more."

She mutters something under her breath, stands and immediately stumbles.

I catch her, mutter a curse myself as I walk her in and close the door.

She holds her glass out again.

Instead of pouring for her, I take it from her and set it on the counter.

"You said I could have more," she says.

"I changed my mind. Did you eat?"

She thinks. "I forgot."

I shake my head, take my phone out of my pocket and call down to the restaurant. "Send up a sandwich. I don't care what. Just make it fast."

"I'm not hungry," she says as I hang up.

"Our deal, remember? You eat."

She rolls her eyes, walks to the counter and takes the bottle.

I catch her arm. "You've had enough."

"Get off me."

"I said it's enough." I relieve her of the bottle.

"And I say it's not," she says, tugging her arm.

I don't let her go. "You're drunk, Melissa. And you will eat something."

She exhales audibly, turns away, but again, I don't let her go.

"What's going on?" I ask.

"Nothing."

"Not nothing. Tell me what it is."

"No personal effects."

"Yeah, well, now it's interfering with my time."

"Time you bought and paid for."

"Yeah. Something like that. I don't know why you're so fucking secretive. You knew that man. He spooked you. Why?"

"None of your business."

I tug her close. "Like I said, it became my business when it began to interfere with my time."

She gives me a strange look and I wonder if she's trying for a grin but then I feel her hands at my stomach, pulling my shirt out, fumbling with the belt of my pants.

"What are you doing, Melissa?"

"Making sure you get what you paid for." She slurs the words.

"Is it that bad?" I ask. "This secret?"

Her hands stop their work and she looks deep into my eyes, searching them, then resumes, shifting her gaze downward as she succeeds in undoing the belt, the pants.

"You really want the waiter who's about two floors away to see you on your knees sucking my dick when he gets here?"

Her eyes fly up to mine.

"Didn't think so," I say, redoing the fly of my pants, my belt.

On cue, the elevator doors slide open and a waiter pushes a tray inside.

"Sir," he says, pretending not to see a drunk Melissa stumble her way to the couch.

"Thank you," I tell him and hand him a fifty-dollar-bill. "Don't worry about cleaning it up tonight."

"Thank you, sir," he says and a moment later, he's gone.

I go to the coffee machine and make her a mug of black coffee. When it's ready, I hand it to her.

She takes it and I watch her drink a sip. When I set the plated club sandwich with fries on the coffee table in front of her, she picks at the fries.

I stand, arms folded across my chest, and watch her until she finishes the coffee and eats half the fries and a quarter of the sandwich.

"Happy?" she asks.

"Not yet."

She sighs, eats a few more fries.

I open the bottle of water and hand it to her.

She takes it, drains it.

I sit beside her. "Now talk."

"What do you want me to say?"

"Did you know that man?"

She shakes her head, gives a sad little smile. "No."

She's not lying. I can tell.

I think about this and something tells me to ask that question a little differently. "Does he know you?"

"He thought he did, but he was mistaken." Now she's lying. When she lies, she's too smooth and quick to answer.

"You were scared, Melissa. I saw it."

"Not of him," she says and stands up. She's barefoot. That's good. I think she'd topple if she weren't.

She reaches behind her, unzips the dress, pushes the straps off her arms and wriggles out of it, letting it drop to the floor. My gaze falls to her full, naked breasts. She's not wearing a bra.

Hooking her thumbs into the band of her panties, she leans forward to push them off and steps out of them. She straightens and I look her over because she's fucking beautiful, even if she is doing anything and everything to distract me.

I shove the coffee table away with my foot and, without a word, I point to the spot in front of me.

She swallows, gets that flush she gets when she's aroused and nervous at once, then kneels.

"Open your legs wider."

She does and she's kneeling up and I'm hard just looking at her like this, at her pretty, naked body, at the slit of her sex.

I undo my belt, open my pants. I take myself out.

"You want to distract me?" I ask her, touching the already wet tip of my cock to her lips. "You can distract me, but I never forget, Melissa. Never."

I grip her by the hair, force her face backward to kiss her mouth before laying her back on the carpet. I kneel over her, my thighs on either side of her.

"You sobering up?" I ask when she realizes she's not going to be sucking my cock so much as getting her face fucked.

"What—"

"You don't want to talk? That's fine. I'll fuck that pretty face of yours."

She makes a sound, pushes back, but her arms are trapped.

"You can tell me. I'm not your enemy. I won't hurt you. Don't you know that?" I ask, sliding my hand back and rubbing her clit, eyes on her as she licks her lips. "Good. Like that. Just relax," I say, rubbing the swelling nub.

She opens her mouth and I push into her, slow at first,

letting her tongue lick me, lubricate me while I rub her clit, finger her pussy. I draw my hand away and kneel up.

"I'll take care of you after," I say, gripping the end of the coffee table with one hand, angling myself to fuck her face. Finding my rhythm, slow at first, shallow, then deeper and deeper.

I watch her take me. Watch her choke and gasp for breath, feeling her hands on my thighs, nails digging into skin, and I'm getting harder and thicker and when I feel the back of her throat, I cup her head and tilt it and fuck her hard, just a few thrusts inside her hot, wet little mouth. When I come, I hold her to me, buried deep, and I come down her tight little throat, my cock throbbing, pulsing with its release. Her muscles work to keep up, to swallow, urging the orgasm on, intensifying it until I've emptied.

When I'm finished, I release her.

She rolls onto her side, coughing.

I grip her hair again, make her look at me. "Swallow it. All of it," I tell her. "When you do, I'll make you come."

Once she's swallowed, I kiss her hard, tasting myself on her tongue, tasting her and stealing her breath.

Then I turn her onto her stomach and move between her legs. I spread her ass wide and I eat her, all of her, her dripping cunt, her tight little asshole, rolling her onto her back again to take her swollen little clit into my mouth. I suck so hard, she's coming in no time, her gasps almost screams, her hands in my hair, those nails digging into my scalp as she calls out my name, her pussy wet, dripping, her taste the sweetest thing I've ever tasted.

17

MELISSA

Hawk will not let this go. And he's going to find out. One way or another, he will find out.

The man at that party, all those people watching us. They will be curious. They will ask around. Hell, all they need to do is ask that man.

How many people saw those videos? How many others will recognize me?

And what will I do when Hawk finds out? How will I stand the way he'll look at me?

I shake my head. I have to think about my options now because Sean Boyd isn't the only threat.

When we reach the shop, the driver pulls up along the curb and I get out. He climbs out too, but he doesn't follow me inside. Every time he's brought me, he just waits outside for me.

I guess Hawk's still not sure if I'll run or not and right now, I can't say that I won't.

There's one thing I do need to do today, either way. I need to be prepared in case I need to leave in a hurry, and I need two things before I can do that.

Deirdre is ringing someone up when I get inside. Her glance is worried when she sees me and she quickly makes change. A few moments later, the customer is gone and we're alone.

"How are you doing, Deirdre? The pink-eye all cleared up?"

"Yep. But I'm sure that little germ magnet will bring something else home next week," she says, and even now, I can hear how much she loves her granddaughter. It's heart-warming, the way she talks about her.

"Listen hun, something strange happened when I got here to open up shop."

I feel myself grow cold. "What?"

"Some man was waiting outside. Said he's an old friend of yours and asked when you'd be here. Seemed a little odd since you hadn't mentioned any friends being in town so I told him I wasn't sure when you were coming in."

"Who was he?"

"Didn't say. He had dark hair, tall..."

She trails off and I stop listening. Because it can only be one man.

"Did he say what he wanted?" I interrupt.

"Just that he was dropping by to say hello. Left before I'd even unlocked the door. It just felt strange that you hadn't mentioned anyone."

I nod, start to walk away, stop. "He didn't say who he was?"

She shakes her head.

I need to think. I need to figure out what to do.

"Are you taking care of yourself, hun?"

I nod.

"Sure is a nice car you came in." She gestures outside.

"My car is messed up. Turns out duct tape doesn't hold it

together after all," I say anxiously. "I need to run an errand, Deirdre."

"You sure you're okay, Melissa?"

I nod too quickly.

She studies me. "You're not in some sort of trouble?"

I shake my head.

"You can talk to me, you know that, right?"

I nod again. I need to get out of here. I'm on the verge of tears.

"Go on and take care of your errand. I'll be here."

"Thank you, Deirdre."

"You're welcome, dear."

Glancing once at Brian outside who is scrolling through something on his phone, I walk through to the back of the shop and out into the alley behind. Two of the workers from the sandwich shop with whom we share the alley are outside smoking. When they see me, the one leans in to whisper to the other.

I recognize the one doing the whispering. She was there the day of the credit card debacle but I don't care about that right now. I just look away and hurry through the alley and out to the other street where I see the bus coming. I just make it—charging across the street to cars honking their horns.

The driver gives me a shake of her head as I get on and take a seat.

In fifteen minutes, we're at my stop. It's another five on foot from here and soon, I'm turning the corner to my street.

Throughout the bus ride, I think I should just have asked Brian to bring me here. He would have and if Hawk questioned it, I'd tell him I needed a pair of shoes or a book or something. But it's too late for that now and if I'm quick, he won't find out anyway.

Besides, lying to Hawk is hard. I feel like he knows every time I do it and for some reason, I don't like lying to him.

I give a shake of my head. What I'm doing, it's not any of his business. It's not as if it's a part of our agreement. And he doesn't need to know about my private life. My past. He wouldn't want to.

I'm so lost in my thoughts that I don't notice the stranger on my porch until I turn onto the walkway and stop short. But then I remember what Hawk said about fixing the lock when I see his van and realize he's a locksmith. He's working on the door. Hawk said he'd have that done, I don't know if I didn't expect him to or what, but he's actually having it done.

I walk up the drive to the front door. "Hello," I say to the man, sounding much calmer than I feel, holding up my keys so he knows it's my house. "You must be the man Hawk sent."

He nods, stands and wipes his hands on his pants. "Yes, ma'am," he says. "You are?"

"Melissa Chase." The house is under Chase, not my real name. "I live here."

He nods, shakes hands with me. "Hawk didn't mention you'd be here."

"Oh, I just forgot something. Will my old key work?"

"No, those locks were no good. I'll take the new keys to Hawk as soon as I'm finished here. Just a few more minutes."

"Oh, I'll take the keys. It's my house. Can you let me in while you wrap up?"

"Ms. Chase you said?" He digs out his phone.

"What are you doing?"

"I work for Hawk, ma'am."

"It's my house."

He starts to dial a number.

"Wait, are you calling him?"

He puts the phone to his ear, and I can hear it ringing.

"Wait. Stop." But a moment later, I hear Hawk's voice as he answers.

"Hawk, I'm almost done here but Ms. Chase is here wanting her key and..."

He trails off and I know why from the way he looks at me.

"Yes, sir. All right."

"I need to get inside," I try, the man still nodding at whatever Hawk is saying. I have to get the things I need because what if I can't come back here again?

He finally hangs up the phone and unlocks the door. "Ma'am." He gestures for me to go in. "Hawk is on his way to pick you up. He says you're to wait here."

I swallow. "Hawk's coming?" Crap.

He nods, doesn't quite meet my gaze.

"Okay," I say, walking inside because there's nothing else I can do. I was hoping to slip back into the shop unnoticed, no one the wiser.

The door closes behind me and I hear the new lock turn and when I try it, I can't open the door. I'm locked in my own house.

"I'm sorry, ma'am," the man says. He must hear me struggling with it. "Hawk will be here in a few minutes."

"This is...you can't lock me in my own house!"

He doesn't answer though and from the window, I watch him pack up his things. From that same window, not five minutes later, I watch a black SUV, so out of place here, turn onto the street. Hawk climbs out of it.

A sedan pulls up behind it and Axel gets out, leaning against the driver's side door. He lights up a cigarette.

The locksmith walks up to Hawk, hands him the keys—my keys.

When Hawk looks up at the window and meets my gaze, I drop the curtain and step away, my heart racing because I can see from here that he's pissed.

I run up the stairs and into my bedroom. Inside the closet, I shove the empty shoe boxes aside and find the one I'm looking for.

From inside it, I take out an old pair of sneakers and underneath the tissue paper, find the thumb drive and my passport. I shove both into my purse just as the front door opens and I know the instant Hawk's inside because the air shifts, almost like it gets thinner, and it's hard to breathe.

He doesn't say a word as he climbs the steps. I shove the boxes back haphazardly and stand, shoving the closet door closed just as he fills the bedroom doorway, all huge and annoyed looking.

I find myself stepping backward before he even takes a single step inside because I remember well our conversation from the first night. I have a feeling I'm about to find out what the consequences are for breaking one of his rules.

18

HAWK

"You're wearing out my patience."

I step into the bedroom, note how the closet door is open, two shoe boxes having fallen over stopping it from shutting.

She matches each of my steps in the opposite direction, keeping distance between us. She's flushed and out of breath and looks guilty as sin.

"Brian just lost his job."

"I snuck out the back. It wasn't his fault."

I walk toward the closet and she backs away to the foot of the bed. I open the door, look down at the toppled boxes.

"Actions have consequences. As does incompetence." I shove at a box. "What were you doing?"

"I needed something," she starts, her voice different, forced.

I turn to look at her. "What did you need?" She looks guilty as sin.

Her eyes search mine momentarily before she shifts her gaze to a point beyond my shoulder.

"A book."

"You keep your books in the closet?"

She wrings her hands.

I step to her.

She backs up again. "While I was here, I thought I'd get my yoga clothes."

"Did I give you the impression I'm a complete idiot?"

Her back is to the wall by the time I reach her. She stares up at me, wide-eyed but mute.

"I'm going to give you one chance to tell me the truth because I know when you're lying and you're lying now, Melissa. I'll tell you what. I'll even go first and lay my cards on the table."

"What do you mean?"

"I mean I know something bad happened to you at the Boyd house. I mean I know it was Sean Boyd and maybe his father too, although that part I'm not sure about. I know you went to see Liza at the clinic before you agreed to my proposition and I think it's all related. I think the man from the party last night, I think he's somehow related, but I can't put my finger on how. Not yet anyway."

I watch her pale as I talk, watch the color drain slowly and completely from her face.

"So, I need you to tell me. I need you to tell me if I'm hot or cold and just what the hell is going on."

"Just sex," she says, eyes desperate for me to accept that. "We said—"

"I change my mind."

"You can't—"

"And I'll be honest because one of us should be, it's not wholly because whatever you've got going on is interfering with my time. I'll help you, Melissa. I have the means to. But you have to trust me."

Her eyes fill up with tears turning the pretty golden-brown into the palest, softest sand of a pristine beach.

She shifts her gaze downward. I think she's considering her options, but when she looks up at me again, she's closed off.

"Please leave it alone."

"You're in trouble."

She shakes her head. "I'm not."

I feel my anger growing. My anger at her stubbornness. At her unwillingness to trust me, even if on some level, I understand her hesitation.

"I will help you," I hear myself say and wonder why it's so important to me. Wonder why I give a fuck.

But I do.

Another shake of her head is her only response, though, and I make myself count to ten before I speak.

"All right. This is how you want to play it?"

She just stands there watching me, waiting to see what I'll do, I guess.

"You broke a rule, Melissa. I told you, there will be consequences."

"What consequences?"

I reach for my belt, undo it.

She licks her lips.

"Not that kind of consequences, sweetheart," I say, and watch her eyes widen as I tug it from the loops and double it over in my hand, keeping the buckle in my palm.

With a flick of my wrist, I slap it against my thigh, feeling the sting of it.

The sound makes her jump.

"You have a choice. You tell me. Now. You come clean about everything. Or you don't and you choose to lie down on the bed and you take the consequence."

Tears are welling in her eyes and the first of them slips out. "Please. I can't."

"Can't and won't are two different things. Decide."

She shakes her head no. "You said...we agreed. Just sex."

"And we also agreed there would be consequences if you broke a rule, which you did. I'm giving you an out. I advise you to take it. You do not want me to whip your ass, Melissa."

"You want something I won't give. Something I never agreed to give!"

I shift my gaze to the belt in my hand, adjusting my grip. "Get on the bed. Face down."

"Please don't," she pleads, her voice small as tears streak her face.

"Move. I want your ass bare."

Her gaze falls to the belt in my hand, then returns to mine. "I'm sorry. I should have asked the driver to bring me."

"We're so far from that, sweetheart." I gesture to the bed.

"You'll make me, won't you? You're bigger than me. Stronger. It's what men do, isn't it?"

"Is that what happened? Did Boyd make you? Did—"

"Stop!" She covers her ears as if that will stop her from hearing, then scoots to the side to try to slip toward the door, but I block her way.

"God damnit. Why do you make it so fucking hard?"

"Leave it alone. Leave *me* alone!"

"Either get on the bed or tell me the truth. Last time I'm asking."

"Get away from me. I didn't agree to this."

"That's where you're wrong," I say, and the moment I do, she breaks into a sprint for the door.

I catch her by the arm and tug her backward into me. She bounces off my chest and lets out a scream when I toss her onto the bed. She tries to scramble away, but I grab her ankle, tug her down and trap her with my knee on her back. Without another word, I flip her skirt up and tug her panties down. I bring the belt down across her ass.

I don't think she expects me to go through with it, but the moment the belt makes contact with her skin, it's like the air in the room stands still for just the smallest fraction of a second before she registers the pain and lets out a scream.

I expect her to fight me and she does, at first.

She fights like a hellcat.

But then, after three more strokes, she lays there and takes it. Resigns herself to it, maybe, hands fisted, body tense. I still have to keep my knee on her back—she's not that still—but I expect more of a fight from her. Hell, from anyone.

And I don't take it easy on her. The more strokes I lay down, the less she fights, the more I know she's in real trouble. What in hell could be so awful that she'd rather take a whipping than tell me?

But then the act itself takes over. That sound of leather on flesh, that look of her reddening ass as each stroke is met with a breathless scream as if the belt were forcing the air from her lungs.

Fuck, I know it's wrong, but my cock is hard.

After two dozen, she's got her face buried in the blankets and she's fisting handfuls of it sobbing so loud, I'm sure Axel, who's waiting outside, can hear. Hell, the entire neighborhood must hear.

"Enough?" I ask her.

She won't look at me, but she nods, and I hear her sniffle.

I move my knee from her back, adjust my dick because

now is not the time. I watch her slide to her knees on the floor, hands first cupping her ass, then covering her face. She's hiding herself from me as her shoulders shudder with her sobs.

I weave my belt through the loops of my pants and watch her, then crouch down, take her hands away from her face and make her look at me.

"Let me help you, Melissa. I want to help you."

"Go to hell!" she yells, hands on my face, clawing me.

I grip her wrists, pry her off of me and hold her like that, watch her in her rage, in her pain. I want to shake her. To make her talk.

It takes everything I have to let her go. To stand. To look at her like this. Down on her knees, punished. Sobbing.

It takes everything I have to turn away.

And I'm about to go, to walk out, when there on the bed I see her bracelet. She hasn't noticed it's broken off yet and I don't tell her. Instead, I take it and shove it into my pocket.

"Get yourself together. You have three minutes to be outside," I say, and force myself to walk out that door.

19

MELISSA

I don't know if I'm glad or upset that he's already gone when I get outside.

I took longer than the three minutes he allotted me. Hell, it took me twice that to get up off the floor, to stop crying. And still, every few minutes, I suck in a breath and my entire body shudders.

Axel—I guess Hawk's making sure there aren't any more fuck-ups—glances at me indifferently in the rear-view mirror.

Did he hear, I wonder?

Does he know what just happened?

Heat burns my face. I'm humiliated and hurt, and everything is falling apart.

And Hawk's too close. Too close to finding out everything. And being here, as much as I'm safest from Sean, if Hawk finds out, I don't know what I'll do.

When we get to the casino, I'm relieved that Axel just walks me to the elevator and barely looks at me as we ride up in awkward silence. Only once we're inside the penthouse does he speak.

"You'll stay here until Hawk's back. The elevator will be locked. If you need something, you dial the lobby. They'll help you."

"Where is he?" I ask, my voice so small, and my face, I feel it twisting again. I don't want to cry, not in front of him. I don't want to be so pathetic.

Axel studies me, really studies me and he looks like he wants to say something.

All I want to do right now is disappear. I want for him to leave and for me to go into the bedroom and lock the door and sleep under the covers, buried beneath them. Sleep and forget. Just please God for a little bit, let me forget.

"Questions?" he finally asks.

I shake my head and before he's gone, I've already turned and am going into the bedroom.

There's no lock on the door. I never noticed that before. Only the bathroom door has one. But I'm too tired to do anything other than crawl into the bed. His bed.

I'm so, so tired.

I push the button to darken the glass to black. But before I can go to sleep, I remember Deirdre. She's expecting me to return. I get my phone from my bag and send her a text telling her I won't be back and to close up early.

That's when I realize my bracelet is missing.

Panicked, I look around, but then I remember. I remember during my whipping that it caught on the blankets. I remember when it snapped but I forgot all about it. I forgot to get it.

I need to go back and get it.

I can't think about that though. Not now.

Taking off my shoes, I get into the bed, smelling fresh sheets—who has their bed changed daily? My butt hurts so I lay on my belly and draw the covers up to my neck, then higher and all I hear is the ringing in my ears and the sniffles as I stare off into nothing. I'm not sure if my eyes are open or closed, it's so dark in here, until finally, I fall asleep.

When I wake, the clock tells me it's four in the morning. I turn onto my back, wince with pain, look at his side of the bed to find it empty. I get up only because I need to use the bathroom, then climb back into the bed and close my eyes again.

My backside is throbbing and sore. My thighs too.

I've never been whipped like that. What Sean did, it was a different sort of beating. He liked to use his fists. He couldn't do it as often as he wanted though. It didn't look good on the video to have me looking beat up. Look like I was made to.

Although rape sold well, too, didn't it? As well as child pornography?

God.

Jesus.

Hawk wants me to tell him that?

No. No way. I'm doing him a favor not telling him anything about that.

I squeeze my eyes shut against the things I did but those memories, they don't go away. They don't even dull. They're in brilliant color and the details excruciatingly precise. I remember every sound, every touch, and it makes me sick, as sick now as if it were happening again.

I remember the looks on their face, too. All of them.

God.

I was a whore at eleven.

Little Bitch Whore.

His pet name for me. The bitch was because I fought. At least at first. Then I didn't fight anymore. Not even when he wanted me to.

It's so quiet here, it's almost strange. If I stop to listen, it's a sound itself, that silence. And it somehow calms me. Makes things almost manageable when I concentrate on it and that's what I do. I sleep. I listen. I sleep.

And the next day when I wake up, I leave another message for Deirdre telling her I don't feel well and it's not a lie. I tell her I won't be in for the next few days and just to close the shop and leave a note in the window.

By the time I have a shower the next night, he's still not back.

I lock the bathroom door and strip off my clothes then turn my back to the mirror and look at myself. Look at the damage.

My butt and upper thighs are bruised, the welts of the belt distinct and tender to the touch. I don't know how many strokes he gave me. I stopped counting after ten.

I switch on the shower and I don't know if I'm weak from hunger or just sadness. It's hard to even move, to get myself under the flow of water. All I want to do is sleep. I just want to sleep.

But I force myself to stand there, not shampooing or anything but standing under the water for a good five minutes. Afterwards, I dry off and I put on the same dress because it's the thing near at hand.

I don't want to put on new, nice clothes. What's the point?

I'm hungry and I walk out of the bedroom. I'm quiet when I open the door. I listen for him. Listen for any noise.

But I'm alone.

And by the time I get to the kitchen, I've lost my appetite and I go back to bed.

I'm alone that day and the next and the one after that

except for when the maid comes. I don't let her clean the bedroom.

She's hesitant to leave it and tries to tell me it'll only take a few minutes, but I send her away anyway.

Each night without me having to call, a meal is delivered. I manage a few bites before leaving everything. The following morning, when I wake, the dinner tray is always gone and a fresh tray of breakfast is in its place. I think they bring lunch too. I heard the elevator once. But I sleep in the middle hours. Those are almost harder than the nights.

Every time I push the button to call the elevator, nothing happens. I know I need a key, and I guess they all have one. Everyone but me.

It's not until four nights later when I'm standing at the balcony door trying to open it that I hear the elevator doors slide open behind me.

With a gasp, I turn to find Hawk walk in, big as ever, impeccable in his suit, fierce in his expression.

"You need a special key to open it," he says like it's not weird that he's been gone for four days. That he's kept me locked up in here all that time.

I realize I have my back pressed up against the glass, my hands still behind me on the handle.

He steps inside and looks me over and I look down too.

I'm barefoot. Still wearing the same dress. There's a big stain on the front of it. I don't remember spilling anything. I guess I did, though.

I watch him as he walks around the furniture toward me. My heart is hammering against my chest and my throat has closed up and left me mute.

Why don't I rage? Why don't I fly at him? Hurt him like he hurt me. Scratch out his eyes or tear out skin. The scratches I managed to get in have mostly healed.

"Have you bathed?" he asks once he's standing just a few feet from me.

I'm still glued to the same spot. Maybe I've backed up some more, even, because the heels of my feet are pressing against the cool glass.

"Have you bathed, Melissa?" he asks again.

He reaches out and I flinch. He stops, then moves slowly to touch my hair.

I touch it too. I don't know what I look like. I haven't looked in a mirror since he locked me up here.

And no, I haven't bathed. Not since that first day when I stood under the water.

"They said the trays are mostly untouched," he says.

I don't know what he's talking about.

"Melissa?" He peers down at me. "We had an agreement. Eating was part of that."

The agreement.

His rules.

His to change at will.

"You said you wouldn't hurt me." Tears again. My words are jumbled, my closed throat suddenly too full of them. Too filled with words. "You said," my shoulders wrack, sobs now. No soft tears.

Some women cry pretty. Not me. I've never been one of those women.

"You said," I start again, having to suck in a breath. "You asked didn't I know that? That you won't hurt me?"

I see his face for one second. For one split second through the tears and humiliation and shame, I see his face and I think he's sorry. I think he's sad. Sad when he looks at me.

And then I feel his big hand at the back of my head. He's so strong when he pulls me into his chest and wraps his other arm around my shoulders while he holds me like that and lets me sob. I'm ruining his shirt with tears and snot but I can't seem to stop.

In the middle of this sobbing, I feel a hunger so deep it hurts.

A void so empty, it's a black hole.

And when he lifts me up in his arms and carries me to the sofa, I let him. I don't fight. Not when he sits down and cradles me on his lap and I just sob and sob and sob.

It feels good, him holding me like this. It feels good to be in his arms. Against his chest. He's so strong. And when he's gentle, he's so gentle.

Then after all the sleeping of the last few days, somehow, I sleep again. When I'm spent and dried out, I sleep again and it's dreamless. I'm weightless yet I feel him lift me and carry me and when he lays me down in his bed, I feel him lie behind me, and I sleep.

20

HAWK

I tracked down the asshole from the other night. I had to fly across the country to fucking Dover, New Hampshire, but I found him.

I look down at Melissa. She's a mess. Her hair is a giant tangle around her head, she's wearing the same dress she had on the day I left. When I put my hand against her belly, it's concave. Empty.

She hasn't eaten more than a few bites from a few trays. The maid said she wouldn't let her into the bedroom. I could tell when I brought her in here. The bed was unmade, the comforter a heap at the center of it. The glass walls blacked out.

And here she lies, sleeping. Peaceful when I look at her face with her eyes closed, slightly sunken now. Her thick lashes flutter and she mumbles something, then settles back into sleep.

Her color is paler than usual, but it makes her lips look almost redder for it. Snow White in her glass coffin. Cursed. Sleeping until true love's kiss wakes her. Or is that the other one? Sleeping Beauty? I don't fucking know.

I lay on my back and look up at the ceiling.

The door isn't closed so it's not pitch-black in here. I'm still fully dressed, haven't even taken off my shoes.

I still haven't fully processed what I learned.

What I saw.

I know men. I know we're sick—all of us. But I understand now why she said there were worse men than me out there.

Fuck, she's met them. Known them intimately.

Senator Boyd was part of it. He's lucky he's already dead.

But his son isn't.

I quietly climb up off the bed and look down at her. She looks really young. I always thought that, even on that first night. Like there's a little girl inside there and when she doesn't have her guard up, there she is.

I'm trying to understand it. Understand how a grown man can be turned on by a little girl. A child.

Then I think about Marcus and fifteen-year-old Calla.

Melissa was eleven.

My stomach turns at the thought of what I saw, but I make myself stand there. Make myself look down at her. At this broken girl who's managed to piece herself together over the years, at least for anyone who isn't paying attention.

The asshole from the party knew her from the videos.

I saw two.

Well, saw as far as I could stomach it. Eleven-year-old Melissa with those eyes—only they were terrified then. That's how he'd recognized her. Her eyes.

Melissa the child dressed as a child.

Pretty in pink. I remember her reaction to the pink clothes.

Melissa holding her teddy bear, face white as a ghost. At

least her eyes went absent during the terror. Like she wasn't there anymore.

A ghost.

Grown men fucking a child. Making a ghost out of her.

My hands fist now, and rage tightens my chest. I think about the boy-man from the party. I think about his hands on her.

He claimed to only watch the videos. That he hadn't been there when the acts took place. I only believed him because he'd have been her age then. The perverts would probably have stuck their dicks in him too if he'd been there. What a different world he'd be living in. What a different life he'd have.

Prey, not predator.

But at least he'd still have a life.

I walk toward the door and her words come back to me: *"You said you wouldn't hurt me."*

For what I did to that man, I feel no remorse. But what I did to her—whipping her like I did—fuck. I feel like the world's biggest asshole. And even more so for leaving her there afterwards. Leaving her to get herself together alone.

I should have known better.

Hell, I knew she was coming apart, but I was too pissed off that she wouldn't come clean. That she was hiding something from me. That she didn't trust me.

That's what this is about, isn't it? Trust?

I'm about to leave the room when I see her tote beside the door.

After a quick glance at her, I pick it up, carry it into the living room and turn it over on the dining room table. Everything falls out, her wallet, her phone, a small notebook. A smaller bag with some lipsticks inside it.

And a passport.

This wasn't there the other night.

The name on the passport is Melissa Doe and the photo looks a couple of years old. I leaf through it and don't find a single stamp. She hasn't traveled with it. Hasn't even signed it.

Her phone is out of charge so I can't go through that but when I go to put everything back inside, I notice something stuck half-in, half-out of a tear in the lining. A flash drive.

This is new too.

These are the things she went to get from her house. What if the videos are on here? What if she has them?

No. She wouldn't do that. Wouldn't keep those. What would be the point?

I put the rest of her things back and go to my study, the only locked room in the penthouse. I switch on the light, sit behind my desk and plug the little drive into my laptop.

It takes a moment for my computer to register it, and when I try to access it, a password screen pops up.

I think for a minute and try the obvious, her birth date, her name and birth date, the name of her shop but nothing works. I'm thinking of different combinations when I hear her at the door.

"I don't want to be locked up here again," she says from the doorway.

I close my hand over the drive and discreetly pull it free then slip it into my pocket.

Circles shadow the delicate skin under her eyes. She looks tired, and I want to say it's lack of sleep making her look like this, but I know it's not.

I give her a long nod.

She looks around the room, comes inside and sits in one of the armchairs.

"Where were you?" she asks.

"Away on business."

She just nods.

"It's late. Why don't you go back to bed?"

"Senator Boyd, he wasn't a nice man."

I don't move. I don't even take a breath so as not to spook her.

"Neither was his son. Not to Liza either. That's why I did this for her. The first night I mean. I wanted to protect her from you. From those men. But when I went to see her... well, people don't change, I guess."

"Why did you accept the second offer? The month?"

"The driver's license, Melissa Chase." She stops, reconsiders, changes track. "I don't have great memories of that time."

"Your time with the Boyd family."

"Yes."

"And you ran away."

"Yes."

"And you don't want him to know where you are?" She knows who I mean by him.

She doesn't reply right away but when she does, it's not quite my question she answers.

"I don't know what they know or don't know. Growing up in foster care sucks, Hawk. I don't remember anything about my birth parents. All I know is that I was told I had a bracelet with my name on it when I was found. And then I got lucky and got adopted by a wonderful couple, but after they died in a car crash, I was back in the system."

I don't say anything. Just let her talk.

"Everyone wants babies or toddlers. Not kids older than that and definitely not teenagers," she pauses. "But then Senator Boyd...It was an election year and he'd just had a scandal. That's all. He didn't do it out of love for me or any remotely human feeling for a child."

"Did he hurt you?"

It's taking effort for her to keep her expression neutral, but I see through it. I see the little girl she's trying to hide.

To protect.

In fact, I can't get the image of that little girl out of my head.

But I need to be careful I don't let her see it. Don't let her know what I know.

"No, nothing like that," she says, but her answer is too smooth. Too quick.

"Nothing like what?" I press.

Her gaze snaps to mine and I think she's going over what she said. I think she's trying to make sure she didn't give anything away.

"When I turned seventeen, I left. That's all," she says, completely avoiding my question. "I was old enough to take care of myself and I did. I came to Las Vegas and I met Mrs. Adams who owned Wrinkles in Time and worked for her until she died. She left me the shop and I'm continuing her work. And her kids wish they could evict me and make real money on the building, but they weren't able to contest the will. That's about it in a nutshell."

"And you donate about fifty percent of your profits to the homeless shelter a few blocks away. That's the reason you have the low rent agreement Mrs. Adams' greedy kids aren't thrilled about."

"How did you know?"

"I heard the woman at the shop the other day and was curious, so I looked into it."

"Looked into it? Why didn't you just ask me?"

"You're not so forthcoming, Melissa."

She looks around again, then cocks her head to the side. "You don't have any photographs of family either, by the way," she says.

I remember when she found the one in my book.

"Not in here," she continues. "Not anywhere in the entire penthouse. In fact, this place, as nice as it is, anyone can move in. Apart from that tartan I saw the first night, there's nothing personal in it at all."

"My mother died when I was six. My father remarried and it didn't work out for me to stay." It comes out strange. Awkward.

"What do you mean?"

"I was a threat to her. To her son. My father is a wealthy man. Or he was," I pause. "Greed makes devils out of people."

"Was? Is he..."

I shake my head. "He's alive and well. The fortune is what's suffered. I haven't spoken with my father in thirteen years."

"Hawk, you...he's your father. And he's alive and you know him—"

"He made his choice. So did I."

She studies me. "How did you get here? The casino and everything?" she asks, understanding I won't be answering more questions about my father.

"I had cousins in Utah, but I only stayed with them a few weeks before leaving. Most people aren't good, Melissa. Most people are sick bastards."

Her eyes grow wide and fill up and I think how she knows this so well already. Better than me.

"How old were you?" she asks.

"Sixteen."

"You were so young."

"Older than you were when Boyd took you in."

She doesn't comment.

"I eventually made my way to Vegas. Figured it'd be easier to find work here. I worked for Murray Lanigan who owned the casino and the building. He left everything to me when he died, and I grew the business into what it is today."

"Did you go to school?"

"Not a proper school, no, but I learned plenty."

"Do you miss home?"

That question catches me off guard. "This is my home now." I have to force the words.

And she sees right through me. "Is it?"

I stand. "I have something for you," I say, remembering.

She follows me into the bedroom where I take the box out of my jacket pocket. I hand it to her.

"Here."

She looks down at it, then at me. She doesn't touch it. "What is it?"

"Your bracelet. I had the clasp fixed."

She reaches out to take the box, opens it, shifts her gaze back to me as she lifts it out. "Sometimes you do things that are so not in character with who you are."

"You don't know me, Melissa. But then again, how can you get to know me or anyone else when you're so busy guarding your secrets?"

She doesn't answer me but lets me take the bracelet and put it on her wrist.

"It feels heavier," she says.

"I had a better chain put on it," I tell her. That's all I tell her.

I look down at her. She's so much smaller than me especially barefoot. I like this difference in size and for as possessive as I feel of her, I also feel protective. I've never felt this way for any other human being apart from Murray Lanigan.

But he was an old man. A senile old man.

Melissa, she's a woman.

She looks up at me, expectant.

"I shouldn't have left you there, Melissa. Not after what I did," I say.

A flush creeps up her neck and colors her cheeks. "I don't want to think about that anymore."

"Alright."

"I'm hungry."

I smile, hunger is good. "I'll call down for some food, but first..." I walk her into the bathroom and turn the taps in the tub, plugging the drain once the temperature is set. "Take off your clothes. Throw that dress away. I don't ever want to see it again."

She reaches down to lift it over her head, and I look at her, her breasts too full for her almost too-thin body. She hands me the dress and I wait for the panties and together, I put them into the trash can.

I walk around her, see the healing bruises on her ass. When I press on a spot, she pulls away.

I help her into the tub. "What do you want to eat?" I ask her.

"A steak. Like the first night. And potatoes."

"I'm glad you got your appetite back. I'll give the kitchen a call."

It takes me a few minutes to call down and tell them to leave the food in the dining room. I then return to the bathroom and bring the bottles of shampoo, conditioner and body wash to the tub and to wash her.

I shampoo her hair twice, smooth the conditioner into it and rub her down with body wash, liking the feel of her skin slippery with soap. Liking playing with her nipples, feeling them harden.

After she's clean, I empty the tub and refill it, stripping off my own clothes. She watches me as I climb in across from her, some of the water splashing over the wall of the tub when I do.

"Come here," I tell her, pointing to my lap.

She searches my eyes.

"I need to feel you, Melissa. I need to be inside you."

She gets on her knees, more water splashing over the sides of the tub as she makes her way to me. I lift her a little and, as she grips my shoulders, I slide her onto my cock and she feels like home. And I've been away too long.

Neither of us closes our eyes when I kiss her, tasting her softly. I want soft now. I want to feel her and hear her and watch her face while I kiss her, while I suck her nipples, not using my teeth, not yet.

"I missed this," I say.

"You didn't fuck anyone else while you were gone?"

"Don't be stupid," I tell her, holding her to me while I rise to stand.

The bathroom floor is wet now, but the housekeeper will clean it tomorrow. She wraps her legs around me and I carry her into the bedroom, laying her on the bed so her legs are hanging off.

I kiss her face, her cheek and her chin, her throat, her chest and her breasts. I pull out to slide my tongue down her middle and push her legs wide. Kneeling there, I look at her as she lies open and wet, her pussy pink and glistening.

I push her knees back, lick the length of her, circle her clit, dip into her pussy, then tongue her asshole. listening to her gasp as I do.

Rising up, I grip her ankles, spread her wide and push my cock into her cunt.

She's so wet as she bends her knees and reaches for me, lifting her face to mine, kissing my mouth, tongue on tongue and she's so wet, she's dripping as she opens and stretches to take the thickest part of me.

When I kiss her again her breathing is ragged and her hands fist in my hair. Her nails dig into my scalp as I take more, more, more, moving slowly, feeling every tight inch. Feeling her walls squeeze around my cock, her heat burning me up.

When I rub two fingers over her clit, she begins to moan. I claim more of her and move deeper, my thrusts are harder and soon she's whimpering and moaning and coming. I can feel her throb around my cock as I watch her face, her eyes, as she comes.

I watch her take me as I fuck her hard and deep. I'm hurting a little but that hurt sends her over the edge again as she calls out my name and digs her nails into my back. She's breaking skin, tearing my back as I bury myself inside her.

My cock throbs and I fill her up and it's different than before. Different than any other time.

All I can think is that I want my smell on her always. My seed inside her.

I want to keep her filled up with me and clinging to me and crying out my name again and again and again. Because this woman, this broken thing, I'm never going to get enough of her.

21

HAWK

The next three days pass peacefully enough with Melissa accepting a ride to work and back. I've become obsessed with finding the password on the flash drive. Of locating anyone who had anything to do with those videos, including Sean Boyd, who seems to have disappeared off the face of the earth.

If she's realized the drive is missing, she hasn't said anything.

She's settling in a little better. Maybe it was our conversation from the night before. I don't know, but she seems at least a little more at ease. She's still secretive, but knowing what I know, it makes sense she would be.

I'm looking at her on the monitor in my office when the man who's been checking on her house brings me the stack of her mail. She's up at the pool on the rooftop.

I intend to just hand it to her. Most of it is junk anyway. But as I absently flip through, something catches my eye.

It's the envelope addressed to *Little Bitch Whore.*

My eyes narrow.

It's not stamped so it was hand-delivered.

I lean back against my seat and turn it over, then slip one finger beneath the flap and pop the seal. I take out the folded sheet of paper inside and open it to read the three hand-written words:

Been a while.

I look at the envelope again.

Little Bitch Whore.

I dig my cell phone out of my pocket and hit the button to call Axel. He answers on the first ring.

"Are you on property?"

"Yeah, downstairs."

"Come up here."

"On my way."

I disconnect the call and leaf through the rest of the mail but there's nothing out of the ordinary.

Then I think of something.

I open my desk drawer where I'd stored the thumb drive and plug it into the port on my laptop. The password screen comes up and, on a hunch, I type the words Little Bitch Whore.

And...I'm in.

So maybe this isn't the first time she's had mail like this.

I double-click on the single folder on the drive and inside are several documents, with several .jpg files. I open the first of those and a moment later, I'm looking at Melissa's face, younger, maybe eleven or twelve, a kid. Her swollen lower lip has some dried blood on it and she has a bruise on her jaw. There's also a bruise along her right temple.

The next one is zoomed in on her throat and the black and blue handprint. A big hand. And then her scrawny arms and concave belly with the worst mark. Someone punched her hard in the belly.

I open the next one. She's older in this one. I look at the date of the file. She'd be sixteen, I guess. It's not as bad as the last ones because her face isn't as badly bruised. Her clothes are filthy like she's been in them for days. Like she got splashed with muddy water and it dried on her days ago.

Sickened, I open the text files, but they look to be screenshots so I print everything out to be able to read them.

She didn't go to the cops once. She went three times between the ages of twelve and seventeen.

Three times.

How many times did they hurt her, and she didn't go?

My mind goes back to the other day when I belted her ass. How she'd gone almost still. I'd found it strange she hadn't fought me like I expected her to.

Maybe that's what she did then too. Went still and took it.

Because when the instinct to survive takes over, the decisions we make don't always make sense to an outsider.

I wasn't beaten, or worse, as a child. My uncle—the sick fuck—grabbed my ass exactly once and the instant he did, I left. He was a drunk and I still don't know if he thought I was someone else, but I never went back to ask the pervert.

After a knock on my door, Axel enters.

I set the papers face-down on my desk and hold out the letter. "I think this was hand-delivered to Melissa's house. It would have been sometime in the last three days."

He opens it, reads it.

"I'll have someone watching the house."

We should have had someone there all along. "Where are we on locating Sean Boyd."

"No luck yet. He might have left town."

I shake my head. "No." Instinct tells me he's not gone. "Bastard's still here."

In these reports, she accused him and his father of the physical abuse. She never mentioned the fact that they were raping her. That they were letting others rape her.

"When is Liza Boyd's release?"

"No date yet."

I shift my gaze to the security cameras. Look at the one at the pool that's trained on Melissa. I think she's fallen asleep out there.

"I want to find the bastard."

Axel nods. "We will. I've got someone at the clinic 24/7. He hasn't been by." His gaze moves to the screen. "I'm guessing she doesn't know about this."

"No and we're keeping it that way."

Axel opens his mouth to reply, but my phone rings, interrupting him.

I would ignore it, normally, but because it's sitting on my desk, my gaze naturally drifts to the screen and I read the phone number.

It's not an American number. And although it's not a number I have stored on my phone, I recognize the country code.

Scotland.

"You gonna get that?" Axel asks when I just watch it ring and ring.

I should.

Today's a good day. Today, I bought that last of the shares I need of the MacLeod Distillery, gaining control of the family business.

Today's the day my dear half-brother learns he lost. This should be his call to concede because I've won.

But something feels off.

My fingers move without my authorization and I swipe the green bar and put the phone to my ear.

It's not Declan.

The accent is heavier than my brother's. Too hard for many English speakers to understand. It makes something inside me ache.

As the man is talking, I remember how people looked at me when I first got here, asking me to slow down. How Mr. Lanigan got a kick out of it. How easy it was to get women into your bed when you talked nonsense to them just because of that accent.

It's what I'm thinking when I listen to what he has to say. When those few words turn my world upside down.

22

MELISSA

I'm dozing when Hawk's shadow falls over me.

"You're burnt," he says.

He's like a giant, blocking out the whole of the sun.

"You need to put on sunscreen. Where's your sunscreen?" He crouches down to look through the straw bag I brought to the pool with me.

"Relax," I say, sitting up, straddling the seat. "It's here. And I did put it on." I find the tube of sunscreen under my towel and look down at my chest and he's right, I did burn. But it's not bad.

He sits on the edge of the chaise and takes the tube, squeezes some on his hand and starts to rub it into my chest. He's been like this since he got back. Attentive. Sometimes overly so.

And always watching me.

"Hawk, stop. It's fine. It's not bad and I'm going inside anyway." I stay his hand, but he seems anxious. And I realize how totally out of place he looks up here in his suit while people are splashing around in the pool. Pop music is playing probably louder than he likes.

"I hate this fucking music," he says as if he read my mind.

I smile. "It's your hotel. They'll play whatever you tell them to." He's moved on from my chest to my stomach and seems to be taking special care there. His gaze is fixated on my belly button as he gently rubs the sunscreen in. "Hawk, stop. It's fine. I'm going inside anyway. I don't need more sunscreen."

He stands up abruptly like he's just realized where he is. What he's doing. He shoves my towel into my bag. "Let's go."

I reach out, grab his hand. "Wait."

When he looks impatiently down at me, I can't tell what's in his eyes. It's like a storm of emotions and it's strange, that storm. Like it carries him away from me and the feeling that comes over me, it's like a weight settling in my belly.

"Did something happen?" I ask, forgetting what I was going to say.

It's like he's not here, not hearing me.

Like he's a world away.

"Hawk?"

He gives a shake of his head. "Let's go, Melissa," he finally says.

I rise, pick up my cell phone from the table.

He hurries me along as we make our way to the elevator.

When I meet my reflection in the mirrored doors, I look at myself in the skimpy bikini—he didn't even give me time to put my wrap on. My skin gleams with sunscreen and sweat while he stands beside me, impeccable in his suit. Unreadable. Like nothing can penetrate him.

I wonder what it's like to be like that. To be so confident and comfortable and unafraid.

The elevator doors open and we step into the penthouse.

His gaze sweeps over me, takes in the three triangles at the front, one more at the back. It's black, just a simple black bikini. And it's like he's just realized how naked I am.

He pushes my hair behind my ear, then slides his hand down my back and two tugs later, I feel the top of the bikini fall away, just a wisp, and the only thing between us is the tiny bit of fabric between my legs.

My skin is warm and sticky from the sunscreen, but I don't think he cares.

Hawk looks down at my breasts, pale against my slightly burnt skin. He touches one, cups it, weighs it, takes the nipple in his fingers and manipulates it so it hardens, sending sensation down to my belly, my core.

"Wait," I say, putting my hands against him as he pushes me backward into the wall.

He undoes his belt, his pants. "Wait for what?" he asks, smashing his mouth over mine.

The sweet coconut of the sunscreen mixes with his after-shave and I think about the physical differences between us, him big and hard, all muscle, and I think how much I like it. How safe I feel when he holds me.

I feel his cock at my belly and one hand moves to grip my hip as his other cups my jaw.

"Wait for what?" he repeats before lifting me a little, positioning me, his fingers pushing the slip of fabric between my legs aside so he can thrust into me. Hurrying. Like he's desperate.

It's hard and it forces the breath from me. I'm not yet ready, but I like it. I always like the first thrusts. The hurt.

I can come from that hurt alone.

"Look at me, Melissa."

My eyes zero in on his and he's watching me. His pupils are dilated so all I see are the rings of green and blue, that gray banished now as he fucks me, and I wonder how I'm not split in two. How someone so big doesn't just tear me in two.

I dip my head into his shoulder.

With his chest against mine, he keeps me trapped at the wall as he takes my face in both hands.

"I said look at me." He squeezes.

"Hawk?"

His thumbs press into my cheeks. I notice he's not blinking. Something's wrong. I know it.

"What's happened?" I ask.

He shakes his head, shifts his grip to cup my ass, pulling me open. I feel his finger press against my tight hole. He licks my mouth, my lips, then kisses me the way he does when he's going to come and we're so close. Connected.

"You don't know how much I need this," he says.

I never thought I'd like sex. I never thought it was possible for someone like me to like it. Take pleasure from it. But with him, I come. With him inside me, I come.

And when he comes, it's abrupt and almost punishing, that last thrust. He buries his face in the crook of my neck and I feel his breath on me as his cock throbs inside me, releasing, releasing. Filling me up.

I'm panting for breath and when he finally pulls out of me, cum slides down my thighs. Then he's far away again. Silent but holding me close, holding my face, his fingers pressing into my skin.

He's distant again. In that other world. It's as if an ocean divides us and I'm left cold.

He steps backward, looks away from me.

I touch his face.

"What's going on?"

When he finally returns his gaze to mine, it's like he has to drag it.

"Hawk?"

"My father was buried yesterday."

23

MELISSA

We're packed, flight booked and at the airport in record time.

All he's said about his father is that he was buried yesterday. After that, he took a call which I assume was a secretary telling him she'd confirmed our flights and told me I had twenty minutes.

Twenty minutes to shower and pack and leave for *Scotland.*

And somehow, here I am, wet hair in a clip on top of my head, wearing jeans, a long-sleeved T-shirt and the only sweater I have.

Hawk went into my tote to get my passport earlier, which makes me wonder how he knew it was in there at all, but I don't ask him. He's too distracted. Shocked maybe by the news.

He's wearing jeans and a thin, charcoal, V-neck sweater with a sport coat. It's probably the most casual I've seen him.

"Flight leaves in fifteen minutes. They're holding it for you," Axel says as soon as we pull up along the curb at the airport.

Hawk is out and walking to my side with a leather duffel slung over his shoulder. There's a long line at the counter, but we bypass economy and head to the first-class check in counter.

Hawk hands over our passports and tells the woman his name. She's obviously expecting us.

She looks at him a moment too long before doing her job and we're soon escorted through security and to our gate where we're the last to board.

Hawk puts his duffel and my tote in the overhead and gives me the window seat.

It's such a whirlwind that I'm still buckling my seatbelt when he orders a whiskey.

Not fifteen minutes later, our flight is taking off for London where we'll have a short layover before catching a connection to Inverness.

"Get some sleep, Melissa. It's going to be a long trip."

"Are you okay?" I ask.

He swallows the whiskey, signals the attendant for more. "I'm fine."

He's not fine. He's nowhere close to fine. But I remain silent as he orders glass after glass of whiskey before finally closing his eyes and laying his head back. He's not sleeping though. His forehead is furrowed, and I know he's deep in thought.

"Sleep," he says, as if he can see me staring at him.

I do. Or try to at least. By the time we arrive in Inverness, I'm exhausted. I probably got about two hours of sleep on the various flights, and am only staying awake now because of the coffee I managed to drink in London. I'm not sure how Hawk's standing as he loads the duffel into the trunk of our rented SUV.

He walks me to the wrong side of the car, and it takes me

a moment to realize the steering wheel is on the other side here. They drive on the opposite side of the road.

We've barely spoken during the long trip, but once he situates himself in the driver's seat and starts the car, I put a hand on his forearm.

"Should you drive?" I ask. Every time I opened my eyes, it seemed he had a fresh glass of whiskey in his hand.

He looks over at me. "I'm fine."

"I just don't know if it's—"

"I can hold my liquor," he snaps, and I quiet as he expertly pulls out of the tight parking spot, seeming completely at home with this opposite way of driving, shifting gears easily with his left hand, the SUV taking us smoothly onto the road.

It's almost another three hours of driving until we near our destination. The sun and the rain intermingle, each giving way to the other as we near the western coast. There are fewer and fewer cars on the hilly roads as we seem to drive farther and farther from civilization.

And the nearer we get to our destination, the heavier Hawk's mood grows, the quieter he becomes.

I look out the window, take in the beauty of this wild land.

Las Vegas has a dry climate. Here, the hills are the greenest I've ever seen and they seem to go on for miles.

"We're in the Highlands," he says, as if reading my mind.

"It's beautiful."

He makes a gruff sound of acknowledgement. "We're almost there."

"Where is there?"

"The MacLeod home. This is the nearest village. Mallaig."

I sit up when I see the sign marking the boundary of the village.

I've never been out of the country. I haven't seen most of the US and never anything like this quaint village along the coast with its stone houses and small bakery and butcher. A tea shop with pretty cakes displayed in the windows.

But we're through it before I realize and I swear the weather in the direction we're driving is darker, the unpaved road narrower.

Hawk's hands are tight on the steering wheel. We bump along the road and after climbing one of the steepest hills, I see a lone structure in the distance. It's ten more minutes until we reach the long stone bridge that connects what appears to be an island, upon which the MacLeod house is situated, to the mainland.

And I'm in awe.

"This is your...house?"

He only nods once and when I glance at him, I see how his brows are knitted together.

House.

This *house* takes my breath away. It's not a house at all, but a fortress or castle, even. It must be hundreds of years old with stone walls that match the current color of the dark sky. And as we drive over the bridge, I wonder if we should, it's so old.

I glance at Hawk again and I see him differently. In Las Vegas, he's big. He's brutal. He's in command.

Here, he's all of those things, but he's a Highlander first. Born and bred here. It's obvious now. Rough and rugged and fierce, but different.

Less sophisticated, less polished. Wild, like the landscape.

Even his name, it fits.

"Mother-fucker," he mutters, his lip curling as he looks at the house.

The bridge gives way to a large circular courtyard. There are two other vehicles parked here. It's strange, the cars too modern for this ancient place.

I'm distracted by the beauty of the castle that appears to be part ruin. The far walls have crumbled into the water beneath, but there's smoke coming from two of the six chimneys and lights are on in the small windows of the first floor.

There are three floors in the front part of the building, more in that tower in the distance. But is the tower, too, crumbling? I can't tell from here.

Hawk climbs out of the SUV and I open my door. He doesn't retrieve the duffel but comes directly to my side, eyes locked on the castle.

"It's cold here," I say, hugging my arms to myself. It's nowhere near as warm as Vegas.

"It's always cold here," he almost snaps, wrapping his hand around the back of my neck.

I stop, make him turn to me.

"Why did you bring me?"

He doesn't answer right away but smiles a rueful smile and his eyes, even though they're on me, are distant.

He leans down, squeezes his hand around my neck and brings his mouth to my ear.

"Because I'm going to need to fuck the desire to murder my half-brother out of me."

With that, he pulls back.

I know I should be offended but this is the first insight I've had into his life. And it's a big one.

He has a half-brother.

And he hates him.

I remember the photograph I'd found tucked inside his

book. Remember the man holding the baby. Is that his brother?

I open my mouth to ask him more, but the sudden sound of dogs barking breaks into the quiet day, interrupting us. I startle and I don't know if Hawk sees that, but he takes my wrist, pulls me behind him.

We both turn to what a quick count tells me are eight golden retrievers running our way, six puppies and two adults.

"I don't believe it," I hear Hawk say and I see the smile on his face. It's one that makes his eyes shine.

He releases me and crouches down to greet the dogs, petting them and even laughing when the pups lick his face.

When they come to me, I pet them too, but am more curious about Hawk's reaction to them. So different to the cool, collected man I've come to know. The one who doesn't let anything personal show. Ever. A man who is passionate, but so guarded.

I realize I don't know anything about him that doesn't have to do with me.

He finally straightens, giving one of the mature dogs a final pat on the head. "There was a pup I left behind," he says. "I'm going to guess these are the next generation."

"They're sweet," I say, as one of the puppies, tail wagging frantically, licks my face. "And enthusiastic."

I stand, and when he turns to the door, the smile and ease from a moment ago vanishes, replaced by something heavier.

We walk toward the imposing front doors, two heavy wooden doors with black ornate iron hinges and studs, almost as if they came from a century ago. Maybe they did.

He doesn't bother to knock, which surprises me, but

pushes the door open and immediately I smell the scent of wood burning and food cooking.

We step into the entry and stand on a carpet so worn, it's almost threadbare. I can see the stones beneath in some places. The walls, too, are draped with carpets or maybe they're made especially for the walls. I'm not sure, but I don't have time to think or ask about it because I hear footsteps. And soon, a man appears.

A man as tall as Hawk.

As big.

As beautiful.

The one from that photograph, just a little older from when that was taken.

And each man, upon seeing the other, stops, eyes hardening.

Tension thins the air around us.

No, not tension.

This is something else.

Something more.

Hate.

The man must be a few years younger than Hawk but the similarities in features, in stance, in the ferocity of their gazes, leaves no question that these two are related.

"Well, well," the man says in his heavy Scottish accent. "The prodigal son returns."

Hawk releases me and steps toward him. "Prodigal or not, I'm laird of this house."

"Not yet, you're not, brother."

I grip Hawk's arm when he takes another menacing step forward. But when we hear another set of footsteps, he stops.

An older man appears. He must be in his seventies and he's dressed formally in a dark suit. He stops upon seeing

Hawk, surprise in his eyes. A moment later, he smiles warmly.

Hawk takes him in, and nods in greeting.

I wonder if he can speak. If he's able to because his eyes betray his emotions. I wonder if the others can see it. See the loss.

"Welcome home, Hawk," he says, extending his hand to shake Hawk's before moving in to hug him. It takes Hawk a moment to hug him back. "Your father would have wanted you here."

"Don't humor me, old man," Hawk says, stepping backward. "My father turned his back on me." His accent, it's stronger here, that deep burr that belongs only to the Scots making me sit up and take notice.

But maybe it's the anger in his words that makes him sound so harsh.

The brother snorts and starts to say something, but the old man raises his hand to quiet him.

"Now's not the time, Declan. Your brother's had a long journey."

The older man hasn't taken his eyes off Hawk once. When he finally turns to me, when he steps toward me with a warm smile, I see a slight resemblance. It's not as strong as it is between the brothers.

"Miss," he says, coming close enough to shake my hand. "I'm Benjamin. Hawk's grandfather."

"Grandfather?"

I meet Hawk's gaze for one moment before returning my eyes to Benjamin.

"I'm Melissa. Melissa Doe." I wonder if it sounds strange when I say that. The Doe. It sounds strange to me. But maybe that's because I've been using Chase for such a long time and I'm not exactly sure why I tell him my real name now.

"A pleasure to meet you," he says.

Declan snorts and when I look at him, I find him watching me, his dark eyes unreadable.

But then he shakes his head and turns on his heel to disappear into the house. The tension physically lifts from the room once he's gone.

"A bedroom's been prepared—" Benjamin starts, but Hawk cuts him off.

"I'll be taking the master."

24

HAWK

Melissa is taking in every aspect of the house as I lead her through it. Her mouth is practically hanging open, but she doesn't realize she's seeing it at its worst.

It's strange to come back to the house in this state. I knew what I was doing over the last several years, but to see it in person is more difficult than I realized it would be. It's run-down and old. Something that was once grand, reduced. Humbled.

I guess that's what I was trying to do to them. To my father. My step-mother. Declan.

I shove that pang of remorse down deep and lead Melissa up the stone steps to the second floor and to my father's rooms.

Two maids are rushing in and out, carrying his things out.

I push the heavy wooden door wide and gesture for Melissa to enter. She does, quickly scooting to the side to let another of the maids with an armful of clothing out.

I don't recognize the things she's carrying but know

they're my fathers from the colors alone. Our colors. Strange the things you never forget.

He was a proud man. I remember that about him. Proud of his heritage. Of this house. Of what our family name stood for.

I was proud too. Proud to be the first-born son of Hawk MacLeod. Proud to carry the traditional name granted only to the first-born of the first-born.

It meant something to me. Hell. It had meant everything to me.

But that was before my mother died. Before my father married his mistress and made her lady of our house. Before he acknowledged Declan as his—my half-brother—born to him and his mistress just one year after my own birth while he was still married to my mother.

I never learned if my mother knew. I hope she didn't.

Ann, his mistress, had such influence over my father, much more than my mother ever had. She was young and beautiful, and, pathetically, these things seemed to be all she needed to wrap my father around her little finger.

For years, I didn't know Declan was my half-brother. When my father married Ann, I was seven years old. Declan was six. It took him five more years to acknowledge that Declan was his by blood. I guess he was trying to give the impression of being respectful of his dead wife.

By then, I'd come to dislike Ann. Even at twelve years old, I'd started to see through the façade and know the kind of woman she was. Everyone did. Everyone but my father.

Greedy. Superficial. Spiteful. She loved money more than she loved my father or me or even her own son. Loved money more than she did this house. More than she ever understood what this family stood for.

She succeeded in cutting me out of the will altogether.

Succeeded in aiding her son to steal my inheritance out from under me.

And my life's mission since then has been vengeance and all around me is the stain of my success.

I should be happy.

I should be fucking jumping up and down with joy.

"Just make the bed and get the hell out," I snap at one of the maids, annoyed at all the movement, all the people.

I have a headache. I'm fucking dead tired and I have to deal with Declan. I was hoping Benjamin would have gotten him out of the house before my return.

"It's made, sir. I had fresh sheets put on just yesterday," one of them tells me.

The Scottish accent has me enthralled for a moment. I haven't heard it in so long. Haven't spoken like this in so long.

"Thank you," I say more calmly.

She nods and closes the door when she leaves.

I turn to Melissa who appears awestruck in the large room with its thick stone walls and windows in deep alcoves, the glass encased in iron seeming from another time. She goes to the one on the farther end of the room, passing the large four-poster hand-carved bed, fingers trailing over the wood.

I don't think she realizes what the etchings are. People fucking. The marriage bed passed down from generation to generation, blessed to breed a large, healthy clan, the responsibility on the shoulders of the first-born son.

Those times are past though. There is no more MacLeod clan.

I ignore the sick feeling at the thought.

Melissa looks out the window. I watch her take it in

before shifting my gaze to see this landscape again for the first time in thirteen years. Almost half my lifetime.

How have I forgotten how beautiful it is here? Even in the rain and mist. The water, the mountains, the cliffs. She hasn't even seen what's beyond those cliffs yet. Endless beauty. So wild and utterly different from the Vegas strip.

Christ. I remember this. I remember all of it and that longing for the soil of my home. I've not felt it this acutely in too many years.

I've not allowed myself to feel anything at all.

"The Atlantic lies just beyond those cliffs. Climate's very different than Las Vegas."

"I've never seen anything like this," she says, turning to me, then scanning the room, the antique furniture that's been in my family for generations, the tattered rugs on the floor so necessary against the chill in these old stone estates.

I walk into the second room, which should be a sitting room, but I see it's been converted into a huge closet stuffed to the gills with dresses and shoes and bags, all brand names I recognize. All wholly unnecessary and impractical for the Scottish Highlands. Many not even worn with tags still attached.

This is Ann's work. Her pathetic legacy.

I return to the main room, trying like hell to manage whatever the fuck is going on in my head and in my gut.

"There's a bathroom through here if you need it," I say, opening the door to find they had updated the bathroom with modern luxuries.

Melissa walks toward me. "Are you okay?"

I look over her head, out at the sprawling hills and the lush green grass. The wind has cleared the sun of clouds for the moment and the light it casts is more beautiful than that of constant sunshine.

But in the next instant, it's dark again and rain pelts the windows.

She touches her hand to my cheek. "Hawk?"

I look down at her.

She didn't sleep last night, not much at least, but even so, she's still beautiful. Las Vegas, and that first night, and the auction, and everything, all those things, it feels like a lifetime ago.

She feels like a lifetime ago and I realize how much my own thoughts and feelings about her have changed. Have become something strange and foreign to me.

I give a shake of my head.

Now's not the time for that. Now I need to deal with my family.

But I need one thing from her first.

I need to fuck her. To bury myself in the familiar warmth of her.

I walk her to the bed and there, turn her, hold her to me as I undo her jeans with one hand and slide my other hand up her sweater to cup her lace-clad breast. I shove her jeans half-down her hips and push her over the bed. Her panties are askew, and I push them down too. I gaze down at her ass, her perfect ass, as I undo my jeans and take myself out.

Crouching down behind her, I spread her open and look at her, lick the length of her. Dip my tongue inside her and taste her wet cunt before standing, keeping her spread as I drive into her.

She's not ready and she struggles against me.

"Be still," I say, taking her wrists and spreading her arms wide, like she's the Christ nailed to the cross that's hanging over the bed. Like she's the sacrifice.

But she isn't that.

I am.

I *was.*

I lay my weight on her. Looking up at that thing when I fuck her, holding her down, her cunt slickening, wetting the passage for me. This is what I need. Her. To fuck her. To be inside her and feel her.

This fucking, it's like animals rutting. There's nothing slow or sensual about it. It's simple need. And soon I hear her breathing change, coming short and fast. So I fuck her harder and I don't care if she comes, not right now. This is about something else.

I need release.

And being here, I need to stake my claim.

When I'm just a thrust away, I pull out of her, fisting my cock as it throbs, and I come. I come all over their bed, their sheets, their pillows. I cover their bed in cum as Melissa watches.

I know she doesn't understand. Even as orgasm racks my body, I see her, and I know she does not understand.

When I'm finished, I pull my jeans up, look at my work, then at her. I see the expression of shock on her face as if I've just defiled a fucking church altar.

"You don't know what they did to me," I say harshly.

She steps toward me. "I'm sure it's a lot to take in, especially with your father's—"

I chuckle. It's an ugly sound.

"No, I'm not overwhelmed by emotion or sorrow for the loss of my father. I lost him long ago. If he was ever a father to me at all." I check my watch, run a hand through my hair. "Go have a shower. I'll have someone change the bed so you can sleep. I'll come for you after I meet with Benjamin." I don't want her talking to Declan or anyone else.

She reaches down to pull up her panties and jeans.

"What's going on with you?" she asks.

I turn away, and everywhere I look, I see memories. Remembrances. Hell, I almost see him.

And worse than seeing, I *feel* how much I've lost.

Fuck.

It's not supposed to be like this. *I'm* not supposed to feel like this.

"Hawk?"

"I need to take care of some things. Talk to Benjamin. Understand."

"Understand what?"

"Get cleaned up. Shower. Take a nap. Whatever. But you're not to leave this room until I come to get you."

"Why?"

"Because I said so." I walk to the door.

"Hey!" She follows, grabs my arm. I turn and see on her face that she's taken aback by what she sees on mine. It takes her a moment to continue. "Don't take it out on me. I'm sorry your father died and that you had to come back here, but I am not your enemy. You brought me, remember?"

I snort.

She has no idea.

"You're tired, Melissa. Get some rest." I open the door to leave, anxious to talk to Benjamin.

"Tell me why you bothered to bring me if you're just going to be a jerk to me. At least tell me that."

I stop, turn to her. "Do as I say. You know how you'll be punished if you don't."

Her face pales and her mouth opens, but she doesn't say anything.

Fuck. I don't mean that. Not after everything.

"Melissa—"

She clears her throat, shakes her head and when she looks at me, her eyes are different. Wounded.

Crap.

"You're right. I am tired," she says. "Tired of you and your secrecy. You accuse me of it and look at you."

I don't have a comeback. She's right.

A moment later, she turns and disappears into the bathroom. I hear the lock turn.

I look at the closed door, take a step toward it, but stop. I have to deal with my brother now.

I walk out the door telling the maid along the way to change our bedding as I head down the stairs and into my father's old study.

My study now. Almost.

Along the way, I'm looking at everything I pass, remembering everything, the paintings, the rugs, the feel of the stone walls and even their smell. God, I'd forgotten how Scotland smells. How this house smells.

But I can't think about all of that because if I do, it will overwhelm me, and I can't let that happen.

Not now.

Not here.

Not ever.

25

HAWK

"Nice of you to join us," Declan says.

I ignore him.

Benjamin is sitting behind my father's antique desk and a man I don't recognize is standing beside him pointing to something on a document. He's introduced as Michael Smith, one of the attorneys of the estate.

Declan watches me from his place at the far wall. He's leaning against it and has the bottom of his right foot resting on it. His arms are crossed over his chest and he looks so different to how I remember him. Older than he is.

I wonder how he sees me.

Last time I saw him he was fifteen years old. Benjamin has sent photographs over they years, but I threw most away.

When my father married his mother and he became my brother, I was excited about the idea. I liked Declan, we were close, even.

But that was when I'd thought he was my stepbrother, not a half-brother. We were friends before that, too. When my mother was alive

But with my mother's death, everything changed.

And being back here, it brings back all those old memories. Those old betrayals.

"How's the master bedroom?" Declan asks.

I look at him, eyes narrowing.

"Fuck her in the *laird's bed* yet?"

I cross the room in three steps and grip him by the collar. He does the same to me, his grip as powerful as mine. If we fought, we'd be equally matched. Two Goliaths at war.

"You will talk to me with respect."

He gives me a one-sided grin. "Your ears grow delicate, brother?"

"I am not your brother and I will demolish you."

"I doubt it."

"Look around you, Declan. I already have."

"No, you demolished him."

That renders me mute.

"Stop it, both of you," Benjamin orders. "Sit down."

"I tried to shield him from the truth of what you did, you know that? Of what you were doing to your own family."

"He wasn't my family. He chose."

"Imagine that. I had to protect my father from his own son. His first-born."

His father.

"Who was protecting him from your mother? I saw her closet overflowing with clothes they couldn't afford. And look at this house. Look at the state of things."

"No matter what you want to believe, he loved her."

"Oh, I have no doubt of that. She made a fool of an old man. My question is did she ever love him? Love his name? Love his family?"

"You chose to leave. Remember that."

"It wasn't that simple and you know it," I say, releasing

him, shoving him backward. "But you know what? It doesn't matter. I own fifty-one percent of the company and the estate is effectively bankrupt. You'll sign the papers and the house will be mine in a matter of hours. I've won, *brother*. So fuck you."

"Ever hear the term cutting off one's nose to spite one's face? Not sure I'd call what you did winning."

"You can pack your things and get the hell out as soon as the papers are signed," I say.

He grins, adjusts the cuffs of his shirt, his attention to them as he replies. "You tell your nephew he's got no home, then."

"You mean your bastard—"

"Hawk!" Benjamin interjects.

Fuck.

I turn away, grit my teeth.

"What in God's name has come over you?" Benjamin asks.

He's right. The child is what? Four? He's not to blame. Not to be hated.

As if on cue, the door flies open and we all turn to find a boy—my nephew I know from first sight—charge inside. He's got a toy train in his hand and runs directly to Declan who catches him and lifts him into the air.

"I found it! I told you it was under the bed and no one would trip over it."

Declan cradles him, smiles at him in a way I don't think I've ever seen him smile. It's like his entire face softens.

He takes the toy train from his son's hand.

The boy spots me from the corner of his eye, a stranger, and turns his full attention to me. His eyebrows furrow together and it's like looking into a mirror when I see his blue and green eyes.

But for all the innocence inside his, I know the opposite fills mine.

"Who's that?" he asks, pointing so his finger is inches from my face.

Declan's face hardens when he turns his gaze to mine. "That is your *Uncle* Hawk," he says, setting the boy down. "Meet your nephew, brother. James Declan Scott."

James steps toward me and holds out his hand like a little gentleman.

"How do you do?" he asks. "I didn't think you were real."

God. Can I feel like more of an asshole?

I crouch down, take the boy's small hand in mine. "Nice to meet you, James. I can assure you I am very real."

"You don't talk like us."

"No, I don't."

"Do you fly hawks too?" he asks. "Like Grandpa? He said you did. He said you were good at it."

He said that?

My father was a falconer. I had just begun learning the sport when the shit hit the fan so many years ago.

"No, James. Not anymore," I say, straightening. I look at my grandfather. "I'm tired. Let's get this done."

"Go find Alice, James. Help her with lunch," my brother says.

James rolls his eyes. "Alice is so boring."

I can't help but grin.

"Go on," Declan says. "We'll eat together. Make sure she bakes her shortbread."

At that, the boy smiles then turns back to me. "Nice to meet you, Uncle Hawk," he says before walking out. Declan closes the door behind him and turns to me.

"Why don't you let *him* know he'll need to vacate his home? Maybe you can do that after lunch," Declan says.

"Sit down. Both of you," Benjamin says.

We remain standing, glaring, until Declan finally moves, knocking my shoulder when he walks past me to take his seat.

"Declan!" my grandfather's tone is chastisement enough. "You're not boys anymore for Christ's sake! You're men. Declan, you're a father. And whether either of you like it or not, you are family and just about the only family you have left."

Like hell.

Declan and I both take a seat.

I'm tired and meeting James like that, I was unprepared.

I want this done. I want to get out of this room. This house. Clear my head in the crisp Highland air.

Benjamin nods, turns to the attorney. "Michael, let's go over the will," he says, and Michael takes over, explaining the will that leaves everything, as expected, to Declan. Including the debt of the house.

That's where I come in. Because without me and without my money, this place will turn into a pile of rocks and the family distillery which went public under Ann's ridiculous advisement, is now under my control. And that, too, I will drive into the ground.

I want to gloat but then I remember why I'm here. I think about my father. About him in the ground. I think about the little boy who calls me uncle. Who didn't believe I was real. I don't know the first thing about him.

I look around the office, remembering things I'd forgotten. Amazing how the brain works. Adjusts. Protects.

The last thirteen years, life has gone on here while I've been living my own separate one. They all moved on. I guess I did too, but part of me, it's still sixteen years old as I sit here.

And that part of me that, even now, feels a pang of jealousy of Declan.

He slipped right into my place, took over my role like it was his from the start. Stole it right out from under me. Stole both my father and my life.

"Why didn't you name him Hawk?" I ask out of the blue, interrupting the reading of the will.

I look to Declan who looks to me.

"First born male child carries the name," I say. I was disowned. Didn't that erase my existence and give Declan that status?

"First-born of the first-born. The name wasn't mine to give," he says.

Fuck.

Am I supposed to be grateful?

Michael clears his throat. "The distillery is still bringing in some money, but not nearly what it used to."

"Hawk knows well what the distillery is bringing in, Michael," Declan says. "He holds fifty-one percent of the shares, not quite honorably obtained, but well, what can you expect?"

Michael gives me a glance but is clever enough to keep his judgement to himself.

I sit back, take a deep breath in, keep my face hard as stone. "Just business, *brother*."

Declan's hands fist on his lap but he keeps his gaze forward on the wall of shelves behind my grandfather.

When the will's been read, Benjamin slips another document onto the desk. My offer to buy the house. He clears his throat.

"Before that's signed, I want to see the house," I say, standing. "Declan."

"What am I, your personal tour guide? Don't remember where things are?"

"I want to see the state of things. I assume you know it best."

"I have more important things to do like meeting my son for lunch," he says, and walks out the door.

26

MELISSA

After Hawk left, I took a long, hot shower then decided to lie down and close my eyes for a few minutes. Now, as I open them in the almost pitch-black room, I realize I must have slept for hours.

I glance to the other side of the bed, but it's not been slept in. I wonder what time it is but there's no clock in this room. Pushing the covers back, I get up. I'm barefoot and the cold of the stone beneath the old carpet chills me.

I walk into the alcove thinking the walls must be three feet deep. I wonder if that's for insulation or protection in times past. I look out the window at the utter darkness outside. The almost complete stillness.

The moon is full, the wind a whistle that urges the clouds across the sky, the light an ominous silvery ghost-like thing spilling over the water and the hills.

I think if I look hard enough, I'll see ghosts out there.

Finding the latch, I push one of the heavy windows open and lean out. It's a cool night and I inhale the clean, fresh air.

I think how I'd like to go outside, walk out there in the

dark. Feel that quiet. You never have quiet like this in Las Vegas, not even in my neighborhood in the middle of the night. This is nature at its most primal. Undisturbed and serene and magnificent.

My stomach growls and I close the window. I switch on the lamp beside the bed and from inside my tote, I find my phone but it's out of charge and I can't tell the time. I don't have a charger that fits these sockets.

I put on my jeans and a sweater and tuck the phone into my pocket hoping someone has a charger I can borrow.

Slipping on my shoes—a pair of ballet flats—I open the bedroom door and walk into the hallway.

The house is still, as quiet as the night.

As if on cue, I hear the tolling of a clock.

Three chimes.

Three o'clock.

I glance down the hall at all the closed doors, count five in addition to the master. I then head down the stone stairs, taking in a painting on the wall, the tartan of the man pictured the same as the one at Hawk's penthouse.

I remember thinking how generic the penthouse looked. This place, there is nothing generic about it. The opposite. There's history and purpose and family in every square inch.

When I reach the first-floor landing, I see a dim light and walk toward it. It's the living room, I think. A large room with a huge fireplace at the center. I can smell the wood of a recent fire but it's not burning anymore.

I touch the stone of the fireplace and wonder how old it is. How old some of the paintings on the walls are.

Everything here is steeped in history, but all of it, it's tired. Like it's not been cared for and time is eating it away.

It's strange. Sad in a way to lose the past like that but I can't imagine what it costs to keep up a house like this.

Beside the fireplace is a basket overflowing with toys and children's books. I didn't realize there was a child living here. Strange that Hawk wouldn't have mentioned it.

I have to remember he's under an immense amount of stress right now between the death of his father and having come back here, to a place that obviously holds a lot of emotions for him. Painful ones.

Emotions I'm sure he'll refuse to feel or even acknowledge.

There's a sconce along the wall that's lit in the hallway and I follow it toward what I hope is the kitchen. I pass the front doors and peer out of the deep-set windows at that strange light coming and going as clouds obscure the moon.

I get to a door without a handle and push on it. It swings inward and there's a light that's been left on over the modern stove. I step into the large kitchen and it's such a strange place with old and new, the countertops smooth stone, the long, heavy wooden table which looks like it's as old as the house, the newer chairs, plush and comfortable, the appliances stainless steel and gleaming, the refrigerator a Goliath mounted into the wall.

A toy train is the only thing on the table. It looks old, not like the plastic toys you find in the shops these days. More like an antique.

On the wall, I see the light switch and I turn it on. The room is bathed in soft light and the windows become mirrors. Dishes are stacked on the drying rack beside the sink and the dishwasher hums as it runs.

There's a large pot on the stove but I'm disappointed when I open it to find it empty.

I go to the refrigerator and there I find cheeses and

meats and decide on a sandwich. Taking out a few things, I set them on the counter and find a loaf of bread covered by a tea towel on a cutting board.

Using the knife beside it, I cut two thick slices and set them on my dish to make my sandwich at the counter. I'm just sitting down to take my first bite when the swinging door opens.

I'm startled.

But so is he.

Declan. Hawk's brother.

He stands there for a moment looking at me with surprise, but he recovers quickly and smiles, comes inside.

"You weren't introduced to me," he says, and I really have to pay attention to understand him because his accent is so heavy. "I'm Declan MacLeod, Hawk's half-brother." He holds out his hand.

I put my sandwich down, force myself to swallow the bite in my mouth and place my hand in his. "I'm Melissa."

"Melissa. It's nice to meet you. You missed dinner."

"I must have slept through it."

"We didn't want to wake you. The maid said you were fast asleep."

"Where's Hawk?" I ask.

He shrugs a shoulder and moves to the counter. "Who knows?" he asks, opening a cupboard and taking out an unmarked bottle of liquor. "You like whiskey?" he asks, turning to me.

He seems different than Hawk. Not as hardened.

"It's our own," he says, not waiting for my answer but taking two glasses and returning to the table to take a seat across from me. "Don't mind me. Eat," he says, pouring whiskey into both glasses and passing one to me.

I take a bite but have to concentrate on chewing. I can't

seem to drag my eyes away. The similarity in features is so striking, but the differences are just as stunning.

And he's like a window into Hawk's life. A living, breathing part of a world Hawk won't or can't share.

"Are you normally up at three in the morning?" I ask, trying to sound casual.

He gives a sad little smile. "It's been a long few weeks. And now with my brother back, they'll be longer still."

I nod. I don't know what to say.

He picks up the toy train, touches the chipped corner.

"Is there a child in the house? I saw the toys in the living room."

"Aye," he says. "My boy."

"Your son?" I smile, remember the photo I'd seen with him holding the baby. But then I think about Hawk out there in Las Vegas alone in that sterile penthouse and I can't imagine how he'd walk away from this.

"His name is James. He's four years old. I'm sure he'll come find you first thing in the morning, which means in about four hours—if you're lucky," he says, checking his watch. "He's an early riser."

"I look forward to meeting him. Does Benjamin live here with you as well?"

"Yes, the family's always lived together in the house. It's big enough. But Hawk will be changing that."

"What do you mean?"

He watches me, drinks a sip of his whiskey, doesn't answer my question. "You'll need warmer clothes than that," he says. He gestures to my sweater. It's too light for here.

I look down at it. "Oh, I didn't have much time to pack and the climate is so different."

"You live in Las Vegas?"

I nod.

"Constant sunshine?"

"Yes. And constant noise."

"I don't think I could stomach either."

"I guess it'd be hard coming from all this."

"Hawk seems to have managed." He takes a sip of his whiskey. "I'll take you into town tomorrow if you like. It's not far. We'll get you proper clothes."

"Oh, I…Hawk—"

"Hawk's going to have his hands full with the house. Try the whiskey."

I pick up my glass, look at the clear bottle without the label as I sip. It's the same bottle Hawk has in the penthouse.

"It's quite good. Not so…"

"Pretentious," he says, refilling his glass.

I smile. "Yeah, not so pretentious. It's your own, you said? You make it?"

"Family distillery. But I imagine it'll be closing down soon if my brother has his way."

"There's a family distillery?"

"Hasn't Hawk told you anything about us?"

"He doesn't say much about his past," I say, then think I shouldn't have said that.

"I gather he wouldn't."

"What do you mean it'll be closing if Hawk has his way?"

He studies me, eyes keen. They're dark, blue-black. The color is very different than Hawk's but the intensity with which he looks at me is the same.

It's almost intrusive, the way the MacLeod men look at you.

"That's a very long story my brother should tell. He's been the mastermind of the dismantling of all things MacLeod for more than a decade now. I'm sure I'll miss details."

Dismantling?

"Oh." I suddenly think of it. "I haven't even told you I'm sorry for the loss of your father."

"And mother," he says, his expression changing a little, making him look ten years younger for a moment. Like a boy. A lost one.

"Your mother too?" Hawk had left that out.

He nods. "Car accident took them both. She was killed instantly. I think it was a blessing. My father took a few days to die."

"God. I feel like an idiot. I'm so sorry. I didn't know."

"You're not an idiot. I don't imagine Hawk likes to talk about her. And I don't blame him, honestly."

I'm surprised by this last admission. "Can I ask you something?"

"Of course."

"What's the tension between you two?"

He leans back in his chair and studies me. "Now that's a truly long story. And not a pretty one."

"I don't mean to pry."

"Hawk doesn't like me very much, Melissa."

There's a sound I don't recognize but I notice him momentarily shift his gaze over my shoulder.

"He's filled with hate and holds a lot of anger inside him," he continues.

"I've seen that," I admit, remembering his temper.

"You be careful with him," he says.

"She should be careful with me?"

I gasp at the deep timbre of Hawk's voice and turn to find him lurking in the shadows, having come out of some dark corridor like a ghost.

"Melissa seems like a nice girl," Declan says, and a glance

at him shows me he's neither surprised nor unsettled by Hawk's sudden appearance. Maybe he even likes this. He likes goading his brother. "Wouldn't want you to hurt her like you do everything you touch." He casually swallows his whiskey.

Hawk's angry gaze turns to me and when he steps into the room, I see his clothes are wet, muddy even. He's not wearing a coat, and in his hand, he's got a half bottle of whiskey.

Declan stands, turns his gaze to me. "Glad to meet you, Melissa," he says. "Let me know if you want me to take you into town tomorrow. It'd be my pleasure."

I can tell from the way he says it that it's for Hawk's benefit. To irritate him. Taunt him.

And it works because Hawk stalks forward, sets the bottle on the table and lunges for his brother.

But he's drunk and Declan isn't, and he sidesteps him. I let out a scream, jump to my feet.

"Not used to our whiskey anymore, brother?" Declan asks.

"I'm going to kill you."

I grab Hawk's arm when he lunges again but I don't even think he can feel it. Feel me holding him back.

Declan's face hardens and he steps toward Hawk. The two are like giants, nose-to-nose and raging.

"I'd like to see you try," Declan says.

"Stop it. Both of you," I yell.

Hawk takes a deep breath. I can feel how tense his muscles are beneath my hand, but he's not out of control. Not yet.

"This is going to come to fists," he tells Declan in a remarkably calm tone. "But it's not going to be now."

Declan doesn't blink. A moment later, one side of his

mouth quirks upward into a smirk. He turns, picks up the bottle of whiskey.

"I look forward to it," he says. "It's long overdue, isn't it?"

"Long."

Declan turns to me. "Goodnight, Melissa." He walks to the door, opens it, but stops as if he's forgotten something. He turns back, meets Hawk's gaze with a wicked grin. "Why don't you tell her our sordid history, brother? She should know well the man whose bedding her, don't you think?"

With that, he's gone, and Hawk stands there for a moment watching the place where he'd stood. His hands are fisted at his sides but on his face and in his eyes, so many emotions war.

"What's he talking about?" I ask.

Hawk turns to me. "Don't get cozy with my brother, Melissa."

He hasn't shaved since the other night and the scruff that's usually there is thicker, making him look more rugged, older. A little scarier. His clothes too, the mess, it's not him. He's always impeccable. Everything about him is.

"What did he mean with that, Hawk?"

He pauses a moment before answering. "Declan's just being a dick."

"Where have you been?" I ask.

He looks me over and I see how his forehead is creased. He walks me backward until the counter is at my lower back and leans over me.

"Never talk about me with him again. Never. Understand?"

"That's not...I didn't—"

He straightens, eyes intense on me. "He heard me coming."

"He seems nice, Hawk."

"He set you up, Melissa. He knew I'd hear what you'd say."

I realize he's right. Declan had recognized the sound I hadn't. But I can't believe he'd set me up, the way Hawk is implying it.

"That's what he does. He fucks with people. It's a game to him. And I don't want you talking to him. Am I understood?"

"It was nothing—"

"Nothing is nothing. Not with Declan. You don't know what he's capable of. Stay away from my brother. It's the last time I'll say it." His accent comes and goes, and it catches me off guard.

"Where were you?"

He brings the bottle to his mouth, drinks. I wonder how much he's already drunk. If the bottle was full when he started.

I try to take it from him, but he doesn't let me. Instead, he grips my arm to hold me away and purposefully takes another swig.

"Did you miss me?" he asks.

"What's wrong with you? Why are you being like this?"

He releases me, steps away, turning his back to me. He drinks again, goes to the window. I watch his face in the reflection.

"The cemetery's about a mile up the road."

"Cemetery? You went to the cemetery in the middle of the night?"

"I wanted to see my father's grave."

"I would have gone with you tomorrow. In the morning." I go to him, touch his shoulder. "You're soaked, Hawk. Covered in mud. Did you walk there?"

"They didn't even wait to bury him. They couldn't even give me that."

When he won't turn to me, I slip between him and the counter. I touch his face, push the wet hair back.

He looks down at me and what I see is sadness. An immense well of it.

This is a different man than the one I know. The one I met only a few nights ago.

Has it only been a few nights?

With everything that's happened, it feels like a lifetime.

"Go up to bed, Melissa. I need to be alone."

"I've slept all afternoon. I can stay."

He studies me, scans the room, the walls, the ceiling. "I didn't think it'd be like this. All the memories." He drinks again.

"Hey, I'm here," I say.

"Don't be so kind to me, sweetheart. I don't deserve it."

"I see you, you know? I see what you try to hide."

He takes long swallows from the bottle, gulps of the stuff, before setting it down. He's so close, pressing me between the counter and him with his arms on either side of me. With one hand, he touches my hair gently.

He hasn't slept, I know that. Hasn't changed clothes since yesterday. I wonder if he's even eaten.

And all I can do is stand here and watch him.

"What do you see then?" he asks and the way he asks it, it remind me how gentle he can be. How opposite the gruff exterior.

"A good man."

He snorts.

"No, I mean it."

He touches my cheek, brushes hair back behind my ear.

"You're so pretty, Melissa."

"You're so drunk, Hawk."

He ignores what I say, touches his thumb to my lower lip. "And you're the one who's good. You deserve better than what you've gotten."

His words startle me. Confuse me. Take me momentarily out of this reality and into my past.

I should ask him what he means, but I don't want to. I don't want to spoil this.

"I'm not a good man, sweetheart," he continues. "Don't make that mistake."

"It's not a mistake."

I don't think the shadows under his eyes are from fatigue or too much drink even if he hasn't slept since we left Vegas. I think it's from the intense sadness I feel coming off him.

"Hey, I mean it," I say.

He gives me a quick smile, just the lifting of one corner of his mouth, then turns and walks to the door, picking up the bottle on his way, pausing for one moment there but not turning around.

"You don't know what I'm capable of either, Melissa," he says, and walks out.

27

MELISSA

I don't know where Hawk spent the night or where he is this morning, but it's almost ten o'clock when I'm walking down the stairs of the big house because I somehow managed to fall asleep again after the episode in the kitchen.

"She's here!" I hear a little boy's excited, loud whisper.

"James, give her a little space," I hear Declan say as I get to the first floor and see the big fire already burning in the fireplace. Lamps are lit through the room and I think they must need them on all day long because of the weather and thick walls of the house.

The little boy steps up to me with a wide smile on his face and Declan follows with an apologetic look on his.

"Hello. I'm James Declan Scott," he says. "Almost laird of this house."

"James," Declan says in a chastising tone.

I crouch down so I'm at eye level and see that he has Hawk's eyes almost exactly. Their strange color is the same, but Hawk's hold none of the innocence this boy's do.

"It's wonderful to meet you, James. I'm Melissa and I was hoping you'd be here when I woke."

"You were?" he asks, eyes brightening as I straighten.

"I saw your toy train last night and, well, I loved trains when I was a little girl and haven't played with them much since."

"Are you sure? Girls don't like trains, Melissa," he says, his expression very serious, very much like Hawk's.

"You look a lot like your father and uncle," I say.

He smiles broadly again. "Thank you. About the trains..."

I look up at Declan who comes closer, ruffles his hair. "She just woke up, son."

"No, it's fine. And as far as those trains, a lot of girls like to play with them. Just like a lot of boys like to play with dolls."

He makes a face. "Not me."

I laugh.

"Would you like some coffee? Breakfast?" Declan asks.

"I'd love coffee. Do you know where Hawk is?"

"Second time you ask me that in the two times we meet," Declan says as he turns toward the kitchen. I walk beside him. "And my answer is the same. Who knows?"

James comes to my other side and takes my hand in his little one. I'm surprised by this. Warmed by it.

"I saw him this morning, Melissa. He said he was going to the tower," James says.

"You're not to be in that part of the house, James. You know that."

James rolls his eyes at his father and it's so exaggerated, I cover my mouth so as not to laugh. "I didn't say I went with him. He just told me when I saw him this morning. And I told him to be careful."

"Don't roll your eyes at me, mister," Declan says teasingly as he opens the kitchen door for me to walk through it.

"She's pretty," James whispers behind me. At least I think he intended on whispering but it's loud enough for me to hear.

"She's very pretty," Declan says. "And she's too old for you."

I smile.

"How old is the house?" I ask after meeting the cook, Alice, and sitting down with coffee.

Declan sips his while James sits on the counter talking to Alice and eating a cookie.

"Centuries. It was built by my ancestors in the early 1500s."

"That's amazing."

"We've done pretty well with restoring and keeping up renovations, but as you can see, things aren't what they used to be. These houses are expensive to keep, and the estate is now bankrupt, but that's my brother's problem now."

"What do you mean?"

"I signed the papers this morning. At least we'll keep the distillery open."

"I don't understand, Declan."

He puts his cup down and looks at me. "Do you know why Hawk left Scotland?"

I shake my head.

"Has he told you anything at all?"

I look into my cup, embarrassed that my answer is no.

"Alice," he says, his tone authoritative, different than when he talks to me. "Take James inside. Get him dressed and ready to go into town."

"Yes, sir."

"Will you come with us, Melissa?" James asks.

"Go, James. Or we'll be late," Declan says.

I don't get a chance to answer as he's ushered out.

Declan waits until the door closes before speaking.

"You asked what the tension is between my brother and me and I'll tell you. You should know and it's not only Hawk's story to tell. It's mine too.

"My mother and father were having an affair while Hawk's mother was still alive. While she was lady of this house. My own mother, Ann was her name, was a maid. I'm the result of that affair.

"Hawk's mother died young and when my father married my mother and claimed me as his own blood, everything changed between Hawk and I. We were less brothers then than we were before either of us knew we shared blood."

"That's why he left?"

Declan shakes his head. "My mother was much younger than our father. And she was not as committed to our father as she should have been," he says, looking away momentarily. "Hawk was trying to protect his father, but he went about it wrong."

"Protect your father against what?"

"Having his fortune squandered. Having his new wife steal Hawk's legacy out from under him," he pauses, sips the last of his coffee. "When Hawk exposed one of her many affairs, I'm sure he thought that would be enough. That our father would divorce her, and they could go back to being their own little family mourning for his long dead mother. But Ann, well, I'll just say she had a great deal of influence over my father. I think she could get away with murder when it came to him. And after the accusation, my father chose Ann over Hawk. He disowned his son."

"How old was Hawk?"

"Sixteen."

"That's why he left."

Declan nods. "And why he's so filled with hate. Why he's done what he's done over the last decade of our lives."

"Which is?"

"Look around you. This house was grand when I was a boy. Look at it now."

"He'll fix it, I'm sure. He has the means—"

"It's not only that, Melissa. The family has lived in the house together for centuries. I've lived here since I was born, in the servants' quarters to start, then as the laird's son. My son deserves to grow up here. It's his legacy as much as mine or Hawk's. But my brother will be taking that away from the boy."

My mouth falls open. "He wouldn't..."

Declan shakes his head, stands. "I've said too much. I don't mean to upset you."

"I'm not...it's not your fault. I appreciate you telling me."

"I'm going to take James into town. He needs to see the eye doctor. You're welcome to join us if you like. You need a jacket if you don't have one. And better shoes. Those won't do here, not if you want to stay dry."

"Hawk—"

"Hawk isn't here, is he?" Declan points out, gaze locked on mine.

The door opens and James enters the kitchen wearing a rain coat and galoshes and holding a small umbrella. "Ready! You'll come, Melissa? I'll even take you to get the best chocolate cake in the whole world."

Declan moves to stand beside James as they wait for my answer.

It only takes me a moment to reply because Declan's

right. Hawk isn't here. And because Declan's been more open with me in two short meetings than Hawk ever has.

"I'd love to. Just let me grab my bag."

I don't run into Hawk on the way back upstairs and don't see him anywhere in the house. Declan lends me a jacket which is about five sizes too big. When I slip my arms into it, I realize it's his from the scent of aftershave clinging to it. I find myself glancing back to be sure Hawk isn't coming around a corner because if he was angry about me talking to Declan yesterday, he'll flip when he sees me wearing his jacket.

We climb into Declan's older model Range Rover and head into town.

"This bridge scares me," I say as we cross it.

Declan smiles wide, glancing over at me. I see two dimples beneath the scruff along his sharp jaw. His dark hair is messy, and he looks like he hasn't shaved in two days. He's wearing a Barbour jacket that looks well broken in and all I can think is how opposite he looks to Hawk right now. How this is the side of himself that Hawk hides beneath his expensive suits.

"Bridge is fine. It'll be here long after we're gone. Don't fret, Melissa."

James tells me the story of how they figured out he needs glasses just a few weeks ago and how he'll have them before starting school in the fall. The first day apparently falls on his fifth birthday. He also tells me that he's going to be getting a nanny soon. One he hopes is as pretty as me.

I smile at him.

Declan rolls his eyes and gives me a wink at James' stories. I see he's proud of his son, though. I wonder about James' mother but am not quite brave enough to ask about the woman I'd seen in that photograph.

It's raining softly when we get into town and Declan rummages through the trunk for an umbrella.

"I don't mind the rain," I say as I help James open his little one.

"You can borrow my umbrella," James says when Declan doesn't find one. "I know girls don't like getting their hair wet."

"You make a lot of assumptions about girls, little man," I tell him as we walk into town.

I'm looking into every shop window we pass and listening to the language I should understand but struggle to with the accent.

Declan and James seem to know everyone we pass, and I'm introduced to curious eyes, made more curious when they hear Hawk's back in town.

"This Hawk's woman?" an old man asks, openly looking me over. It's not in a leering way though, and at the end, he gives an approving nod. "She needs more meat on her bones but otherwise, she'll do."

"He realizes I'm standing right here, right?" I ask Declan when the man walks away.

Declan laughs and we enter the eyeglass shop where James goes directly to the doctor. I follow with Declan as the doctor brings out a box. Inside is a small pair of round red glasses.

James' face lights up when he sees them, and he looks at himself in the mirror as the doctor positions them. He gives himself a nod of approval before turning to his father.

Declan crouches down and James steps toward him, peering into Declan's face.

James touches the scruff on Declan's jaw, seems to search his face as if it's the first time he's seeing it. "Is this how you see, dad?"

"What do you mean?"

"Not so blurry."

Declan laughs again and hugs James. I see how his eyes glisten. "I can't believe it's taken me this long to figure out you need glasses," he says.

"It's not your fault. I didn't know either," James says like a little man. He turns to look up at me, gives me a nod like the old man did. "You're even prettier now, Melissa."

"Well, thank you," I say with a blush.

We head out to a clothing store where I try on a jacket similar to the one I'm wearing but a woman's model.

"I'm not sure how long I'll be here," I say to Declan. The jacket is quite expensive, and it may not be worth my buying it if we leave in a few days.

"You'll be here a little while, Melissa. There's much for my brother to do." He turns to the sales lady. "She needs a smaller size, I think."

The woman looks at the inventory on her computer, but they don't have my size at the shop. She arranges to have one sent directly to the house from a shop in Inverness that afternoon, though.

I end up with that and three sweaters. I also choose a pair of boots that Declan suggests but when we get to the counter, he takes out his wallet to pay.

"I can pay for my clothes," I say.

"You're our guest, Melissa," he says.

"Declan, it's expensive—"

He looks down at me. "Put your wallet away."

I try again, but he nudges me aside and the woman runs his card through. I thank him, making a mental note of the amount to send him a check.

"Let's get cake!" James yells once we're outside.

The sun is just peeking through a break in the clouds and it's bright on the wet streets and rooftops.

"The sun is amazing here," I say.

"When it deigns to shine on us," Declan says, squinting up into it.

I look at him with his wide smile, my bag in one hand, James' hand in the other and again, I find myself wondering about James' mother.

"Cake," James urges, tugging a little.

"You have a sweet tooth," Declan says, and gestures to the tea shop across the street. It's the one I'd noticed as we drove through town yesterday.

We walk inside and the waitress, an older woman, immediately smiles brightly at James who hugs her tightly.

"Don't you look handsome," she says to James. She shifts her gaze up to Declan, then me, looking me over from head to toe.

"Well, well," she starts. "The girls around here will be sorry to hear you weren't alone."

"You shouldn't be gossiping with the girls around here, Mary," Declan says, giving her a hug and a kiss on the cheek. "This is Melissa. She's my brother's girlfriend."

The word girlfriend catches me off guard and I have to remind myself that's not what I am. Not at all.

The woman looks shocked. "Hawk's back? Well of course he is with your father's passing. Of course, he is."

I notice she doesn't mention Declan's mother's passing and a glance at Declan makes me think he's noted it too.

James tugs on Declan's sleeve. "Better get this boy some chocolate cake, Mary."

"Come with me, little man, and you can slice your own," Mary says, and I'm left alone with Declan.

Declan places a hand at my lower back, and we walk to a

table. I hear Hawk's warning of last night. That I don't know what his brother is capable of. But when I look at Declan, it's not danger I sense. Actually, it's a similar sadness to what I see in Hawk.

They're more alike than Hawk realizes.

"Declan, can I ask you something?"

"Of course."

"When you said Hawk was changing things, did you mean you and James won't be able to live at the house anymore?"

He nods and I see the worry in his eyes when his gaze shifts momentarily to his son.

"Does he know you want to stay? He won't kick you out. Why would he?"

"You don't understand our past, Melissa."

"When he goes back to Las Vegas—"

"Do you think he'll go back?" Declan asks it like it's a question, but I think he's trying to tell me Hawk will be staying.

I look at him. I just assumed...

"This is home to him. To all of us. Being a Highlander, you're tied to this land. This wild, unforgiving country. No place is home but Scotland no matter how long you're away."

"This is my home now."

I remember when Hawk said that a while back about Las Vegas and even then, I didn't believe it for a second. Maybe Declan's right.

"All right now, James," Mary says, and we look up to see the two of them return with three giant hunks of cake, setting one in front of each of us.

"Can you eat all that?" I ask James.

He nods, enthusiastically digging in.

Declan breaks off a piece with his fork. "You'll understand why when you taste it."

I smile and am about to take a bite of my own slice when I hear the door open and feel the cool wind it blows in.

Declan's expression changes immediately and my back suddenly goes rigid.

I hear Mary's surprised gasp and I don't have to turn to know who it is.

I feel him. I always feel him.

"Uncle Hawk! You came!" James yells happily, oblivious to the tension.

I look up to find Hawk towering over us, eyes locked on Declan who sits back, puts the bite of cake into his own mouth and gives him a mocking grin.

"Welcome, brother," he says around the food.

Hawk turns to me and I think I'd wither if it wasn't for James' excitement.

"Uncle Hawk, you should try this cake. It's the best ever, I mean it. You can try a bite of my dad's."

Hawk walks around me to take the seat next to mine and looks at his nephew.

"Nice glasses, James," he says. "You look very handsome."

"Thank you," James says proudly.

"And I'd rather try a bite of yours," Hawk says.

James hugs his cake closer.

I see Hawk's smile.

"Double espresso," he tells Mary when she comes to the table.

She studies him with raised eyebrows. "Well, hello to you, Hawk."

Hawk looks up at the woman, maybe surprised by her reprimand.

"Hello, Mary. Good to see you," he says.

"Same." She smiles. "How about a plain-old coffee, Mr. Fancy with your *espresso*," she makes a face as she says the last word and even Hawk has to smile.

"Coffee's fine, Mary. Thank you."

She lingers. "You've grown, Hawk. Changed."

"Thirteen years will do that to you."

She nods. "Well, it's good to see you've returned home." She pats his back. "I'll get you a slice of cake with your coffee. I remember you used to love it."

"All right. Thank you."

She looks between the brothers and walks away.

Hawk takes us in. "Cozy."

Declan smiles and puts another bite of cake into his mouth.

Hawk turns to me, wraps a possessive hand around the back of my neck. "You and I will have a talk when we're home."

I feel Declan's eyes on me. Feel my face heat up.

Before I need to respond, though, Mary returns with Hawk's coffee and cake.

"James, go get us some whipped cream," Declan says, never taking his eyes off his brother.

"Really?" James bounces excitedly out of his seat in an instant.

"I figure you have something to say," Declan tells Hawk as soon as James is out of earshot.

Hawk leans toward him. "You're not stealing from me again. I'll kill you before I let that happen."

Declan leans forward and all I can think is how flimsy the table between them is.

"That's twice you've told me you'll kill me. Do I look worried to you?"

"Where's the boy's mother?" Hawk asks. "Ran for the hills when she got to know you?"

Declan's eyes darken. He sits back in his chair and puts his fork down. "Sarah passed away two years ago. Doctors found the tumor days after James' birth."

I cover my mouth in surprise and glance to Hawk to see he's shaken too.

"Not what you expected?" Declan asks.

Hawk looks down at his plate, rubs his forehead.

"Fuck." He looks up at Declan. "That was—"

"Cold?" Declan inserts. "Unfeeling? Cruel?"

Hawk takes a deep breath in, nods. "All of those and more. I'm sorry for your loss. And for what I said."

Declan nods too, any accusation vanished, only weight left behind, the weight of a heavy loss. "So am I," he says.

James returns with Mary behind him holding on to the bowl of whipped cream.

"It's even better with cream," he says.

"I bet," Hawk says, looking at James, really looking at him and giving him a smile. He heaps a generous spoonful onto James' cake, then mine, then his own.

Declan pushes his plate forward and Hawk scoops some on his too. We sit there eating cake and drinking tea and coffee in awkward silence but for James interjecting his thoughts on this, that and pretty much everything.

When we're finished, Declan and James stand. "You'll want to take Melissa home I assume?"

Hawk nods.

With a quick goodbye, Hawk and I are alone, and he turns to me.

"You're a jerk to him, you know that?" I say.

"You don't know anything about us."

"I know a little now. And if you're planning on kicking them out of their house—"

"It's not their house. It's my house."

I shake my head. "If you're planning on kicking them out, then you were right last night."

"Right about what?"

"That you're not a good man."

Hawk's face tightens. "Did my brother put you up to this?"

"No, he didn't put me up to anything. He just lost both parents and he's a widowed father worried about his son."

Hawk stabs his cake with his fork, breaks it apart, and when he turns to me, I see that weight of sadness in his eyes too.

"Just think about it," I say. "There's James to consider."

"I thought it'd be easier," Hawk says, looking beyond me.

I reach up, touch his face. I want to tell him I understand. I want to tell him to keep talking, but then he looks down at the sleeve of my borrowed jacket and his eyes narrow dangerously.

"You have his scent on you," he says, his voice hard.

"He lent me his jacket. I didn't have one."

"I'm sure he did. He's marking territory.

"No, he's not. He's just being nice."

He chuckles. "Oh, Melissa, you are so naïve." He stands, pulls my chair out. "Take it off," he orders.

I get to my feet and before I can protest, he takes it off me himself. I try not to look at the other patrons in the restaurant. Try to pretend they're not watching.

He puts his own jacket over my shoulders before taking my arm and walking me out, carrying my shopping bag and Declan's coat, refusing to put it on even in the rain that's falling once again.

28

HAWK

"Why did you bring me here?" she asks when we're in the car. "I thought you needed me, but you just seem really pissed off with me every time you see me."

"I'm not pissed off with you. Being back here is harder than I thought it would be. That's all."

"Then let me help you."

I turn to her. "Stay away from my brother. That'll help me."

"You're wrong about him. He's really just being nice."

"What did he tell you about me?"

She looks straight ahead as we drive. "He told me about your parents and Ann."

I snort. "What did he say? Paint her to be a saint?"

"No, actually, he didn't. He told me about the affair and finding out he was your brother by blood. And he told me how much influence his mother had over your father. He gave the impression she was unfaithful, and you tried to protect your father and that it backfired."

I'm silent for a moment because it's the truth. And I

guess I didn't expect Declan to tell the truth. Or maybe that his version would be different than mine.

That's twice in one day now that I'm surprised. Caught off guard.

First, it was my grandfather this morning giving me the one thing my father did leave me. I feel the weight of it in my pocket and it deepens my already heavy sense of loss. And now this. Now Declan telling her the truth about what happened. Declan knowing it.

"And I get the impression no one seems particularly bothered that his mother died too, along with your father," she continues, and I'm grateful to be drawn from my thoughts.

"She wasn't a nice person," I say.

"Still, she was his mother. I'm sure that's painful for him."

"Don't worry about Declan. He'll be fine. Always is."

We get to the bridge that connects the small island upon which the house is situated to the mainland and I see how Melissa sits up.

"It's safe. I wouldn't take you over it if it weren't."

I park the SUV and climb out. "Wait here," I tell her, getting the boots I saw she'd bought out of the trunk. "Put these on."

"Why? It's just a short walk to the house."

"We're not going into the house."

I wait for her to put on the new boots and take her arm to walk her around and behind the house. Two of the dogs follow us part of the way as we make our way through the moist fields and I try to ignore the rain soaking my sweater.

It's about ten minutes before I hear the sound of the sea. It grows louder as we climb over several hills and get to the cliffs. I stop when we do because even in this rain, I can't not stop. I can't not look at this.

Melissa hugs her free arm around herself and I watch her take in the view. The vast gray sea, the wild waves in the constant wind.

"This is unbelievable."

"It's the most beautiful place on earth."

She turns to me. "How did you leave it?"

Her question reminds me why we're here and I tug her along, walking fast, catching her when she trips on the jagged rocks. A few moments later, we're inside a small opening in the cliffs, sheltered from the rain but with a view of all of it.

But it's not that I look at. It's her.

I think about what I felt when Alice told me the three of them had gone into town. How James had been so sweet holding her hand. I think about how they were together, cozy in the bakery. A ready-made family.

Melissa turns to me and her smile vanishes. I'm not sure she's aware that she's taken a step away from me.

"What is it?" she asks.

She puts her hands against my chest when I step toward her, walk her backward to the wall.

"I don't want you to go anywhere with him again."

"What?"

I unzip my too-big jacket that she's wearing and open it, unbutton her sweater and open that too, then take her breasts out of the cups of the bra, tucking them underneath the heavy mounds. I cup them, weigh them. Knead the nipples into hard points.

"What are you doing?"

I meet her eyes and keep them locked as I unbutton her jeans, unzip them and tug them down to mid-thigh.

I look at her like this and it's almost pornographic, her half-dressed, half-naked. My gaze slides from her eyes to her lips to her breasts and finally, to the slit of her sex. With a hand at the back of her head, I pull her to me, kiss her.

"You're mine, Melissa. Mine. This mouth, it's mine," I say, crushing my lips to hers, sliding my hands to her breasts again, taking them in my palms. "These breasts are mine. This pussy," I start, lowering one hand to cup it while with the other, I undo my jeans, push them down only as far as I need to.

"Hawk—"

"This pussy," I say, bending at the knees to get underneath her and thrust hard into her.

She gasps, nails digging into my shoulders.

"This pussy is mine," I say against her mouth, pumping into her once, twice before pulling out.

I take her by a handful of hair and spin her around so the side of her face is at the cave wall and with my other hand, I finger her pussy and drag the moisture there to her back hole.

Because that's mine too. And it's time I claimed it.

"Every part of you is mine," I say, bending my knees again, pushing against the tight hole. "You belong to me, Melissa."

I rub against her, using my fingers to collect more of the moisture, rub it into her. I tug on her hair and she watches when I spit into the palm of my hand and rub my dick.

"Mine. Not his. Not anyone's."

When I take her clit between my fingers, it's like pushing a magic button because her muscles relax, and I push the head of my cock into her ass and it's tight and hot and all mine. All fucking mine.

"Hawk," she starts, gasping for breath.

"And when you see him again, you'll feel me inside you. You'll remember me inside you. You'll remember you belong to me."

The last part I say as I thrust deeply and thoroughly.

Her head is bent backward, and I kiss her mouth, her throat, bite the curve of her neck.

"Hawk," she starts, almost panting, and I hug her to me, fucking her harder, faster. She fists her hands against the wall and when she comes, she calls out my name again.

I thrust once more, deep and hard, and as I feel her throb around me, I come too, and it's with a roar that's more animal than human.

Because I am an animal and I'm staking my claim when I empty inside her.

Melissa is mine.

All fucking mine.

29

MELISSA

My knees give out and he holds me up as he slides out of me. He pulls up his jeans first, then tugs mine up because I can't seem to move. He's rougher than he needs to be, and I feel his breath at my cheek.

I turn to look at him and I think about what he said. About being his. Belonging to him. And it feels like this is different than our strange arrangement.

"When I went to my father with my allegations against Ann, I was naïve," he starts, surprising me with this.

He walks away, sits on a stone.

I remain where I am and watch him even though he keeps his gaze outside.

"I should have waited to have solid proof although who knows what he'd have done even with that. He was so completely in love with her and she just had him wrapped around her manipulative little finger. She made him choose. Me or her. It couldn't be both. And my father chose. And then I chose. I don't think he expected me to leave."

He's quiet, but he's not finished.

"I vowed vengeance. It was all I could think of."

I go to sit beside him. "Hawk—"

He shakes his head to quiet me.

"The distillery is the main income generator of the estate. It's been privately held within the family for more than four-hundred years. But Ann convinced my father to go public. When he did, I saw my opportunity. I bought shares. I had others buy shares and bought them back. It took me years, but I now own fifty-one percent of MacLeod Distillery. And I've been driving it into the ground since I started. The more money they sank into it, the more they lost. I made sure of that."

"Oh, Hawk." I touch his face, push his hair back and make him look at me.

"You see, Melissa, this is what I'm capable of. So you're wrong. I'm not a good man."

"You were hurt."

He shakes his head, gives a sad little smile. "He tried to make contact with me over the years, but I never allowed it. Ignored his calls until he stopped calling."

He looks away again.

"And what did I care about Ann? What pleasure would it give me for her to see that her son would inherit nothing but debt? But none of that matters because they're both dead now. My father is gone. It's too late for anything."

"It's not too late," I say, taking one of his hands between mine. "There's your brother, your nephew. Your grandfather."

He doesn't reply or even acknowledge that he heard me at all.

"I know every inch of these cliffs, you know. Grew up

playing in the wild. Never thought I'd lose it all," he pauses. "I don't want to lose it again."

I think about what Declan said about Scotland being in his blood. In Hawk's. And I realize something.

"You're staying, aren't you?"

30

MELISSA

I'm alone when I wake up the next morning.

He never did answer my question yesterday. And I can't stop thinking about the cave. The way he took me, it was different than any time before. Like an animal marking his territory, this was him marking me.

But what he said afterwards, about losing this. About not wanting to lose it again.

I wish I could talk to him now. Make him tell me more.

I wish I could stop thinking about going back without him.

I take my phone and head downstairs hoping to find a charger for it. I have an iPhone and I'm sure at least one other person here has one. First thing I do is go into the kitchen where I find Alice wiping down the counters.

"Alice, do you know where I can find a charger for this?"

She turns to look at the phone. "Oh, yes, dear. In the study. Check the desk. Third door to your left." She points and I go, counting the doors, taking in the faint musty scent of the ancient house, imagining how old the stones that make up the walls are.

When I reach it, I knock on the door, just in case someone is inside, but there's no answer. When I turn the knob, I find it's empty.

I switch on the light, looking around at the large room. Bookshelves line the wall behind the enormous wooden desk, and I wonder how old it is. If it's an antique. It must be.

Leather-bound books take up most of the shelves. One houses empty whiskey bottles.

I walk over to it, read the labels. MacLeod Whiskey each with a year on it. I follow the row and notice how the logo has changed over time. See how the colors of the tartan, the only thing from here that was at Hawk's Vegas penthouse, are somewhere on each label.

The mahogany leather chair looks like it's been here forever. Two windows overlook the lush green back of the house and a large armoire takes up the space between them.

On the desk are piles of papers, not neat but not messy either. I think about Hawk and wonder if he's twitching being here. He likes order and things put away. Everything in its place. This house is the absolute opposite of that.

I open the wide, thin drawer at the center and inside it, I find pens and pencils, paperclips, no phone charger. I close it and open the one on the top right. There are some folders and papers, and I pull it out farther but don't find a charger here either.

Closing the drawer, I open the next one and when I see more folders, I'm not optimistic. I've almost closed it when I see a charging cable at the back of the stack.

"Bingo," I say out loud and reach for it. I plug my phone into the wall socket and sit back down to wait. Once it has enough juice, I'll call Deirdre to check on things.

But when I go to close the drawer, one of the folders catches. There's so much stuff in the drawer that I have to tug it to get it out and when I do, something slips out and falls to the floor.

I look down and it takes me a moment to process what it is.

An American passport.

I pick it up, open it and see the photo of me taken hastily in one of those booths at the mall. I remember Hawk hadn't given it back to me after our flight. I open the folder wondering if his is in there too. Maybe for safe keeping? Makes no sense though.

But when I open the top flap to see what's underneath, the air in the room suddenly becomes thinner.

My missing flash drive, I'd forgotten about it. So much has happened that the last few days feel like months.

But this, what I'm looking at, it reminds me. Abruptly and absolutely, it reminds me.

And it's not the flash drive.

This is worse.

It's what's on the drive. It's all those files printed out. The police reports. The photographs. Everything.

I think I would be sick if I had any food in my stomach.

I'm unprepared for this.

I know these photographs. I've memorized every detail, and yet, every time I see them, the power they still have, it's like those years between now and then are just stripped away.

My face is that of a child's. My hair shorn. I remember when I'd crudely cut it, not wanting the pretty long locks they liked so much. That's what had gotten me into trouble. They needed me pretty and my butchered hair was anything but.

I remember when it was taken. How nice the lady had been at the police station, how gentle and sweet.

And then I remember how she'd looked at me after Liza had lied to her and the Boyds had ushered me out. I remember the car ride home—no, not my home.

Their home.

My prison.

I remember how they'd punished me, and I can't seem to drag my eyes away. Can't stop remembering.

Because the past, it's here.

Liza knows where I am, and Sean knows too because that man who came to the shop, who gave Deirdre the creeps, I know it had to be Sean. Nothing else makes sense.

And as much as I want to avoid this truth, as much as I want to bury my head in the sand and pretend it's not happening, pretend the fact that I'm here on another continent, across an ocean, here in front of me is reality in full color. Here is proof that no matter how far or where I run to, the past will always be just a few steps behind.

Hawk knows. How long has he known? Since that day at the house? The files were password protected, though. How did he break the code?

But maybe he doesn't know everything. Maybe he doesn't know about the rest of it. The worst of it. There's nothing about those videos on the flash drive.

Why in hell does he have these pictures? How did he get my password? Or did he get the files from somewhere else? Is there still a record buried somewhere?

I make myself look at the photos, the first one, then the next one. Whenever I open these files, I make myself look. It's like a ritual. I make myself see. Make myself touch the bruises, the ones on my face and neck. The one on my belly.

I remember how that one had hurt.

No, they had all hurt. That was just the meanest, to kill any spawn when he got the idea I might be pregnant. Christ.

I didn't even have my period yet. I didn't get it until I was fourteen and by then they'd been raping me for three years.

By fourteen, I had the birth control shot. The doctor didn't even ask my permission. But then again, Senator Boyd made me out to be some sort of slut.

I turn to read through the reports, read through Liza's lies, her betrayal.

She'd been afraid of them too, though. I have to remember that.

But was it fear that drove her to lie? Or the promise of adoption. Of belonging to that family. She was desperate for it. Desperate to belong. And look where it got her.

I turn the last page over thinking that's it, that's all there is, but then there's one more thing. One more thing which tells me how Hawk guessed my password.

I recognize Sean's handwriting. It's a little feminine. He hit me once when I said that. Just backhanded me right there at the kitchen table. I hadn't been in their house that long then and it was the first time he struck me.

For a long time, I wished I'd never said it, never teased him about it but I realize now the violence was always coming. Me having made the comment or not, it was coming.

Here's that familiar handwriting again on the envelope.

Little Bitch Whore.

My hands shake, and sweat drips down the back of my neck.

I'm able to block this out for months at a time. Years. But when it comes back, when there's any hint of him, of them, something on the news like when Senator Boyd died, or walking by a man who happens to wear the same cologne, any random thing, it's like it sends me back in time and traps me there.

From inside the envelope, I take out the folded sheet of paper and read the three little words written there: *Been a while.*

31

MELISSA

My phone comes to life, startling me.

I catch my breath, put the sheet of paper down.

Taking my phone, I absently enter my password and look at all the missed calls.

I listen to the first from Deirdre telling me she she'd work extra hours until I got back, then another from Jim at the garage telling me about a newer model Ford Escort that he just took in to sell and would I be interested? He says it's a good car without too many miles and makes a crack about my duct tape fender.

The next two are disconnects. Probably wrong numbers.

I think the one after those must be a wrong number too because it's silent at first but there's something different about this silence. It's not empty. I can hear whoever is on the line breathing.

And when the caller clicks his tongue, I feel myself go rigid, feel myself grow cold as every hair on my body stands on end.

How can a sound, the simple clicking of a tongue, have that kind of power over someone?

How can it just erase years?

Because it does just that. It simply wipes the years between us away and transports me back in time. Back to when I was a little girl.

A scared little girl at the mercy of monsters.

"Been a while."

The phone slips from my hand, clatters to the floor and I know if I wasn't sitting down, I'd fall.

I know he's talking again. I hear the mumble of words while I just sit looking at the phone down there and thinking how modern it looks against this old floor, this wasted carpet.

Minutes pass until finally, I hear the recording telling me my options and I reach down to pick it up. The recording repeats, and I choose the option to listen again.

And there it is again. The silence, the breathing, that clicking of his tongue. Those same words he'd written on that sheet of paper that Hawk somehow intercepted. Probably in my mail. He's had someone pick it up. He's got this whole thing all sorted out.

"You look good," Sean says, drawing the words out. "Just got a glimpse at the shop. Can't wait to have a real close look."

I shrink into myself.

"And I'd love to see you, since I'm in town. Hell, since all three of us are in town. When's the last time that happened?" He takes a deep breath in. "You and me and Liza will have a family reunion."

I can't breathe.

"And besides, I miss you."

I want to disconnect. To delete the message. Bury my head in the sand.

But Sean Boyd won't go away, though. Even if I delete a hundred messages. Even across an ocean, I'm not safe.

But what he said about seeing me. The shop. I think about Deirdre alone there.

"Guessing your boyfriend won't like sharing you though, huh? He doesn't know what a little whore you are, I bet. Or does he know you cream yourself having your mouth and cunt stuffed at once? I wonder if he's seen the videos."

"Stop," I say weakly, but I'm not sure to who.

Even my voice, it's that of the little girl and my eyes are wet. I am her again. That powerless little girl.

"I miss my Little Bitch Whore."

The taunt has an edge of hate to it and I make a choked sound at those words.

Little Bitch Whore.

That's his name for me. Was from the first time he raped me.

"You'll meet me, Melissa. Or I'll make sure your boyfriend and all his buddies see what a dirty pervert you are." His voice is hard now. He's not playing. I know this Sean. This one's the meanest.

"I'm at the Palazzo. I'll leave a key for you in an envelope marked L.B.W. What do you think?"

Shouldn't the voice mail have cut him off already? Why is he going on?

"Tomorrow at noon. A nooner. I miss those, don't you? I'll see you then, Little Bitch Whore. Don't be late. I don't want to have to start in on Liza without you there. Bruises are a pain to cover up. You remember that, don't you? And she's already in bad shape. Can you believe she came out here to find you? Says she wanted to reconnect. I guess she missed you, too. Honestly though, I just think she needed some cash." There's a pause before he continues, his tone more threatening now. "Don't make me come get you, Melissa."

With that, he disconnects.

I sit there for a long minute listening to the racing of my heart. Trying to stop my hands from shaking.

I dial the shop, but the recording goes on and I remember the time zones. It's the middle of the night there.

Liza. I have to call Liza.

I find the number of the Brewster Clinic and dial. Someone answers there. I assume they have someone on twenty-four hours a day.

"Hello, I'm looking for a patient, Liza Boyd."

"Ms. Boyd is no longer a patient here, ma'am."

"You mean she was released?"

"I'm afraid I can't give out personal information."

"Do you have contact information for her?" I ask.

"Ma'am that is all confidential. We take care to protect our—"

I disconnect, frustrated, then remember the other messages.

One more of those is disconnected right away, but the next one, it's from Deirdre and it takes her minute a speak like she doesn't realize it's time to.

"Hey hun, I was hoping to catch you. I have something here for you. That man from the other day was back. Honestly, he was more than a little upset when he heard you weren't here again. Left something for you. An envelope addressed strangely to L. B. W." I can almost hear her shaking her head. "Just a sec, dear." I hear her say something to someone and I assume it's a customer. "Anyhow, I have to go but you just call me back and let me know if you want me to open the envelope and read it for you. I'll talk to you soon, dear."

I check the date of the message. It's from yesterday. The one from Sean is from two days ago. Did he get pissed that I didn't show up at his hotel room?

And what about his threat to share those videos with Hawk?

The final voicemail comes right after Deirdre's and the time stamp tells me it's from minutes after her call. It's him again, but I knew it would be.

"You think you ever had a fucking choice? You don't show up and I'm going to have to hurt the old lady after I send those videos to your boyfriend. You get one more chance, you little bitch."

His voice is so full of loathing, I think he almost spits the words.

My heart pounds and I call Deirdre, but I get her voice mail right away. It's the time difference. That's all. Just the time difference.

"Deirdre, it's me. Listen, I want you to stay home. Do not go back to the shop, understand? That man, he's not my friend. Just stay home. And if you see him, call the police. God. I...please call me as soon as you get this. I'm on my way back."

I get up, look around. I pick up my passport.

I need to go. I need to get back. If he hurts Deirdre because of me, I'll never forgive myself.

I'm so distracted with shoving the bundle into my bag that I barely register the sound of James talking. I don't see his toy train on the floor, either. I step right on it and let out a little scream as I go sprawling backward, all those pages flying from my hands, scattering all around me. I land right on my tailbone, catching myself on the heels of my hands as

I watch the little train slide across the floor and crash against the far wall.

"Melissa!"

James comes running around the corner, a toy airplane in one hand, another train in the other.

I turn to him.

His little face is shocked, eyes filling up with tears.

I look around me at the papers all over and all I can think is he shouldn't see those. Shouldn't see the pictures. They would terrify him.

Tears start to fall from his eyes, and I sit up, wiping off my hands.

"It's okay, James. I'm okay." I get on my knees, pushing through the pain, and quickly gather everything up.

"I'm sorry, Melissa," he says through his tears. "I'm sorry."

I get up, go to him, the papers I've managed to collect in one hand as I hug him.

"Shh, it's okay, sweetheart. I'm fine. See, look, nothing is broken," I say, standing back, ignoring the throbbing in my tailbone.

He looks at me, drags his eyes to mine. Hawk's eyes. He has Hawk's eyes. It strikes me again and I think about Hawk and how he's seen these photos, read these files.

"I'm in trouble," James says, starting to cry again.

I bend down, hug him to me again. "No, no sweetheart. You're not in trouble. It was an accident. I wasn't watching where I was going. It wasn't your fault." I draw back, wipe away his tears. "And I'm not going to tell anyone," I say, forcing a smile because I hear Alice calling for James. "Our secret, okay?"

He nods.

The kitchen door opens, and Alice comes out wiping her

hands on her apron.

"What's happened here?" she asks when she gets a look at us.

James looks at her and she looks at him and I get the feeling this isn't the first time someone's slipped on one of his toys.

"I tripped and fell," I say. "I wasn't paying attention and James was helping me pick up the things I dropped."

"I hope it wasn't one of your toys—"

"It was my fault, Alice," I say, putting one hand on James' shoulder and saving him from having to lie. "Is that shortbread I smell?" I ask to change the subject.

Alice smiles proudly at me. "Recipe comes from my great-great-grandmother," she says. "I've made some tea. Come on and have some."

"Is Hawk here?" I ask.

"He went for a walk early," James says.

"I'm sure he'll be back soon. The sky's going to open up any minute now," Alice says. "Come have some tea."

"You and James go ahead. I have to take care of something first."

James is hesitant, but Alice takes him into the kitchen.

Once they're gone, I walk to the front door where a glance out the window tells me the rental is still here.

There are two sets of keys on the table beside the door where I find the one for the SUV and I walk outside.

But what if I'm already too late?

No, I can't think about that.

I start the engine and the clutch screeches as I put it into reverse, but I manage it. Glancing in the rear-view mirror when I'm on the bridge, I see James standing at the front door and Alice running out behind him. The look on his face is so defeated, it brings tears to my eyes.

32

HAWK

I'm walking back to the house from the cliffs beneath a heavy sky. The air is cool and damp. How I'd forgotten this. Vegas couldn't be more different and every moment I pass here the farther my life there feels. The emptier.

At that, I think of Melissa.

She's become important to me. A part of me. And it has nothing to do with our arrangement.

My brother signed all the papers last night.

I got everything I wanted.

The house is mine as it should always have been. But even the text from Axel telling me they've finally picked up Boyd doesn't help.

I'm not in the mood for celebrating.

A sound breaks into the perfect silence. I stop, turn my face to the wind and listen. It's coming from some distance, but it's there. And I know where it's coming from.

Without consciously deciding, I begin to walk toward the source of the noise.

The music grows louder and mixed in with it is the sound of a hammer pounding against wood.

As I near the peak of the hill, the broken-down mews comes into view. I haven't seen it since the day I left. Growing up, this was a source of pride for my father. For my entire family.

Falconry has always been a part of our lives. It's the reason for my name. My father's name. His father's name and so forth going back to the very beginning of our lineage.

Strange to think that I know every detail about every member of my family going back centuries and Melissa doesn't even know who gave birth to her.

I give a shake of my head and look at the wooden structure. It's smaller than I remember it being but maybe that's because the roof's caved in on the far end.

The music grows more distinct, and the hammering begins again.

I walk toward it, trying to place the song. AC/DC. I used to listen to them when I was growing up. I haven't heard this music in years.

Declan walks out, oblivious to my presence, hammer in hand, two nails sticking out of his mouth. He heads to his toolbox which is resting on a boulder and swaps out the nails.

"You should turn down the music. Anyone can sneak up on you," I say.

He turns his head like he wasn't caught off guard at all. "What makes you think you snuck up on me, brother?"

Brother.

I look at him, at the man he's become. Dark eyes, dark hair, built like me. A Scotsman. A Highlander. Nothing left of the friend I remember.

I think about James and what Declan said about the boy's mother and wonder what his life's been like.

"It's early for this, isn't it?" I ask, gesturing to the mews.

"Not too early." He drops the hammer and nails into his toolbox and wipes his hands on his jeans. "We'll be out of your house by the end of the day if that's what you're here for."

Fuck.

"And if you're just here to gloat, then you can go fuck yourself," he adds on, hauling a plank of wood up over his shoulder and carrying it into the mews.

I follow him, take up the back half of it.

Declan glances at me, surprised, I guess.

"How long has it been like this?" I ask.

"Broken down?"

I nod.

We set the plank down and he crouches down to measure and mark the wood.

"More than ten years."

I don't speak, just watch him as he straightens, turns to me.

"He didn't set foot in here but to release the hawks the day you left."

My father loved the sport. He was a born falconer. And I was following in his footsteps. Another part of my legacy gone.

"You shouldn't have left like you did," Declan says as if he just read my mind.

"I had no choice."

"Yeah, you had a choice. Stay and fight. Or just stay."

"My father chose."

He snorts. "You know, after all those years, those last days, he thought I was you. Kept calling me Hawk. *My boy*."

Something flashes in Declan's eyes. It's not anger or taunting or anything like that. It's hurt. "I didn't correct him or tell him it was me. Figured it didn't matter anymore. And you're right in that my mother had a grip on him that none of us could match, but he loved you. He would have forgiven you."

"Forgiven me? I'm the one who told him the truth."

"You always have to be right, don't you? Let me ask you something. You think he didn't know the truth?" Declan asks, stepping closer and cocking his head to the side. "You think our father was that stupid that he didn't know his wife who was twenty-five years younger than him had lovers?"

"If he'd known, why did he let her get away with it?"

"What would you let Melissa get away with?" he asks, gesturing toward the house.

"What the hell does that mean?"

"You don't even know how lucky you are, do you? Life is short, brother, and you've wasted enough of it, haven't you?" He turns back to the wooden plank. "Get the other end."

I pick it up, help him line it up and slide it into the slot. I walk out to pick up the hammer and a couple of nails.

He watches me as I secure the plank of wood.

"Are you staying?" he asks.

I don't look at him. "Don't know. I'll repair the house. Make it like it was before."

"So you can sell it. More money for the man who has enough to burn," Declan says, stepping outside and watching the sun peek around a dark cloud.

I follow him. "Just as I don't know you, you don't know me."

"And isn't that a shame."

We look on in silence and I don't want to walk away but I'm not sure how to continue.

"You're not the only one who lost when you left, you know," Declan says. "And neither was he. I lost, too. I lost my brother."

And I mine.

I look down at the glen, remember the stories grandfather would tell about fairies and the like.

"You tell James the stories?" I ask.

Declan follows my gaze, smiles. "He loves them. I've promised to take him camping down there when he's older and big enough that the wee people don't snatch him up."

"You scare the boy."

"He's not so easy to scare." He walks back to the mews.

"You don't have to go," I call out, my voice sounding strange. Thick.

"I won't live on your charity."

"No, you won't. You'll run the distillery like you've been. You'll more than earn your keep. Even if I stay, the house is big enough."

When I turn, I find him watching me. "What about all that talk of murdering me?"

"I didn't think I would care when he died. Didn't think I cared about anything. Being back here has shown me how untrue that is. You're right about wasting life. Wasting time. I've lost too many years. Lost my father. Never got to meet my nephew's mother. I don't know the man you've become. I don't know my nephew. And I'd like to."

He studies me, doesn't answer just yet.

"I may still want to kill you, though," I add, my lips trying for a smile.

He smiles back. "Same goes for me, brother."

We stand like that for a minute in that perfect sunshine just before the clouds come and obscure the light again, dumping rain onto our heads.

"Uncle Hawk! Uncle Hawk!"

We both turn to find James running madly toward us, Alice trailing so far behind she's a dot in the distance.

"What is it?" I call out, and Declan and I go running toward him. He's out of breath and wet from the icy rain when Declan reaches him, wrapping his arms around his boy.

"What is it, James?" he asks.

James looks up at me. "Melissa," he says, tears welling in his eyes as he casts a guilty look to his father. "She fell on one of my toys and she must have really hurt herself—"

I don't hear the rest. I dash to the house, running at full speed, almost knocking Alice over as I charge past her and into the house.

"Melissa!"

No answer. I run to the steps, call out.

"Melissa!"

"She's gone, sir," Alice says from the door. "She took the car you came in and left."

"What? Did she say where she was going? Why?"

"She dropped this," Alice says, handing me Melissa's passport.

Fuck.

She found the printouts.

"Poor James thinks it's his fault," she starts. "He's very upset."

Why did I put those papers in there? I shouldn't have even brought them with me. I should have destroyed them.

Declan walks inside, looks at me.

"How long ago did she leave?"

"Maybe an hour. Not long," Alice says. "James wanted to come get you sooner, but I told him to wait until—"

"Go," Declan says, cutting her off.

He picks up his keys from the table beside the door and tosses them at me.

I catch them, look at them stupidly.

What must she think?

"Go get her. The roads will be slick and she's not used to driving here."

I nod and as I walk out, I hear James softly cry.

"It's not your fault, James," Declan says.

No, not his fault. My fault.

"I'm sure Melissa will explain."

Once outside, I get into Declan's Range Rover and start it up. I switch on the tracker, glad I had the chip put on her bracelet when I'd had the clasp repaired. She's got a head start, but I can make that up.

33

MELISSA

My phone keeps losing reception and I'm lost. It doesn't help that the rain's picked up again and it's cold enough that the roads are slippery.

It's been ages since I've driven a stick shift and never with my left hand.

The gears scream as I shift to drive up the next hill, trying to load the map on my phone again, my attention split.

It happens so fast, the turn coming out of nowhere, the rain at its heaviest, the boulder on the side of the road. I look up and it's too late, I know it even as my foot instinctively slams the breaks.

The tires screech, the car slips and swerves.

I scream, clutching the steering wheel, realizing I'd never put on my seatbelt as the SUV collides with the boulder, the sound of metal crushing and my own screaming all I hear as something pops and my forehead collides against the windshield, the pain sharp and instant just before I lose consciousness.

34

HAWK

The car's stopped moving.

She's not much farther, but I'm stuck, cursing as I wait for the shepherd to clear the herd of sheep across the road. It's a fucking eternity before he does and gives me a friendly wave I'm unable to return.

I hit the gas, the Rover lurches forward and I take the turns faster than I should, but I don't care. She's still not moving and I have a bad feeling.

A car honks its horn as I narrowly miss sideswiping him when I take the turn off to where, according to the tracker, Melissa should be. As soon as I'm over the hill, I see it.

"Melissa!"

I stop the Rover, pull up the parking break and leap from it. I don't even close the door. Rain pelts me as I run to the smashed SUV, and I don't see her. Not until I get to the driver's side.

There's blood on the cracked windshield and she's slumped over the steering wheel, passed out.

"Melissa!" I call out, but she can't hear me.

The door's locked, they all are. I run back to the Rover and open the trunk. Inside, I find a toolbox—this Rover is so old I imagine Declan has to stop often to make repairs. From inside it, I take the biggest wrench I can find and when I'm back at the rental, I check on Melissa once more. She's still out.

I walk to the back seat opposite where she is, raise the wrench over my head and smash the window in. It shatters on the first hit, but it takes another to clear the glass enough to unlock the door. I ignore the cutting shards as I reach around to unlock all the doors then run back to the driver's side.

"Melissa?"

She groans and relief floods me as I gently draw her upright.

Blood streaks her forehead and she's going to have a hell of a bump, but she looks at me, blinking, lifting her hand to touch her forehead. She looks at the blood on her fingers like she's not quite registering what it is.

"Hawk?"

"Are you okay?" I ask her, looking her over.

She blinks. "What happened?"

"You crashed." I pat her arms, her legs. I don't think anything's broken.

"My head," she starts as I slide my arms underneath her and lift her out. "It hurts."

"I'll get you home. We'll get a doctor out there."

At that, she seems to remember what she was doing. Why she'd left.

"No," she starts, trying to get free of me. "I need to go."

"Where are you going to go?"

She looks up at me and I see into the cabin of the car at her tote on the floor of the passenger side. The papers there.

"Melissa?" I ask her.

But her eyes roll back and her head lolls into my chest as she passes out again.

35

MELISSA

I'm lying on a bed when I open my eyes. I don't know exactly where right away, though.

But then I see him.

Hawk.

He must have been standing nearby because he's coming over now. His hair is disheveled, and he looks tired.

I look at his shirt, at the blood on it. And I remember. I remember the papers I found. I remember the messages on my phone.

"I need to go," I start, but as soon as I try to sit up, pain like nothing I've felt before has me on my back again.

"You put a crack in the windshield with your head," he says. "You're in no condition to go anywhere."

"How long have I been out?"

"Most of the day."

I shift my gaze to the far window, realize it's dark out.

"Deirdre," I say.

"Deirdre?"

"Sean..." How will I explain? "I need to get to the shop."

I try to sit up and Hawk comes to my side. "Lie back, Melissa. You're not going anywhere."

"You don't understand."

"I understand more than you know."

"Deirdre's in trouble."

"Who's Deirdre?"

"The woman who works with me. Sean...He said if I didn't meet him...He said he'd hurt her."

"Sean Boyd won't be hurting anyone. Axel picked him up the other night."

"What?"

"He went looking for you. I've had a man on the shop."

"Because of those pictures you found. The reports."

He knows. God, he knows all of it. Shame fills me as tears blur my vision.

Hawk studies me and before he can answer, there's a knock on the door.

"Come in," Hawk say. James pushes the door open and peers around the door. "Come inside, James."

He's wearing striped pajamas and is barefoot. In his arms is a worn teddy bear. His eyes grow huge as he looks at the bandage on my forehead and I think he's going to cry.

"It's all right," Hawk say, going to him, taking his hand. "Melissa's fine. And she'll tell you herself you're not the reason she left. Melissa?"

I look up at him. "What?" Why would you think that?" I ask him as Hawk lifts him up to sit on the bed.

"You hurt yourself because of me and then you had to lie to protect me." He sniffles.

"Oh, sweetheart," I reach out to touch his face, wipe away a tear. "No, that's not why I left. Not at all."

"And she shouldn't have left like she did, should you have, Melissa?" Hawk adds.

I look up at him and I see a firmness in his eyes, hear it in his voice. I turn back to James.

"No, I shouldn't have. I'm sorry you thought it was your fault, James. It wasn't, not even close."

James smiles and a moment later, he throws himself into me and I feel every bruise as he hugs me hard and I hug him back, loving this little boy already.

"Go on to bed now, James. If your father finds out you're out wandering the halls at night, you know he won't be pleased with you."

"All right, Uncle Hawk."

"Shall I take you back?" Hawk asks.

"No, that's all right," he says, sliding off the bed. "You stay with Melissa." He turns to me. "I'm glad you're home, Melissa."

His words strike me and all I can do is watch him walk away in his striped pajamas and little bare feet.

The door closes and Hawk returns to my side, looming over him, hands folded across his chest.

"You and I need to talk."

36

HAWK

I give her that night and the next few days to rest. And all I can think about any time I look at her is what I'd thought, what I'd felt, when I'd seen her slumped over the steering wheel.

It's five days later when I decide it's time we had this talk.

"How long have you known what's on that drive," she asks when I enter the bedroom.

She's sitting up and Alice has just cleared the tray of food she'd brought up. Melissa's on bedrest. My orders.

"Long enough. You shouldn't have left like you did. You should have waited for me. Talked to me."

"I thought Deirdre was in trouble. I thought—"

"You should have talked to me!" I slam my fist into one of the bedposts.

Melissa jumps.

I hold up my hand, mutter a curse under my breath. I don't mean to frighten her, but I do because she gets that look in her eyes, that one from the first night.

"I don't want to talk about it. Ever. I don't want to think

about it. You can't understand what...I just...I wish I could forget. Why can't I forget?" Her voice breaks.

I go to her, sit on the edge of the bed. When she turns her face away, I touch her chin to make her look at me.

Tears well and overflow from her eyes and what I want most of all is to wipe them away forever. I touch one with my thumb, smear it across her cheek.

"The past is exactly that, Melissa. Past. But if you let it have any power over you, it will destroy you."

She sniffles, turns her face and wipes her hands over her eyes.

"When I went on my trip, I went after that man at the party."

She won't look at me as she cries quietly.

"I know what happened, what they did to you. What the Boyd's made you do."

She makes a sound, tries to draw herself away and she still won't look at me.

"Look at me," I say.

She shakes her head.

"Melissa. Look at me."

I take her face in both hands and hold her, make her look at me. And the look on her face, it breaks something inside me.

"They raped you. They raped a child. You're not responsible for anything that happened. You know that, don't you?"

She squeezes her eyes shut and tears flood her face. I'm not sure she can talk right now. I pull her to me, hold her against my chest and let her sob.

"And you don't have to talk about anything you don't want to talk about. But know this. I'm going to punish every one I get my hands on. It's over, sweetheart. No one's ever going to hurt you again. I swear it."

It takes her a long time, but I hold her until finally she puts her arms around me. They're soft at first, weak, but soon, she's clinging to me, and I lift her up and sit her on my lap and hold her. I just hold her until the sobbing stops and she quiets.

Her eyes are puffy and red when she finally looks up at me.

"Why?" she asks.

"Why what?"

"Why are you still here? I'm a mess, Hawk."

"You're not a mess, Melissa. You're mine."

37

MELISSA

I stare up at him. At this man who stormed into my life just weeks ago.

Has it only been weeks?

This man who bought me not once but twice. Who I expected to be brutal and although he was, he was also gentle. Gentler than any I've ever known.

"How did you find me out there?"

He touches my bracelet. "I had a tracking device put in here. A chip. It's tiny but you felt the weight difference."

"Why did you...Never mind." I shake my head. No point in asking why he did that. He's Hawk MacLeod. I'm not surprised at all. "What now?"

He stands up, walks away, rubbing the back of his neck with his hand. When he turns back to me, he runs that hand through his hair and it stands on end.

"When I saw the crashed SUV, Melissa, I was scared. For the first time in a long time, I was scared. I thought—"

"I'm sorry," I cut him off. "I'm sorry, I just—"

"I've wasted a lot of time. I don't want to waste any more. And I don't want to lose you. I can't lose you. I love you."

It takes me a moment to register that. Then another to really understand it. And I think I misheard him. I must have.

"What did you say?"

He smiles, comes to resume his seat on the bed.

"I said I love you." He touches my face softly. "I love you."

"I don't...When...why..."

"I don't know when or why, I just know I do."

"You saved me," I say. "In so many ways. I've never felt as safe with anyone. As protected. You're not what I expected and I love you, too, Hawk."

He wraps his big arms around me, pulls me in to him. I wince, my ribs bruised, but I hug him back because the pain is worth it, worth this. I love him. I don't want to be anywhere but in his arms.

That thought reminds me of something. I draw back.

"You never answered my question the other day," I say.

"What question?"

"You're staying here, aren't you?"

He studies me, cocks his head to the side and gets a familiar glint in his eyes. Like he's up to no good.

"I have another proposition for you, Melissa."

38

HAWK

Another's devil's bargain.

"Our month isn't—" she starts.

"I don't care about the month. It's not enough. This is my home. It's been my home from day one. Declan's right. I should never have left. But past is past. And I'm finished with it.

"I'm staying here, Melissa. Reclaiming my place. I want to watch my nephew grow up. I want to be here with my grandfather. I will rebuild the house to what it once was. No, even better. I will make it grand, as it should always have been."

I lift her hair over her shoulder before brushing her cheek.

"And I want you to stay here with me. Make this your home too."

"You want me to leave everything behind—"

"What is everything? What is the life you've built in Vegas?"

She shifts her gaze away and I watch her eyebrows furrow.

"What life?" I ask again.

She looks up at me. "The shop."

"You don't need the shop. I'll make monthly donations to the shelter."

"It's Mrs. Adams' legacy, Hawk. I can't just shut it down."

"Then I'll buy it outright. Buy the whole building. Or back you financially if that's what you want. You'll promote Deirdre and let her manage it. Hire someone else to help her. Hire anyone you need. Your house is a rental. Your car, well, don't get me started on that car. And as far as friends, I think you and I are in the same position there."

"Do your bodyguards count?"

I smile because I think she's joking. "Just Axel."

"What about the casino? The hotel?"

"Axel will manage both. It's not important. Don't you see, I've lost too many years. Half my life. I want to start living how I was meant to live. And I want you by my side."

"You want me to live here with you?"

I smile wide, touch my thumb to the delicate skin beneath her eye that's already wet. She's so sweet. So innocent. She never lost that, even after what those bastards did to her.

"That won't do, Melissa. Not for this proposition. I want more. I want everything. You'll marry me. You'll be my bride and my wife, and I'll be your husband. I'll give you a proper last name. I'll be your family. And together, we'll fill this house as it was meant to be filled, with children and laughter and family and joy."

Her mouth falls open and she's staring up at me and all I can think is how right this feels. How perfectly right.

"Will you marry me, Melissa?"

EPILOGUE

Melissa

Three Months Later

I realize something about Hawk that I guess I should have known all along. I mean, it's in keeping with the man I've come to know over the last few months.

When Hawk makes up his mind, you can consider it a done deal. He's the same in business and his personal life.

We flew back to Vegas together a few days after that proposal a very different couple than the man and woman who arrived here not a week earlier.

A happy one.

That's not to say he wasn't sad over the death of his father. Of everything that time stood for. He was. And I don't think Hawk will ever forgive himself for the loss of those years. But he has a way of taking things in stride and in this case, making up his mind to be happy.

I've made up mine too.

We never discussed Sean Boyd again. I know the day Hawk went to him. I know the day Hawk hurt him. Maybe did worse to him.

Does it make me a terrible person that I don't feel remorse over it?

Deirdre happily accepted my offer to become manager of Wrinkles in Time. I wasn't sure she'd want it with her granddaughter being so young, but she surprised me when, in accepting, she began to tell me of the changes she'd be implementing. Things she'd thought about in passing but never had the ambition to do. I just had to promise her a trip to Scotland to attend our wedding which I happily did.

Fifty percent of the proceeds of the shop will still go to the homeless shelter and that's on top of the generous donation Hawk made in Marjorie's name.

That was a surprise. I hadn't expected him to do that and wouldn't have even found out if it weren't for the woman who manages the shelter dropping the hint.

I didn't tell Hawk I knew but every time I look at him, at my Highlander, home now and happy, I think about the kind of man he is and I feel more blessed than I ever thought I would in my life.

"Don't cry," Deirdre says to me. "You'll ruin your makeup."

But I can't help it.

I'm standing at the back of the church where Hawk is waiting for me at the altar, his brother at his side, his grandfather standing in the first pew.

Deirdre, like the grandmother she is, licks her thumb and wipes at what I guess is a smudge of eyeliner on the corner of my eye before rearranging the veil to cover my face.

"Ready?" James whispers up.

When we told him our news and he learned I had no family, no father to walk me down the aisle, he immediately stood up and offered his hand and I'm so happy I'll be a part of his life. He's a very special boy.

I look down at him dressed like his father and uncle in traditional Scottish clothing, the kilt displaying proudly the colors of Clan MacLeod. It's still amazing to me the amount of history here. The amount of family.

"Ready," I say to him.

He holds out his hand and I slip mine into his little one. He clears his throat like Hawk does and straightens his shoulders. I see Declan at the alter with his proud smile as his son walks me down the short aisle of the chapel.

My eyes are locked on Hawk's and it seems the past weeks flash before my eyes as I take each step. The moment I first met him, that first night, the next day when he showed up at my house, and all the ones that followed when he wouldn't just take what he had a right to but instead cradled me in the protection of his arms and wouldn't let me go. Not even when I fought like hell to be free of him.

When James hands me off to Hawk and Hawk lifts my veil, he wipes away the tear that has managed to slide down my cheek. He leans down to kiss me and whispers in my ear that I'm beautiful and that he loves me. All I can do is stare back at him and try to hold it together.

He knows this too. I see it in his eyes.

The priest clears his throat to begin the ceremony and when it's time to exchange rings, Hawk takes my hands in his and I look down at the ring he's holding. A family ring, his mother's once.

Strangely, his father hadn't given it to his second wife. Instead, after the passing of Hawk's mother, he'd set it aside for Hawk to give to his bride. Hawk only found out about it after his father's death when his grandfather had given it to him and explained.

When we say our vows, he slips that ring onto my finger and I slide a gold band onto his and it's like everything comes together, it's complete and right and how it should be. How it was meant to be from the moment we came into each other's lives.

Because I realize I've always belonged to Hawk.

And he's always belonged to me.

And together, we're home.

The End

THANK YOU

Thank you for reading ***Devil's Bargain***! I hope you enjoyed Hawk and Melissa's story.

Declan MacLeod will have his own story to tell soon and Axel and his brother, Hugo, whom you met in ***Killian: a Dark Mafia Romance***, will tell theirs too.

If you'd like to keep updated on dates and news, please sign up for my newsletter and consider joining my Facebook Group, The Knight Spot.

And if you loved Devil's Bargain, flip to the next page to read a sample from ***Taken***, of the Dark Legacy series.

SAMPLE FROM TAKEN

Helena

I'm the oldest of the Willow quadruplets. Four girls. Always girls. Every single quadruplet birth, generation after generation, it's always girls.

This generation's crop yielded the usual, but instead of four perfect, beautiful dolls, there were three.

And me.

And today, our twenty-first birthday, is the day of harvesting.

That's the Scafoni family's choice of words, not ours. At least not mine. My parents seem much more comfortable with it than my sisters and I do, though.

Harvesting is always on the twenty-first birthday of the quads. I don't know if it's written in stone somewhere or what, but it's what I know and what has been on the back of my mind since I learned our history five years ago.

There's an expression: *those who cannot remember the past are condemned to repeat it.* Well, that's bullshit, because we Willows know well our past and look at us now.

The same blocks that have been used for centuries standing in the old library, their surfaces softened by the feet of every other Willow Girl who stood on the same stumps of wood, and all I can think when I see them, the four lined up like they are, is how archaic this is, how fucking unreal. How they can't do this to us.

Yet, here we are.

And they are doing this to us.

But it's not *us*, really.

My shift is marked.

I'm *unclean*.

So it's really my sisters.

Sometimes I'm not sure who I hate more, my own family for allowing this insanity generation after generation, or the Scafoni monsters for demanding the sacrifice.

"It's time," my father says. His voice is grave.

He's aged these last few months. I wonder if that's remorse because it certainly isn't backbone.

I heard he and my mother argue once, exactly once, and then it was over.

He simply accepted it.

Accepted that tonight, his daughters will be made to stand on those horrible blocks while a Scafoni bastard looks us over, prods and pokes us, maybe checks our teeth like you would a horse, before making his choice. Before taking one of my sisters as his for the next three years of her life.

I'm not naive enough to be unsure what that will mean exactly. Maybe my sisters are, but not me.

"Up on the block. Now, Helena."

I look at my sisters who already stand so meekly on their appointed stumps. They're all paler than usual tonight and I swear I can hear their hearts pounding in fear of what's to come.

When I don't move right away, my father painfully takes my arm and lifts me up onto my block and all I can think, the one thing that gives me the slightest hope, is that if Sebastian Scafoni chooses me, I will find some way to end this. I won't condemn my daughters to this fate. My nieces. My granddaughters.

But he won't choose me, and I think that's why my parents are angrier than usual with me.

See, I'm the ugly duckling. At least I'd be considered ugly standing next to my sisters.

And the fact that I'm unclean—not a virgin—means I won't be taken.

The Scafoni bastard will choose one of their precious golden daughters instead.

Golden, to my dark. Golden—quite literally. Sparkling almost, my sisters.

I glance at them as my father attaches the iron shackle to my ankle. He doesn't do this to any of them. They'll do as they're told, even as their gazes bounce from the closed twelve-foot doors to me and back again and again and again.

But I have no protection to offer. Not tonight. Not on this one.

The backs of my eyes burn with tears I refuse to shed.

"How can you do this? How can you allow it?" I ask for the hundredth time. I'm talking to my mother while my father clasps the restraints on my wrists, making sure I won't attack the monsters.

"Better gag her, too."

It's my mother's response to my question and, a moment later, my father does as he's told and ensures my silence.

I hate my mother more, I think. She's a Willow quadruplet. She witnessed a harvesting herself. Witnessed the result of this cruel tradition.

Tradition.

A tradition of kidnapping.

Of breaking.

Of destroying.

I look to my sisters again. Three almost carbon copies of each other, with long blonde hair curling around their shoulders, flowing down their backs, their blue eyes wide with fear.

Well, except in Julia's case.

She's different than the others. She's more...eager. But I don't think she has a clue what they'll do to her.

Me, no one would guess I came from the same batch.

Opposite their gold, my hair is so dark a black, it appears almost blue, with one single, wide streak of silver to relieve the stark shade, a flaw I was born with. And contrasting their cornflower-blue eyes, mine are a midnight sky; there too, the only relief the silver specks that dot them.

They look like my mother. Like perfect dolls.

I look like my great-aunt, also named Helena, down to the silver streak I refuse to dye. She's in her nineties now. I wonder if they had to lock her in her room and steal her wheelchair, so she wouldn't interfere in the ceremony.

Aunt Helena was the chosen girl of her generation. She knows what's in store for us better than anyone.

"They're coming," my mother says.

She has super hearing, I swear, but then, a moment later, I hear them too.

A door slams beyond the library, and the draft blows out a dozen of the thousand candles that light the huge room.

A maid rushes to relight them. No electricity. Tradition, I guess.

If I were Sebastian Scafoni, I'd want to get a good look at the prize I'd be fucking for the next year. And I have no doubt there will be fucking, because what else can break a girl so completely but taking that of all things?

And it's not just the one year. No. We're given for three years. One year for each brother. Oldest to youngest. It used to be four, but now, it's three.

I would pinch my arm to be sure I'm really standing here, that I'm not dreaming, but my hands are bound behind my back, and I can't.

This can't be fucking real. It can't be legal.

And yet here we are, the four of us, naked beneath our translucent, rotting sheaths—I swear I smell the decay on them—standing on our designated blocks, teetering on them. I guess the Willows of the past had smaller feet. And I admit, as I hear their heavy, confident footfalls approaching the ancient wooden doors of the library, I am afraid.

I'm fucking terrified.

Available in all stores now!

ALSO BY NATASHA KNIGHT

Dark Legacy

Taken (Dark Legacy, Book 1)

Torn (Dark Legacy, Book 2)

Twisted (Dark Legacy, Book 3)

Benedetti Mafia World

Salvatore: a Dark Mafia Romance

Dominic: a Dark Mafia Romance

Sergio: a Dark Mafia Romance

The Benedetti Brothers Duet

Killian: a Dark Mafia Romance

Giovanni: a Dark Mafia Romance

The Amado Brothers

Dishonorable

Disgraced

Unhinged

Standalone Dark Romance

Deviant

Beautiful Liar

Retribution

Theirs To Take

Captive, Mine

Alpha

Given to the Savage

Taken by the Beast

Claimed by the Beast

Captive's Desire

Protective Custody

Amy's Strict Doctor

Taming Emma

Taming Megan

Taming Naia

Reclaiming Sophie

The Firefighter's Girl

Dangerous Defiance

Her Rogue Knight

Taught To Kneel

Tamed: the Roark Brothers Trilogy

ACKNOWLEDGMENTS

Cover Design by Clarise Tan, CT Cover Creations

Cover Photography By Wander Aguiar

Cover Model Zack Salaun

ABOUT THE AUTHOR

USA Today bestselling author of contemporary romance, Natasha Knight specializes in dark, tortured heroes. Happily-Ever-Afters are guaranteed, but she likes to put her characters through hell to get them there. She's evil like that.

Want more?

www.natasha-knight.com

natasha-knight@outlook.com

Printed in Great Britain
by Amazon

43547104R00177